Jane Two

Jane Two

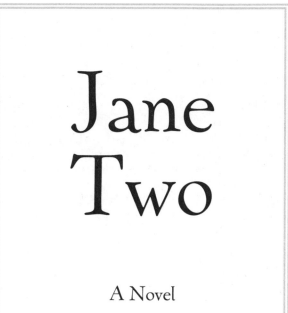

A Novel

Sean Patrick Flanery

CENTER STREET

New York Boston Nashville

Copyright © 2016 by Sean Patrick Flanery

Cover design by Diane Luger
Cover copyright © 2016 by Hachette Book Group, Inc.

Center Street
Hachette Book Group
1290 Avenue of the Americas
New York, NY 10104
CenterStreet.com
twitter.com/centerstreet

First Edition: April 2016

Center Street is a division of Hachette Book Group, Inc.
The Center Street name and logo are trademarks of Hachette Book Group, Inc.

The publisher is not responsible for websites (or their content) that are not owned by the publisher.

The Hachette Speakers Bureau provides a wide range of authors for speaking events. To find out more, go to www.HachetteSpeakersBureau.com or call (866) 376-6591.

Library of Congress Cataloging-in-Publication Data has been applied for.

ISBN 978-1-4555-3943-7 (hardcover); 978-1-4555-3942-0 (ebook)

Printed in the United States of America

RRD–C

10 9 8 7 6 5 4 3 2 1

For her

I believe there are only ever a handful of moments in a child's life that truly shape who he is or who he is to become. There are plenty of moments for fine-tuning, but only a handful that mold the sharp, memorable features of the face...and also the soul. This is my handful.

Jane Two

Chapter One

So, here we are again. You know, most people check their mailbox to see what's inside it, but I think you know that I check mine to see what's not. I would tell you to stop me if you think that you've heard this one before, but I already know that you've heard it before. Bear with me. Sometimes I just need to hear myself say it again—to get it out.

I went home to try and touch the things I left behind, but they just weren't there anymore. Other things were. I needed to go back to that place again. I just needed a return trip to my childhood to pack up rubble memories to take with me before someone else occupied that space. I had to. I wanted Texas to be more familiar than it was when I went back. I wanted everything to reflect my memories exactly. It seemed like an eternity since I'd gone back to the mileposts and cairns of my past. But, adults have slag lenses, and we all learn to breathe through filters. I wanted everything back the way it was. My Grandaddy always told me I'd come back home looking for my porch, and here I was, looking. I just didn't want it to be too late.

I had a cab pick me up from the church and the cabbie asked me who got married, eyeballing my suit. "Nobody," I said. As I rode in the taxi with that package next to me, I asked the driver to take a detour and stop on the farm road right outside my old junior high school. I just needed to see it again, to see if I could understand what I had missed. I told the driver that I'd only be a minute, and asked him if I could leave my things in the back. I could see he was staring at me in the rearview mirror before he asked me, "Nothing dangerous in that box, is there?" I remember looking at it and wondering the same thing, but then I just stepped out of the cab and started down the long gravel driveway to the front of the school, where it looped around and went right back out to the farm road. With every step I took, it grew and grew, until I found myself at its base, right in the center of that circular drive where kids are dropped off for school 180 days a year. There it was, the flagpole that gave me perspective, standing right where it left me. It wasn't until I was stranded up there in the middle of a dewy school night that I had truly seen a crystal clear picture of all the puzzle pieces that were to become my life. And with a mixture of trepidation and desire, I longed to climb it once more, to see it all again.

You know, most memories have a sort of swelling effect. Just about everything from my youth that I see today is just a little bit smaller, or less important than my memories' scale. I now know of only two things that defy this rule: that flagpole...and Jane.

I knew exactly whose sneakers they were. Those Vans, the new and impossibly rare 95s, belonged to a unicorn. There was a sixty-foot nautical-type flagpole dead center in the front of my new junior high school, and the sneakers dangled from the crossbar about fifteen feet from the top. Two weeks later, my Grandaddy was asking my part in all of it, closing in on the truth because he knew I'd lied to my parents about the shoes up there on that flagpole. He knew everything. The old, retired deputy sheriff sat on his rickety lawn chair on my front porch, staring out at the angry thunderhead accumulating on the Texas horizon, silently probing my truth. When he talked to me, he rarely ever looked me in the eyes. But when he did, it was something special. He was seeing something special. He was recognizing something in me.

This time, his not looking me in the eye hurt a little until it hurt more when he turned to me with gunmetal flinting out of his pupils—eyes that had drawn a confession from many a crook and lowlife. He said, "You can only ever assuage a mistake and benefit from it if you pull three lessons out it." And even though my Grandaddy's coon-ass bayou French made *fix* come out as *ass-you-age*, I knew exactly what he meant.

I had to tell him the truth about the sneakers.

When I arrived at school on that first day of sixth grade, I spotted her 95s through the cool wall of water gushing out of the furnace that was my Texas sky. Despite the blurring rain, I knew. I knew because every single day of that previous summer during swim team practice, I had seen her walk by the pool. With the discerning eye that only adoration can bring, I watched her glide across the parking lot every day clutching a Frisbee. So I knew, and I was immediately consumed with how I might get the 95s down and return them to their rightful owner. They were hers. She was the only person I knew with 95s, and they were almost as perfect as she was.

"Who threw the clown shoes up onto the flagpole?" vibrated out of the speakers during the morning announcements. Our principal's voice paused for a moment afterward, as if Mr. Totter really expected an answer. I pictured him, his suit smelling of mothballs over the pilled-up gray wool vest, sticking his shiny head out of his office into the hallway awaiting an echoing confession. Obviously, one never came, so following a death-rattle cough, he finally concluded: "Lest you forget, this constitutes vandalism, and will be treated as such" and "No one defaces our wonderful school" and "I will have those shoes down immediately."

Minutes later, with a crowd of students around him on the front lawn, Mr. Totter was holding a pellet gun, patiently pumping it and firing it up at the shoes, trying to tear the laces and bring down those 95s like big game. The flagpole was a solid chrome monolith of sixty feet, over a foot in diameter at its base, and with two opposing arms jutting out from each side about fifteen feet from the top, like a ship's mast. Both arms had a chrome ball at the end, and the sneakers were about two feet from the end of the right arm, swaying in the sultry breeze. I remember preparing to viciously tackle Mr. Totter to the ground if he were to accidentally damage her shoes. I don't know if he realized his idiocy, or if he just gave up, but after a few more volleys, Mr. Totter scurried back into the building gripping his rifle.

All summer long I had seen the flyers at the local Piggly Wiggly for Frisbee lessons at my junior high, so every day when I saw her pass the pool, I knew exactly where she was going. And every time I saw her pass again, going home, she would walk barefoot in the shallow creek that ran right next to the pool, letting her feet cool. Her 95s hung around her neck like a scarf, the same way I always wore the red scarf Mom made me for Halloween a few years earlier. Nothing changed the first half of her journey on that last day of summer, but on the way back she just ran through the pool parking lot barefoot. I didn't see the 95s around her neck that evening, but I do remember that she did not stop to smile at me. Something had happened, and when I got to school that first day and saw those 95s dangling on the flagpole, my gut confirmed there was a new person on my hate list.

Houston, Texas, is about 1,700 miles from California, so things took a bit longer to arrive on our shores, and 95s were no different. I'd seen the icon Alva's feet in skateboard magazines, though, so I was well aware of the 95's hallowed significance. The fact that she not only knew what they were, but actually owned a pair was a testament to her unicornness. I would have staked my life on the fact that I was the only person in school who knew exactly what was dangling on that chrome cross in the schoolyard. Not just 95s...but 95s that her feet had graced. Those shoes weren't up there a week before someone drew a huge Wanted poster on the bathroom wall.

MISSING: ONE PAIR OF RED AND BLUE CLOWN SHOES! $500 REWARD!

—THE CIRCUS

Graffiti popped up everywhere referencing those shoes, with various rewards. Each taunted me for the safe return of the 95s. The doggerel lit a fire under the school's ass, and there was rumbling that Mr. Totter had arranged to have the fire department come and extract the unpatriotic eyesore as soon as possible, though the colors matched the flag.

It didn't take long before rumors spread that Jonathan was the culprit. He was in eighth grade that year, and widely regarded, at least by me, as a complete jack-wagon. One of those big-talking verbal bullies who had never actually been in a fight in his life. His brown-bodied, white-billed John Deere hat had never left his head in all the years I knew him. Jonathan had stolen her shoes while she was playing Frisbee barefoot on the field behind the gymnasium. Then, with the help of two of his idiot buddies, they slingshotted those sneakers up into the sky and onto that cross with a surgical-tubing water balloon launcher. Jonathan even bragged that he had yelled to all the Frisbee girls on the field until they each turned and stared at him holding up the sneakers, then saw a "weird little hippie girl in a yellow dress" react, shot her the bird, and sprinted away with "the stupidest-looking shoes I'd ever seen on a girl."

I was in the restroom one day after word had spread, and I even heard Jonathan changing his story to say that he actually climbed up there and hung them, by hand. What a lying sack of shit! I knew that fat fuck couldn't get four feet up that pole if his life depended on it. I just stood there at the urinal, pretending to pee, feeling the hatred rise up my entire body in a heat wave from my feet all the way into the root of every hair in my scalp.

Jonathan had to pay. There was no way around it.

"Lying faggit, tub of shit!" Oh, sweet baby Jesus, I couldn't believe that I actually said that out loud, and that huge tile bathroom repeated me word for word. In all honesty, my indictment was intended for my enjoyment alone, but now it was for everyone's.

"The fuck did you just call me, you little pussy?" Jonathan squealed in his fat-fuck little squeaky voice. I panicked, and rushed to zip up my jeans, realized that they were already zipped as I had finished minutes earlier, and just stayed at the urinal to hear that pig lie, then slowly turned around to face the giant. Jonathan was a good fifty pounds heavier than me, and I'll be honest, I lost a bit more pee in the moment he hollered at me. I apologized to Jonathan for saying my thoughts out loud, but even when he backed me up against the urinal, I refused his request to "take it back!"

"You don't think I could climb that fucking pole?"

"I don't."

The other boys awaited Jonathan's rebuttal.

"Prove it, you little pussy." Jonathan stuck his finger in my chest, and turned and started to head out of the bathroom as if he had just "shown me." I remember thinking that out of all five words I let accidentally escape my lips that day, he had only contested the first. The only word that wasn't absolutely subjective was the one that he found fault with. I couldn't believe he didn't swing on me. I certainly didn't want to fight him, but I was surprised. How did he expect me to "prove" that he couldn't do something? I stared at the ground while tucking in my shirt. And that's when I saw it. Right where Jonathan had been standing. I saw it and it dawned on me. My answer lay on the floor in a puddle of pee.

I'll have your shoes back by Monday.

My Grandaddy liked to say that a *how* was always tailgating a good *why*. He said that a real man always finds it harder to short-change others than he does himself, so I should make my dreams public—that way I'd be letting others down if I failed. And a real man doesn't let others down.

That Wednesday, I excused myself from math class to go and use the restroom. My junior high had three separate lunches, one for each grade, and the eighth-grade lunch was during my math class. I saw Jonathan at his corner table surrounded by his platoon of dunces, and let go of my red scarf before they figured out I was wiping my sweaty palms on it.

I interrupted Jonathan's mouthful of pizza to blurt out, "I'll prove it to you by Monday." Then, I turned around and walked off, my red scarf clenched in my fist to keep me calm. I remember waiting to be clocked in the back of the head with a fist, or food, or something, but the blow never came. A trail of questions and profanity faded out as I made my way back to math.

That Friday night was the first night I'd ever sneaked out of my house. I was petrified. Petrified of getting kidnapped. Petrified of getting attacked by drug addicts. Petrified my parents would find out I was a hoodlum on occasion. Petrified of someone else getting her 95s back to her before I could. My dog, Steve McQueen, slept on my bed with me, always had to be touching me ever since I was a toddler, and he would wake up if I left, so I had to take him with me. But in truth, I was just too scared to do it without my best friend. It took us almost two hours to get to the school that night, because we ducked from every pair of car headlights that approached, and I'm telling you a Weimaraner is not an easy dog to conceal. Big as a pony, his telltale gray coat reflected in headlights. In a town that small, there was a good probability we'd be picked up and forced to call my parents. About twenty times we had to hide behind broken-down cars on cinder blocks in neighbors' yards or behind abandoned shacks where Steve McQueen tiptoed gingerly around broken glass.

We made it to the school around one a.m., and I stood in front of that monument of threat and promise for an eternity before attempting ascent. A long gravel driveway came off the main road, so the school was a good distance from any potential witnesses. Steve McQueen lay there, frog-style, with no idea what a naive pup his partner was. I hugged that pole hard. I hugged it as if my life depended on it, long before it actually did. I made it about twenty feet up before I was absolutely crushed with panic. I slid down The Pole much faster than I should have, my red scarf flaring up from the speed of it, and I collapsed on the ground in desperation. I was overwhelmed with fear from the height I'd attained, although it was less than halfway up to the arms, but I was absolutely devastated from the fear of the realization that what I had claimed I would do was completely impossible under the circumstances. I sat with my legs crossed next to Steve McQueen and just stared up at the mast, like a lost sailor, willing a true bearing to come with the prevailing westerly winds. And come to me it did.

I had simply arrived too late. My little Texas town was one

of the most humid places on earth, and by one o'clock in the morning, everything was coated in a veil of dew. That pole was no exception. I must arrive no later than twelve thirty a.m. to have the needed friction to reach the top. I also realized I possessed another secret weapon for my next attempt. It occurred to me as Steve McQueen and I walked home. We took the back way to avoid traffic, crossing playing fields and the stand of trees with The Hole, and the football field under lights where we got to play one game per year, where I had scored my very first FUN Stadium touchdown. That's where I remembered it.

A few years earlier, when I was about eight years old, I scored on an end-around pitchout that left me all alone in the end zone. I had eyeballed the stands for my family until I found them clustered together way up on the top bleacher bench, and I slowly raised both my hands to wave at my mom and dad and my whole clan; Grandaddy, Mamau, James, even Lilyth and Magda came to see me play. I had been elated to stand under the uprights, but shocked to see the ball still stuck to my chest as both my arms waved at my parents. Stickum, although outlawed by the NFL in 1981, was an aerosol spray that turned you into walking flypaper. Stickum prevented fumbles. Stickum increased receptions. Stickum would grant my ascent to her 95s.

The next night I went to sleep early with a "headache," so Steve McQueen and I were at the school by midnight with two full cans of Stickum. As we took the shortcut across the field of diamonds, the raw gash in the earth that so terrified me there drew a sharp snarl from Steve, but I raced on past The Hole, and urged him not to stop. When we finally reached The Pole, I caught my breath and unloaded my cargo. If I sprayed my T-shirt, it would just get pulled out of my jeans when I climbed, so I took off my red scarf, shirt, shoes, and pants and sprayed my entire bare chest, arms, hands, inner thighs, calves, and feet. I intended to attempt the ascent in my underwear. I had to let each coat of Stickum dry before reapplying, so it was twelve thirty before I was ready to climb. I had already collected about ten mosquitos on my body, guests who had checked in for a quick drink and realized too late that they could never leave.

I gave Mr. McQueen a good-luck pat on the head and came away with a palm full of short hairs, so I had to respray my right hand a final time, losing precious moments. I stuffed what I needed to stuff in the back of my underwear, and I was ready. I could feel the dew in the air, so I knew I had to hurry. I had to hurry to do what is arguably one of the stupidest things I have ever attempted in my life.

When I first stepped up to that flagpole, I gave it a big hug, rested my chin on it, and looked straight up the long chrome tube that penetrated the sky. Her shoes seemed a mile up. The clear view made me absolutely paralytic with fear, so I decided to focus solely into the distance and use my peripheral vision to guide me. My periphery was always just a little bit blurry, and tended to help me hide life's horrible realities. I wouldn't look down. I wouldn't look up. I looked for my Grandaddy's horizon, straight out into that nothing, lit up by a Texas butter moon, until I felt the crossbar.

I must have been about halfway up when I realized that as much as the Stickum was keeping me on The Pole, it was making it extremely difficult to pull my limbs off and up once they were stuck. Just as I was starting to realize my exhaustion, my head hit a metal arm. It was at the peak of an up-pull, so my head hit hard. I had made the climb so much more difficult in my mind that I was only mentally halfway up when my skull cracked the crossbar. Blood dripped into my eye from what I knew must be a pretty big gash right at my hairline. You couldn't see it from the ground, but there were little steel supports under each arm right at the point where they connected with The Pole, and my head had collided with a little steel burr on that support bar, causing it to sink straight into my scalp and rip it open. Steve McQueen sensed that something was very wrong and barked up at me. I looked down to shush him.

It wasn't until I looked down that I realized that I hadn't made the climb more difficult in my mind at all. It was difficult. It was high. It was far higher up than I had estimated from the ground. If I fell, I would die. I knew it. Steve McQueen smelled it. And the blood obscuring my vision was magnifying the probability of me falling. I wouldn't allow myself access to any mature logic at all, and went instead with my abundance of youthful idiocy to calculate the risk-to-reward ratio of retrieving her 95s. I must've spent about four one-thousandths of a second on this estimation.

Yeah, she's worth it.

Now, everything up to this point was nothing but an athletic endeavor. But what happened next was one of the most surreal, hyper-focused adrenal experiences of my life. Time, and every one of my senses, seemed to slow way down. The pain at my hairline was gone, my lungs no longer burned, and my blood droplets seemed to float to the ground, peppering the concrete all around Steve, who was still smiling up at me, his barking muted, flickering in time lapse.

I would get her shoes.

I'd climbed this mast a thousand times in my head, and knew exactly how I would navigate every millimeter. So, I set out across the steel arm for her shoes, fifty feet up, going backwards, hand over hand, hanging with only my arms, my legs dangling into nothing, until I was about four feet out. I swung back and forth until I could snake my legs around the horizontal bar right where it joined the vertical. I hung up-side down, and felt the vertical with my foot. I managed to hook their intersection with my right foot, just as I had in my mind's rehearsals, and slowly I inched myself to right-side up. Creeping all the way out across that steel arm, I touched my very first pair of 95s. I touched *her* 95s. They were double-looped around the end of the spar, so I had to fling them around twice until they were freely draped over the arm, one shoe on each side. Both sneakers were suspended in a perfect balance for a moment, defying gravity, until one shoe dragged the other higher and higher and it leapt over the arm, set free. They landed about five feet from Steve McQueen with a clunk, but Steve never took his hunting-dog eyes off me.

Once her shoes were free and I was out at the end near that big chrome ball, I realized that the top of the horizontal metal bar was coated in fine Texas clay dust. And, as a result, my ad-hesion was gone. The Stickum had picked up every molecule of debris. I could feel the boom swaying. I could feel myself rotate just a bit with every sway. I could feel my heart throb-bing. I could hear the blood leaving through the hole in my scalp. I could see the Dairy Queen in the distance. I could see the Shakey's Pizza. I could see FUN Stadium by The Hole. I saw my entire life as a child concentrated into one singularity. I reached in my underwear and I pulled out the hat—the hat that had fallen off that fat tub of shit's head in the bathroom as he jammed his finger in my chest, the hat that I saw on the floor in a puddle of pee as I stared at the ground—the hat that I had tied a length of my mom's thread to with a noose on the other end.

Carefully, I slid that noose over the chrome-plated ball that glittered in the moonlight. I cinched it tight. I watched it dangle. It was the first time I actually read what that hat said. *Nothing Runs Like a Deere* twirled in the breeze. I was about forty-five feet off the ground, and I remember thinking, *Well some things probably do, but certainly not a fat fuck like Jonathan.*

I was hugging that chrome beam with my arms and legs like a little tree monkey, but the chrome spar's sway grew more and more severe, like a snap reverberation of my passion to survive. I could see my moonlit Weimaraner moving to and fro underneath me as I clung to that arm, but Steve McQueen sat perfectly still, staring up at his errant protégé. The motion was mine. The top of The Pole probably wasn't moving any more than a foot in either direction, but when it would stop and snap back in the other direction, the acceleration was enough to make me slip and rotate on the steel arm. I clasped my hands together around the horizontal arm of The Pole and tried to cross my feet, but as gravity pulled me down and I rotated completely upside down, my feet came apart and I hung by my prayer-clasped hands, swinging by the sheer force of inertia from side to side.

Not a single fiber of my being doubted that I was going to die in the next thrust of that pole's torque. I would die because I knew I would have to separate my hands on the horizontal in order to hand-walk back to the vertical pole. And I knew that if I did, my hands would no longer hold. In that moment, I wondered if Steve would stay by my body all night like those World War II army dogs. I wondered if she would think that I had stolen her shoes, and had just died trying to get them so I could brag about my thievery. I wanted her to know that I was trying to *save* her 95s. I wanted her to know that I saw her every day by the pool. I wanted her to know that every single time we crossed paths, she had embossed an indelible image on the back side of my eyelids. I wanted her to know that I thought about her more than I thought about race cars or fighter planes or sports. And that I thought about her through every piece of music I cherished. But really, in that moment there on The Pole, swaying out of control, I just wanted my mom and dad. I wanted them more than I had ever wanted anything in my life. I was embarrassed to end my life this way. I did not want to die an idiot's death.

I threw my legs up to try and regrab the horizontal, but the debris that had collected on my body made my feet too slippery to hold. Slick from Stickum coated with dust, my hands were too slippery to unclasp in order to walk them hand over hand, and I knew in that instant that the Stickum that had assisted me in my ascent would now most certainly cause my death. I had to try to keep my knuckles squeezed together in prayer-lock in order to maintain my slowly faltering grip. But, in my failed attempt to swing my legs up, the sheer momentum of my kick had slid my clasped hands about an inch closer to that pole. What I thought was going to kill me might actually save my life.

It must have taken me fifty kicks to come within reaching distance of that pole of life, but when I got close enough, I flung my lower body around the vertical like a newborn to his mother. I got my legs wrapped around The Pole while my hands still kept me up, prayer-gripping that metal arm. I knew how slippery I was, and that as soon as I let go of the horizontal bar I would slide much too quickly straight to the ground no matter how hard I hugged. I knew it would hurt, but I also knew that I would not die. I looked out at the city in front of me, and this was the most reassuring sight that my memory provides to this day. It was the view that no one else has ever seen of my Dairy Queen, my Shakey's, my stadium, my church, her house, and my life.

As soon as I let go of the horizontal arms, I slid down at what seemed like fifty miles per hour. I hit hard. A sprained ankle was of little notice to a boy who had just transcended fear and lived to know he would see his parents again. Steve licked my face, and all my senses came back into a much more recognizable acuity. Time accelerated. The crickets seemed to be chanting. The Pole's shadow seemed to be dancing, and the 95s were the most brilliant shade of faded blue and red I'd ever seen. I looked up at The Pole and saw streaks of my blood from top to bottom, and all the way out smeared in blotches and drips across the right arm. I looked at the ground around Steve and me, and it looked like it had been sprinkling blood just like fat raindrops before a Texas storm. I had no idea how I would explain my forehead to my mom and dad. But I was alive. I was alive, and I had her 95s.

I wore my Speed Racer baseball cap the very next day to hide that huge gash, and I put those 95s in her forest green mailbox on Sunday after sleeping with them clutched in my arms. Grabbing my bike from under the giant bean tree in my front yard, I rode right up to her curbside mailbox and stuck her 95s inside. I took my time, hoping she would see me as I retied her laces perfectly. And I rode away without looking back.

I wanted her to know it was me. I prayed for her to know it was me. All through school I never found out. But I did see her walk down that creek, barefoot again, with the 95s dangling around her neck. This time, she smiled *at me*, every time she smiled.

When my mother dropped me off for school on Monday, the whole lawn was filled with kids and teachers alike. Standing outside Mom's smoke-filled car, I looked up at what everyone knew was Jonathan's most prized possession. It had never before left his head in public till that day in the bathroom, and it was now flapping in the wind sixty-five feet up, out of his reach, with a big red *LIAR* written across the white bill. Everyone stared at his hat, knowing he had no way of getting it back. Jonathan never said another word to me about those 95s.

"Who put the baseball cap up on the flagpole? WHO PAINTED MY FLAGPOLE RED? Lest you forget, this is my school, and heads shall roll, you buncha ingrates, unless someone steps forth!" Mr. Totter's voice rasped over the intercom. All Jonathan's buddies at his lunch table that day knew it was me, but even as rumors spread, I never said a word. Not even to Firefly. When the rumormongering finally rippled the truth to the principal's office, Mr. Totter called my parents to school for a conference. When Mr. Totter asked if I was involved, I lied. I looked my mom and dad right in the eye and I lied. This is the first they will read of that lie.

I'm sorry.

My Mamau and Grandaddy arrived a little late at our house that same night after the Totter conference. Smelling like a real man in his Pinaud gentleman's powder, my Grandaddy was groomed to the nines, his brown shirt pressed and tucked in his brown polyester trousers. His whole life, he'd never wear a T-shirt except under a proper shirt, because he said it was like wearing your underwear on the outside. Mamau was all gussied up in gold as usual with good gold jewelry and a gold hair thingy securing her mass of freshly dyed brown-ish golden maroonish hair, humming "My Sweet Lord." I never saw my Mamau without makeup. She always looked perfect for my Grandaddy. He called her his unicorn. They were with us most weekends and often after school if I had practice. My Mamau set to making her fried chicken every-body loved while Mom, Dad, and my sister were arguing. My Grandaddy called me out onto the porch, same as always.

"Seedlin', get the hell out here!"

My ankle was aching and swollen, and I tried not to limp. I ran outside and sat right next to him in the lawn chair that his best friend James usually occupied. He took a moment be-fore he spoke, glancing at the Speed Racer baseball cap glued on my head. He eyeballed my leg, then kept staring out at the horizon. No one conveyed more information with fewer words than my Grandaddy. Nobody.

"Your daddy told me about that flagpole." I just looked at him. He kept gazing out at the horizon. "You know, your daddy rolled a fifteen-foot Civil War cannon out and left it in the main intersection when he was a boy, your age, and I asked him the same goddamn question I'm 'bout to ask you. I reckon you got the same goddamn answer." My Grandaddy never once asked me if I had done it, but instead said, "I can think of some good reasons to climb it, and some bad reasons to climb it. Which one did you have, son?"

As I stared at him watching out over the land, I took a very careful moment to decide exactly what I'd tell him.

"A good one," I said.

My Grandaddy turned to me and looked clear into my soul, then slowly he nodded his head up and down before going right back out to the horizon. He took one of his trademarked gargantuan inhales of air, held it, and let a tiny little grin escape.

"Go get your Grandaddy a wing."

"Charlie?! Where's Charlie?!" My Mamau came yelling, clutching her giant breasts draped in her gauzy gold dress as she stuck her head out onto the porch. She called his name in a panic the same way she always yelled out for him when she lost sight of him for more than five minutes. "Oh, that man gon' give me a heart attack one'a these days. Charlie, here ya go." She handed him a plate with two small bits of chicken and retreated to the kitchen, where my sister was still scream-ing at my dad.

"And, Seedlin', give your Mamau back that saucer."

I'd brought my Mamau that same plate back many times, and I asked my Grandaddy about those two bits, and why he never ate one. He told me that those two pieces were called the Bull-Yawn. He said it was the absolute best part of the bird, and that if you could measure the "delicious" in a fried chicken, 90 percent of it would be in those two tiny pieces. I loved the imagery of that term: A vicious bull, violently pulling at the ground with its front legs, suddenly so tranquil-ized by something that it just gives in, relaxes, and yawns. I asked him why my Mamau got them every time, and why he never wanted one for himself. He just looked out at the horizon for a moment like he was trying to find something, something that had been there for years and suddenly vanished. And whenever he would do this, I knew that as soon as his lips were to start moving, another piece of life would slip out. Some of the absolute best things I know came from that porch. Then he began, and he said, "You know, son, it's always better to live without good stuff than it is to live without someone you wanna give all your good stuff to."

I wanted to bottle every single thing he taught me on that porch.

"You gotta deserve 'em to taste 'em," he said. "Your Mamau deserve 'em, now go get your Grandaddy that wing."

Chapter Two

Jane came into my life headfirst in the early 1970s when I was eight years old. I was staring into my bowl of Cocoa Pebbles, listening to my new 45 of Simon and Garfunkel's "The Sounds of Silence" when I heard a repetition of small, passion-filled breaths. My eyes followed the sound through the sliding glass window, across our backyard, up the fence, and collided intermittently with what I can only describe as the perfect embodiment of everything that I find wonderful about this life. Even doing my timed laps around the block on my Sting-Ray every morning, I had never noticed anyone moving into the house out back behind us, much less that they had a trampoline, or a lot much less that Jane would bounce on it. My hatred of gravity was punctuated by the fact that it would only allow me short glimpses of Jane's face before calling her back down, never failing to notify her long black-brown hair last so it hovered in the air just that much longer, like an echo, before it fluttered below the slats of the brown wooden fence. From that moment on, Jane would be the catalyst for all my ideas, secrets and dreams, never allowing my passions a moment's rest.

The next day, although she was completely unaware of it, Jane became the star of my very first short film. I documented her rhythmic bouncing on an old windup Bolex movie camera that my Grandaddy had confiscated off a criminal and given me—one five-minute shot of the top of my fence with Jane's head appearing at regular intervals. I crawled, completely hidden in the bushes, slowly pulling branches out of the way of the lens.

I kept the film in an old Charles Chips container in my closet along with all my other prized possessions. Either projected on my bedroom wall or out my back window, Jane bounced all through my youth to "The Sounds of Silence."

I don't know how he always knew, but he just did. "Seedlin', get the hell out here." So, out I'd go, straight to the front porch, where my Grandaddy was perched in his lawn chair next to his friend James as always. James was a second Grandaddy of mine, a black man who was born on the bayou about fifty yards down from my Grandaddy and exactly four months after him. They had been best friends and sheriffs together for more than half a century. My Grandaddy looked at me. "What you filmin' back there?"

"Oh, uh nothin' really."

"Well, thing ain't got no zoom-up lens on it, so you want that 'nothing' to be in focus, you gonna have to get closer, hear me? A lot closer." James shifted his big butt in that rickety lawn chair the same way he always did before he spoke. "Ya Grandaddy know."

22

That boy was filming me today so I jumped higher.
  And pretended I didn't notice him.
  Fed Donovan, and then he layed there and watched me paint
in the garage. A lot of purple and orange.

———————

If I couldn't see Jane jumping when I looked out my bed-room window, she was in her garage painting. I knew. Al-ways. And I always went. Jane must've just come from the shower, her wet hair hung tousled and wavy around her face and jumbled down over her olive-tan shoulders to her waist. Watching her through the bushes as she painted, my heart swelled listening to her. She had a beautifully unconscious rendition of "Song Sung Blue" by Neil Diamond. She'd sing a bit and then break off mid-lyric as she considered a brush-stroke or choice of color. On her head she wore big padded black phones whose spiral plug connected her to the old turntable on the concrete floor. She was restricted, and when she'd reach for the darker colors at the far end of her paint palette, the headphones would come unplugged. She would escape for those colors. She would escape the tether of her headphones—even escape music for those colors—whereas I would have escaped colors for music. She'd swirl fresh globs of deepest cobalt blue oil paint into solar yellow. The isolated beauty of each slowly became a rich rainforest green. At times the purple hippie fringe along her sleeve would drag through the paints accidentally, so, unperturbed by the fact of indeli-bly stained clothing, she'd deliberately drag the leather tassels across her canvas, striping it with all colors.

Jane's soundtrack was as constant as mine. As soon as a record ended, she would select another. With her headphones on, I could never tell what song she had selected until she sang a line or two. I would watch her small cupped hand hovering under the brush from her makeshift cinder block pallet that displayed cadmium red, vermillion, lead white in the rainbow spectrum of heavy metals, beside Ball jars of linseed oil and turpentine and other solvents. Jane's voice rang out "The Sounds of Silence," and I always wondered why they hadn't recorded her mellifluous, off-key version. It was my favorite song. Her brush traveled the short distance to the right lower corner of a finished canvas where she signed it: *Jane*. Her left palm held the globule of green, while her brush just kept dipping into her makeshift cup, before finally traveling back up to the canvas to add the word *Two*. *Jane Two*. I looked at my own palm and wondered if the green paint Jane held in her hand would remain in the crevices of her palm to mark Jane's life line and heart line. And how that hand would feel in mine.

Jane was my dream. She defied logic, but it was the faulty logic that came from underestimating my abilities. I now know that real dreams require unreasonable actions, like my Grandaddy always said, and that is why I despise my reasonableness with gusto.

My mom yelled, "Supper!" so I slipped away from the bushes shrouding Jane's garage, back around the block, up Sandpiper to Bentliff, and inside my house. To exist in Jane's presence was all I wished for. I hadn't a clue what I could ever conjure to say to such a unicorn. I walked inside my house for dinner and straight into a fog of the sickening perfume that my sister Lilyth had coated herself with and my mom's cloud of cigarette smoke at the huge chopping block with little drawers that contained postage stamps and paper.

Most nights right before bedtime, Dad would time me with my silver stopwatch racing my bike around the block. I'd relinquish its leather thong from around my neck, and I'd set off on my Schwinn Sting-Ray. Often when I was out at the second corner of the block, I'd see Lilyth smoking with Magda on the far corner. Next morning, before school, same thing—Dad timing my laps and Lilyth out smoking. My red scarf just like Speed Racer's never left my neck and my dad had put an *M* on the front of one of his old racing helmets with red electrical tape. My Sting-Ray was my Mach 5, and I wanted to break a record every single day.

My dad would cheer me on like I was in a tight battle for the lead on the last lap of the Monaco Grand Prix. He would yell to me about braking for the corners, and proper apexing to shave tenths. And he always said that the biggest gains were hidden in the most overlooked areas. He always said that my goal was to improve, whatever the size of the improvement. And above all, to never quit, because *that's not what winners do.* I'd scream by in cutoffs and bare feet, the hot wind pulling at my hair, hoping to shave a tenth or even a couple hundredths of a second. The speed of my progress was less important than the progress itself, so I had to make sure it was always there. There was no rush—even with Jane, I only had to get a little bit closer to her every day. I just couldn't quit. And every day, I hoped Jane would see me as I was screaming by on my Sting-Ray.

I heard my father's words, but I was far too literal as a child. Maybe it was the things I stuck to that kept Jane at a distance. I wish I had understood at a much earlier age all the wonderful things that my Grandaddy told me. It all seeped down from my Grandaddy. And my Grandaddy contradicted just about every sentence from any parenting handbook ever written. He was the only person in my life to ever contest all those lies. He'd say, "Winners *do* quit, ya little seedlin', they quit doing the shit that makes 'em lose," and, "Winning *is* everything, and forget what all those other pansies say, because they don't even know what the goddamn competition is." He told me, "Progress, and progress alone, gonna point to the winner, and without it, ain't gonna be no pointing at all."

Sports defined my absolutes in life. Sports framed a definite game plan. In sports I relied on no one else; the absolutes were clear. For me, sports were straightforward mathematical equations that, if approached with the right work ethic, could almost always guarantee success. It was easy to outwork people who I knew weren't working. But Jane was different. With her, it wasn't just up to me. The uncertainty of love was hard for me to process. I couldn't intentionally bend physics with Jane. But I could with sports.

My Grandaddy showed me my first magic trick of life when I was eight years old—a magic trick that I just had to find a way to apply to Jane. I was sprinting down the sideline of the soccer field during a game against Crestview when I chased after a ball that a teammate had passed to me just a little too hard. The ball was racing out-of-bounds, and my body did something instantaneously that no stopwatch, slide rule, or measuring tape could match. My instincts immediately and accurately calculated that the ball would cross the sideline and out-of-bounds a good two seconds before I could reach it. So, I slowed down. I gave up. I'd heard my Grandaddy say many times that "most people think that they's two possible results for every endeavor, success and failure, but they's wrong. They's three, but only one you gotta be scared of."

My Grandaddy taught me to learn from both success and failure, but he always told me that quitting would affect my life far more than anything else.

At halftime, my Grandaddy walked up to me, and I saw the absolute worst thing that a child can ever see in an elder's eyes.

Disappointment.

Grandaddy told me that he never wanted to see me quit again. He told me to chase every ball out-of-bounds with the true belief that I could keep it in-bounds.

"Even if you eyes is tellin' you that you won't make it, well goddammit, you keep sprinting, 'cause at the very least it will tell all those on the other team that even in the face of certain defeat, *you* gonna keep going. And they gonna know in they heart that they cain't defeat that level of determination. And at the very most, you gonna find that that level of determination gonna bend physics, and you eventually gonna catch that ball."

I had no idea what he was talking about, but I knew I would sprint for every single ball just to avoid my Grandaddy's disappointment.

"Up ta you. You can spend your life checking things off your impossible list, or you can spend it adding things on, but you gonna learn real quick when you find ya self wantin' somethin' you ain't never had. And at *that* moment, you better get goddamn ready ta do something you ain't never done."

As my Grandaddy spoke, Steve McQueen snuggled up next to me shoring up my courage, and the image of Jane bouncing, defying gravity, kept obscuring the image of that soccer ball. From that day on, I never let anyone see me give up on going after a ball headed out-of-bounds. In game after game, I chased every wild ball with a level of focus and intent that I previously couldn't match. Then one day, in a game against Westbury, Clatterbuck passed a ball to me. That ball, by my calculations, would go out-of-bounds about three seconds before I could reach it. The conundrum was that I ended up missing it by only a millisecond. It was at this point that I started believing that I could catch these balls.

Now, I'm the last person alive to believe in any hocuspokery, but this much I do know: Either those balls started to slow down, or I started to speed up. I don't know if they coincidentally started finding a certain patch of grass that held them up just long enough, but I started catching the balls after my usually reliable instinctual calculations had deemed it impossible.

It was on the first day I caught the ball that my internal calculator underwent a correction. It had to recalibrate. Because, of all the criteria that it used to instantly determine success or failure, one crucial thing changed: my belief. You see, up until that first day that I saw my Grandaddy's disappointment, my body was inputting my lack of belief in the equation. My Grandaddy told me that belief can make a liar of your own eyes. But not to worry, he said, "Your eyes gonna catch up. That goalpost gonna move. What was impossible yesterday, but 'came possible today, gonna seem goddamn normal tomorrow. Then, there gonna be a new impossibility in ya life that 'ventually gonna fall under the constant bludgeoning of a certain determination. And once them impossibilities start to fall with practiced regularity, then space and time gonna contort all up, and the noise of life gonna be shrunk up into more a manageable volume. This is when physics gon' bend, and it gon' bend to your will. You gotta believe. Because getting your hand raised only make you a winner in one aspect of life. What *really* count is what you do after the goddamn crowd go home. It ain't ever what you get for puttin' in all the hard work, it's what all the hard work gonna make you become. That's the shit that make you a winner, and you better goddamn believe it, son . . . it's everything."

That boy fell out of a car trunk in his driveway, so I painted a new painting with a lot of blue and listened to 'Sounds of Silence' on my headphones. Finished embroidering one dinner napkin to put in my hope chest. Geraniums in cross-stitch. Mom said 11 more and I will have enough for dinner with all my brothers and mom and dad and invite five friends. But I don't have five. I have my cousin but he's far. And maybe I have another idea but I won't say or then it might not come true. Good night.

I came face-to-face with Jane for the first time when a brainstorm told me to confront my claustrophobia by locking myself in the trunk of my father's car after figuring out how to open it from the inside. I was determined to stay in for ten minutes, and I was halfway through the first five seconds when panic began to set in. My brain was on sabbatical somewhere near the engine compartment, and I couldn't get the latch—whose mechanism I had committed to memory—to be my friend. I imagined that this was what it must be like to be trapped in The Hole. I hollered and yelled as I flailed around in the sauna the trunk had become, when I heard a car pull into our driveway. I heard my sister saying good-bye to Kevin. I knew the engine on his Firebird. I hollered again and Kevin's car revved, so I hollered even louder as tires squealed out the driveway. My sister Lilyth yelled something at me as she passed, but I could make out only the words *re-tard* and *dumbass*. Then she drummed on the trunk and kept right on going into the house, but I could've identified her without even hearing her voice because the smell of a nause-ating new perfume crept inside the trunk to savage me. I had to get out. I thrashed and screamed again in a full panic un-til the latch finally popped open, at which time I burst out, wringing wet from sweat and gasping for clean air, right into a perfect face-plant on the driveway. My sneaker was caught on the latch, so I remained dangling at a bad angle as my eyes adjusted to the sunshine.

Why fortune sent Jane walking home by my front sidewalk on this very day haunted me for decades, but she stood there staring at me from no more than ten feet. Still as a bell in the shadow of my giant bean tree by the sidewalk, Jane was everything. It wasn't until then that I realized that Jane was nothing less than an alien being who had been beamed down for the sole purpose of making a mockery of our female pop-ulation. Her presence caused me to slip into inarticulateness, and after an inordinately long pause, I searched my vocabu-lary for a word while we looked at each other and came up with, well, "Hi" with my laces still twisted around the latch.

Jane looked like she was aware of so much magic that peo-ple haven't yet discovered, like she knew all the secrets. Like she inhabited a secret room walled in velvet, like the lit-tle boxes that expensive jewelry comes in. I bet her velvet was purple. She took a moment, then answered back with an equally if not more gusto-filled "Hi," the only difference being that it was followed—what seemed like three weeks later—with a devastating "Bye." She took a step backwards and then a step forward, as if to wind up a little extra speed before her shadow followed her out from under my giant bean tree . . . and Jane was gone.

———

My mind never left Jane as my mom smoked up a storm next to me while she drove me to school in the Dodge Dart. I hung out the passenger window for air and stared at the houses in various states of disrepair. Most of them had broken-down cars in the driveway and trash. Mom reminded me that my dad wasn't coming home today until after practice, so he'd pick me up from football. The radio knob was broken, so I asked Mom if the guy at the gas station could fix our car radio.

"We'll see, Mickey."

"When's that new school open, Mom?"

"Couple weeks, maybe before Halloween." We pulled up to my school. "And, Mickey, in lieu of me driving you to practice today, Miss Flinch's driving you, so you be sure to tell her thank you for driving. Hear? We won't see her after today."

"Why does Miss Flinch have to go to the new school? She's so nice."

"You'll have a new homeroom teacher, darlin' and I'm sure she'll be just as nice." But I didn't want a new one.

"When can I ride my bike? Everybody else rides their bike."

"You're not everybody else, Sug." My mom patted me lovingly. "And every day a bike gets stolen from this school. We'll see." We stopped in front of the school as kids of all ages filtered in from buses and cars. I hugged my mom good-bye. "Wait, don't you want to take off that—Sug, your scarf!"

I heard her, but I was already committed to a dead sprint toward the front door of Missouri City Elementary School, straight to homeroom, minutes late for my first day. And school or not, I liked to wear it for Speed.

"Okay, Lawrence, you can sit right down, thank you for that poetry," said Miss Flinch to the fat redhead. "And Emmalyne, you're next." Unruffled, Miss Flinch smiled and swept her feathered Farrah Fawcett hair dramatically as she turned to see me enter, out of breath, and gently close the door behind me. I waited at the door for Emmalyne to finish reciting her poem. When Emmalyne was done quoting "The Night Before Christmas" I proceeded to my chair, but my head was immediately jerked to a stop because I had accidentally closed my scarf in the door. About thirty students at folding-top desks gaped back. While my feet had kept going, I was momentarily hanging by my neck. Giggles assailed me. Finally, I was able to right myself. I reached my hands behind my back to open the door and freed my scarf. Breathless, I gently shut the door behind me. I glanced over by the windows and saw the kid with the red crew cut who looked swollen all over. He and his friends had stopped mouthing off and throwing paper airplanes, and just stared. I did my best to hide my embarrassment as I continued on to the last empty chair during a long, uncomfortable silence all the way to the far row by the window.

"Mickey, you're next. So Mickey, make us smile, please," said Miss Flinch.

No sooner had I sat down and escaped the stares and giggles, I had to stand again and start all over. Awkwardly, I disentangled myself from my desk, slowly stood up, and searched my memory banks. The entire class stared at me, awaiting something...then, I blurted out some words about a loon and a balloon, as if the quicker I went the less mortification I would endure. Everyone stared as if I had just spoken a foreign language.

"Oh, it's by T. Rex." I immediately sat down again, willing the teacher to just move on.

The room was utterly silent.

"Who's T. Rex?" blurted the inflated kid who kept fuzzing his red crew cut with the palm of his hand, over by the windows behind me.

"Shut up, Firefly," said Emmalyne.

"Lawrence, did you mean to raise your hand first, dear?" asked Miss Flinch sweetly. Before I could reply to what struck me as a completely stupid question, a voice came from the back of the class, soft as velvet.

"Marc Bolan." And just like that she spoke.

I turned around slowly to find, way in the back...Jane, her raised hand gracefully descending to her lap. She never even looked up after she spoke. I didn't want her to catch me staring, but I couldn't get my eyes to leave her. I wanted to know every detail of her world, and I wanted to start yesterday. Jane was mine—mine alone to translate.

"Who's Marc Bolan?" persisted the loud, fat kid with the red brush-top, Firefly. "He's the singer of a rock group called T. Rex," Miss Flinch replied. Before Firefly could tell me I was a stupid shit, Miss Flinch interjected. "Lawrence, you might've heard 'Bang a Gong (Get It On)' on the radio?"

"That duddn't count!" pouted Firefly.

"Of course it counts," declared Miss Flinch cheerfully, and I sighed in relief. Just at that moment, Jane lifted her eyes and looked right at me with a sliver of a smile. She didn't scan the room and eventually find me. No, she lifted her head, and her eyes came right to me. "Songs are just poetry put to music. Just because it's something you hear..." Miss Flinch kept on explaining somewhere off in the far distance.

It only lasted a moment, and it was gone. Jane sat back there drawing on a sketch pad. She didn't look up again after that. I wanted to know everything about her, and I would've asked if it weren't for the sudden paralysis that gripped my body when I saw her. I hoped it would go away by the time class ended, and that maybe I could follow her down the hall to some place quiet and ask her... about her. But suddenly, another voice slammed into my head, preceded by the smothering stench of mothballs.

"Jane?" Wooden paddle in hand, Mr. Totter stood in the doorway, drab as death, smoke from the cigarette he had just quashed right outside the door shooting from his nostrils as he spoke. Practically bellowing, the principal continued, "Jane, we need to get you through registration and into a homeroom for the people transferring to the new school."

And then Jane just floated out the door without a sound. She glanced back at something very near my desk just as her eyes crossed the doorframe, taking her from my view. I wanted it to have been me. I'm almost positive that other things happened that day, but I don't remember any.

Jane mattered, and I knew she contained a lot of things I needed. That night I sent her a letter. With care, I put it in my favorite mailbox on the corner of Bentliff Street and Sandpiper Drive, where the two intersected before Sandpiper curved around in a ninety-degree dogleg that eventually posed Jane's house directly behind mine. I looked at that mailbox every day on my way to school because it was tilted, and one of its four legs was bent inward at a weird forty-five-degree angle so it almost looked like it was dancing... or dying. But I'd always chosen dancing. I'd never seen a happier mailbox. And my Grandaddy had always said that happiness is the only magic in the world. That mailbox had to be magic. I patted the happy, federal blue box as I fed it and thought that Jane's unicorn magic might even mend its leg if it delivered my letter. Even though I deliberately sent it to the wrong address, I hoped for Grace to stand and deliver. I hadn't a leg to stand on, really, but I reasoned The Dancing Mailbox had three.

Chapter Three

S ome might say it was cowardly of me to send Jane's letter to a pretend address. At the time, it was a magic precaution that, with time, just sort of stuck. But there comes a time in every young dude's life when he's got to reach down between his legs and see if there's actually anything down there—anything that'll make him realize that there might just be something that's more important than what he's afraid of. That night, at my Grandaddy's behest, I reached down. After that utterance from Jane in Miss Flinch's homeroom—after I'd almost hanged myself by my red scarf caught in that damn door right in front of Jane. I'd ride a wheelie on my Schwinn Sting-Ray every night when I rode past her house, and not once did I ever see her watching me. But if ever I slipped and let my real self out, she was there to see me in all my ordinariness. The "me" that only I knew. The "me" that locked myself in my dad's trunk. She saw a lot of those moments that contained the type of humiliation that only tenure can cure. That first day of school, I had just gotten back from football practice and raced out of my Grandaddy and Mamau's Cadillac Coupe de Ville because it turned out Dad had to work late again. Mamau smooched me, told me to stay off the concrete, and promised me her best fried chicken, like every time they visited.

"Goldie, goddammit, stop flappin' y'jaws and waggin' y'tongue and let that boy go play. He ain't no sissy, woman!" And with that, he went to join James, who was already in his lawn chair and waiting for my Grandaddy.

"Y'all gon' be the death of me, Charlie." Mamau straightened up to face him with her usual worried pout, but her eyes were full of amusement and she squeezed my face before she let me out of her mother-bear embrace.

I ran under my giant bean tree and across the street, past an orange VW Vanagon parked in our neighborhood, and over to Trent's front yard, where I could play more football, because in Texas there is no such thing as too much football. So I joined in on a game with twelve or so local boys and my tomboy neighbor Kim on the sideline, who always begged to play but who no self-respecting Texas boy would tackle on account of her being a girl. The gang was already playing "tackle the man with the ball." Mr. and Mrs. Milan were sitting right next door to Trent's, holding hands, watching from their Kmart aluminum lawn chairs on their manicured grass. They didn't seem to mind if our tackles spilled over onto their lawn, which Mr. Milan kept so nice. They didn't have any kids of their own. So when we did tumble over and tussle on his grass—which was always remarkably softer than Trent's scrubby lawn—Mr. Milan would laugh and cheer and raise his can of Miller to us and take another swig, then lean over and kiss Mrs. Milan. I really liked them. And their smiles told me more than our handful of conversations ever could. My Grandaddy said they were "good folk," and that was enough for me.

Back then there was no such thing as flag football, except when the cheerleaders would play their annual game of "girl-ball." There was only one kind of football, and that was full contact. No one wore pads, and we tried, sometimes very successfully, to hold off tackling a guy until he was right on the sidewalk for added pain and lacerations. The goal of the game was to get the ball and scramble around for as long as you could until you got tackled or stripped of the ball. Most of the kids were older than me, and all were bigger. I did have one thing in my favor, and that was speed. While collision presented a fairly big problem due to my size, collision avoidance was easier for me.

It wasn't long before I scooped up a fumble and eluded my pursuers. On my third or fourth lap around the yard, with my bigger pursuers running out of diesel, Eddy—who was ten at the time—reached up just as I screamed past him and grabbed a handful of hair on the back of my head. My upper body stopped right in its tracks, while my legs and lower body flew out from underneath me until I was completely horizontal before slamming to the sidewalk. My head hit the concrete first and I was dazed for a moment.

Now this sort of completely illegal way of bringing an opponent to the ground was always frowned upon, and even had a name. It was called "red-necking." It was like clothes-lining, only with a fistful of hair. I got up off the ground with tears in my eyes and told Eddy that that was "no fair" and not to do it again. He just laughed at me for crying and told me to shut up. Every part of my body was willing the tears to creep back up my cheeks and into my sockets again, but I could already taste them.

"There's a hardheaded boy, Mickey!" hollered Mr. Milan

encouragingly over his potbelly as I ran home past him and Mrs. Milan, the orange Vanagon in my way, and my bean tree. When I ran crying all the way up to my front door, I smelled Grandaddy's Pinaud French men's powder as I was rounding the hedges to go inside. From the front step right behind a row of bushes, he had been watching Eddy's battery and bullying play out. After I explained what he had already seen, I learned exactly the correct way to deal with this same situation when I would someday be a father. My Grandaddy didn't march over there and give Eddy an earful of, "don't treat my grandson that way" crap. What he did was this: He simply wiped my eyes with one giant, scarred knuckle, told me he'd give me a one-time profanity exemption and to go back over there, look Eddy right in the eye, hold my trigger finger an inch away from his nose and say, "If you do that again, I'll crack you in the fuckin' face." I heard James shifting, still in his lawn chair, muttering, "Uh-huh, you tell dat granbabby."

My Grandaddy then held up the calloused palms of his hands, his life line so deeply visible despite the calluses, and let me throw a couple combinations at his hands. It was a crash course in boxing right there on my front step. After my quick lesson in fighting and philosophy from Grandaddy, I marched under my bean tree, back across the street past the orange Vanagon with the fluttery little curtains in the back window, past the Milans, and right up to Eddy. I pointed my tiny trigger almost straight up his nose, as I was a head shorter than he, and said exactly what my Grandaddy had told me, minus the "fuckin'." I don't know why I left that part out, but it just didn't seem right in front of the Milans. Eddy giggled and walked away calling me a crybaby. Although most of the kids there were my friends, no one stood up for me since

Eddy was the biggest kid in the neighborhood. He usually got away with picking on whomever he wished undeterred, because all the parents thought he had this squeaky-clean persona like Eddie Haskell, the kid in "Leave It to Beaver." Like you'd expect him to come out and say, "Hi, Mr. Cleaver," all polite and polished.

That day, the only adults who knew what a shit Eddy was were Mr. and Mrs. Milan and my Grandaddy. The game resumed and I soon found my opportunity, grabbed a loose ball, and swept right past Eddy knowing that he couldn't catch or reach me unless he grabbed a handful of my hair again. Well, he did just that. This time I was dragged back to the ground with a patch of hair missing, leaving a bloody mottled spot right behind my right ear. Immediately, I started crying again.

"I told you not to do that again, Eddy!" I wailed.

"Or what, you pussy?" I wanted to know what my *or what* was, but I just didn't.

You see, there comes a time in every kid's life when he either starts on a path of responsibility and self-sufficiency, or becomes just that—a pussy. And what did I do? I ran home crying again. And my Grandaddy was right where I had left him, looking through the ficus bushes. He checked out my head and wiped the blood off with his kerchief this time.

"Y'want me t'go over there?" A question whose tone translated to: *What the hell kind of a man will you end up becoming?* Although I knew my own dad would have gone over there if I wanted him to, my Grandaddy never would. I could see in his eyes what needed to be done, and I answered without flinching.

"No, sir."

"Time you tell 'im how ta pull out tha' nigger-cock," said James in between sips of his Miller pony.

"Now you hush that, Jame', it too early." But I had to know. And so he told me.

Finally, I asked Grandaddy to hold up his hands again, took another couple swings, and headed back across the street. This time I couldn't hold back the tears. There was nothing "macho" about this. I was petrified. Again, I walked past the orange VW Vanagon, then on past Mr. and Mrs. Milan—on the edge of their lawn chairs now, holding hands, Mr. Milan clapping his Miller can on the aluminum chair arm and hollering, "Go get 'em," at me—and up to Eddy, pointing right in his face and delivering the exact same line as before. But this time, I took my Grandaddy's PE. I couldn't help it. That *fuckin'* just became necessary, and no other word could've replaced it. Eddy slapped my hand away and giggled. I looked over my shoulder to see if Grandaddy was there, but I couldn't see through the bushes. I turned back to Eddy.

"Let's play," I said, trying to sound as tough as I could between sniffles.

"Start running, pussy," sniggered Eddy, and then he Joe Namath'd a spiral right into my chest, which I surprisingly caught without getting the wind knocked out of me.

At this point I had overestimated Eddy's speed, because he was nowhere near me. So I immediately turned around and ran right past him again. Without hesitation, he grabbed a handful of hair from the back of my head and leveled me onto the ground. Now, the image of what happened next will be tack-sharp in my memory forever, because I saw a Picasso-esque portrait of the definition of false bravado. I yanked Eddy's hand off of my head before I even hit the ground, sprang back to my feet immediately, and turned to face him. The purity of the venomous rage displayed on my face turned his laughter and finger-pointing instantly into him running the hell away from me. It only took me a couple milliseconds to catch that lunking tub of shit and tackle him right there on the sidewalk. I straddled Eddy, forgetting every single punch my Grandaddy had shown me, and proceeded to hammer-fist him in the face until his nose completely exploded. He was screaming and crying and flailing his arms as I was beating him with the pinkie sides of my fists. I was so enraged that I was bawling my eyes out while bludgeoning this kid.

I heard Mr. Milan yelling, "That's enough, boys" and my Grandaddy echoing him, but swearing his head off. Grandaddy spoke Cajun, the Frenglish ghetto talk of the bayou.

The next thing I knew, I was swept up into the air with my arms still pinwheeling wildly but connecting with nothing. My Grandaddy had watched, then lumbered across the street to stop the fight before it got uglier. When we got back home and I finally stopped crying, he tried to teach me the difference between standing up for myself and actually maiming someone. However, in my freshly released fury, I could tell no difference.

When I finally stopped heaving and sobbing, and at my Grandaddy's request went back outside, I walked across the street to apologize to everybody for having lost my temper. Now, I had seen the look on all their faces every single time I walked back across the street after having been run off by Eddy, but this time was different. What I saw in their eyes this time was completely different. They saw me as a different person. The same way adults view others who stand up for themselves, ones who don't suffer fools gladly. That evening, there was only one person who could solve my problem right then and there, and that was me. No words to Eddy from my Grandaddy would've done anything except make him a bigger bully next time. And yes, it's a shame that bullying happens, but it exists, so my Grandaddy taught me to deal with it head-on, and with a fist, right between the eyes.

That evening changed the trajectory of my life. It was that cathartic moment. It's a moment in life when a boy reaches down and either finds balls, or he finds a useless, generic, Barbie-and-Ken-smooth plastic bulge. Blood was shed that day, but sometimes blood needs to be shed. I'm a better man, and so is Eddy. I guess it was Grandaddy's way of kicking me off the teat. I had clung too long, and that was the dawning of self-sufficiency. It was that very day I reached down there and I was lucky enough, thanks to my Grandaddy, to find two solid rocks. Well, I was only a kid, so maybe they were more like pebbles, but they were there, right where they were supposed to be. That very next Sunday, Mr. and Mrs. Milan, fingers intertwined, drank Miller beer with their free hands, kissing and smiling to each other as they witnessed the front-row drama unfold.

"There's my soldier!" bellowed Mr. Milan.

I was chosen to be a team captain and got first pick for my team in Trent's front yard. My first draft choice? Eddy, who is still a dear friend today.

Over the years, I lost count of how many times I got knocked down and dazed. But every time, I'd get up and dust off and keep going. I was the youngest on the team, and still the smallest, but almost always the fastest. Flat on my back, I'd stare up through the grille of my football helmet into the faces of my teammates all suited up for football and looking down at me.

"I think he's dead," Firefly would announce, picking his nose right above my face. "It looks like he got flattened by a T. rex!"

"He ain't dead. Practice ain't over till we're all off the field. Off yer ass, son! Tell you one thing, Tommy wouldn't have been caught like that. We need some more 'Tommy speed' on this team's what we need," said our head coach Gasconade, eyeballing my Grandaddy disapprovingly as Grandaddy lit up a cigarette and yelled "off the field" through a puff of smoke, his neck muscles flexing powerful as a dragon.

On the days he was able to be at practice helping out, my Grandaddy never played favorites and worked me even harder than the other boys on the team, but Coach Gasconade directed every play around Tommy. Cars and parents awaited their sons returning from battle on the turf, a cluster of eight fields that served both football and baseball, depending on the season. On the other side of a winding four-foot hurricane fence was a border of trees that marked a stone-hard mud crevice in the ground—that crevice was The Hole.

As I dusted off, I looked over at the only field that still held a baseball diamond where a red Firebird was idling, driving in a circle. On its roof sat Kevin, looking right at me with his left leg hanging through the open driver's window, nonchalantly steering his car with his foot and smoking while his other foot dangled over the windshield of his bright red trophy. Kevin stared at me like he had known me my whole life—like he simultaneously approved and disapproved of everything that I was. Kevin was a mystery, with his wild blond hair, wild eyes, wild manner, and wild outlook on life.

"I tell ya something, we do anything this season, we gonna need more speed in the backfield than just Tommy," echoed Grandaddy's assistant coach, Lew Hoagie, stewed as usual, swilling a Miller out of a can wrapped in a Styrofoam koozie and smoking with the other hand near my dad's car. On Lew's army fatigues shirt lapel he still bore his Purple Heart and Bronze Star Vietnam War medals.

"Faster'n a greased pig in shit, that kid a yours, Paul. Always right behind Tommy on laps, but I be damn if he don't look a lot faster'n him during play," bellowed Lew, even though he was right near my dad. But I knew Tommy was the fastest.

Grandaddy kept right on yelling at the boys like a drill sergeant to get the hell off the goddamn field already so the older boys could get on it to practice. Twenty-one guys stampeded off that field like Texas longhorns, but one of them inexplicably never came back for more football. I never understood why some kids would try football for a couple days and then choose not to play. These kids were aliens to me. The twenty teammates who did return, I knew—these guys always had my back, these guys were my protectors, my tribe. But right now, they scattered straight off the field, straight past their parents, straight to watch the girls' drill team practice. Jane wasn't on the drill team, so I ran over to hug my dad, who'd come right after work. Chewing the fat with Lew, Dad kept his distance since Lew practically had sour beer draining out his pores in the humidity. Lew set up with one foot on the bumper of Dad's green '72 Ford Gran Torino.

"Lew says you did great!" Dad picked me up.

Lew confirmed that I ran like hell and that the Red Devils wouldn't be undefeated for long if only more of our boys could keep up with Tommy.

I pointed at Lew's crotch.

"Mr. Hoagie, your balls are hangin' out."

Lew didn't even look down—not that he could've seen over his paunch anyway—and I doubt he even knew that his chicken legs no longer matched his barrel chest. Lew reached down to the hem of his too-short denim cutoffs and gave a squeeze to confirm.

"So they are. Forecast must be for rain." With that new information, Lew scanned the clouds, as his two war medals glistened in the simmering heat. My dad chuckled.

Lew glanced over his tinted cop glasses at the boys taunting the girls on the adjacent field. "Look at 'em, chasin' tail already. How come you ain't a tail chaser, Mickey?" I had no idea what Lew was talking about.

"Mickey ain't no champ, Lew!" Grandaddy had overheard Lew and yelled back across the field.

"That's enough about that, fellas," my dad cut in and ushered me to the car.

"I know he ain't a champ, Charlie! I meant no disrespect," Lew yelled back across the field. "But nowadays, y'cain't be too careful, what with all them *bi*sexual rock stars leadin' our young'ns astray."

"*Bi*sexuals?! Now we gotta worry 'bout champs AND *bi*sexuals?!" yelled Grandaddy right back across the field. "Shit, I ain't even got enough time in my day to be heterosexual with m'woman, how the hell them poofters got time in they day t'be *bi*sexual? They must get nothin' done."

"Done! I'll tell you what they get done. They get..."

"Lew! Your balls are hangin' out!" Dad interrupted deliberately to shut down their conversation in front of me.

"Look to the sky, fellers! I'm tellin you, he's gonna pee on us!" Lew yelled back.

I straddled the Gran Torino's center console. Dad had let me drive ever since I could see over the dash. He got in beside me, ordering eyes on the road as I jabbed the radio button.

"Fly the airplane, don't let it fly you," said Dad sternly.

We got out on the road to home, but my dad always slowed down a bit when I steered, so faster drivers were held up impatiently behind me.

"Hey, Dad, what's chasin' tail?"

"Oh, it's just Lew's way of sayin' chasing girls."

"Free Bird" came on the radio just as Dad yelled out the window at a red Firebird blazing past us in the parking lane, right up close to the Gran Torino's passenger door. "Goddamn drug uh-dikt, Kevin!" When Dad swore, it was like my Grandaddy. They called it taking a PE, Profanity Exemption—a well-placed and excusable piece of profanity used to achieve what no other nonprofane word could. Lightning struck nearby, accompanied by an instantaneous thunderclap. The flash was so severe that Kevin's bright red Firebird paled to a soft pink, and a slash of deep blue paint became visible across the left rear bumper.

"Dad, how come Mr. Hoagie wears his army medals to practice, and Grandaddy and you don't wear your medals?"

"I guess it reminds Lew he done something with his life. He's a war hero for sure, son, and he's a fine football coach. But your Grandaddy and I, we like to focus on making more new great things, not live in the past like Lew, restin' on his mighty impressive laurels." Dad got quiet. Steam came off the hood when bloated Texas raindrops hit the car, and water spewed down the windshield as Dad told me to keep my eyes on the goddamn road or he'd take the wheel.

"Dad, how do Mr. Hoagie's balls know when it's gonna rain?"

"Not at the table, son," said Dad, noticing Mom's look of mock horror as she sat down with us at our little white kitchen table.

I devoured my mom's charred macaroni and cheese, especially after practice. I didn't know any better and she's from Louisiana, so Cajun was her excuse. I shoveled mouthfuls, and Dad pretended to take bites of his as he ambled through the kitchen door into the garage with the excuse that he had to shut the garage door, only to leave his bowl hidden under the back bumper of his '58 British racing green MGA.

"Genie, that was delicious, darlin'. Mic, get out here!" called Dad. My eyes adjusted to the dark garage, and I stretched deep into the foot well to reach the pedals. "Now, rev it, Mic!"

Looking so pretty, Mom watched Dad under the hood tinkering with his race car engine, so she didn't notice Steve McQueen's Velveeta mustache or Dad's empty bowl. As Dad was leaning under the hood, Steve's ears perked up and he came over to whine at me. Dogs hear shit. Moments later, Mom, Dad, and I heard it, too. Tires screeched as the garage door imploded at us, splintering its center, crumpling in about a foot and a half with a sound like a shotgun blast.

"What the goddamn...?", Dad's head popped out from under the hood.

With the garage door now inoperable, Mom, Steve McQueen, and I followed Dad as he raged back through the kitchen and out the front door to the driveway to find a mop of blond hair intertwined with a sheaf of feathered brown inside a red Firebird now coupled intimately with our garage door. Oblivious, Kevin and Lilyth were making out in the front seat of Kevin's '73 Firebird SD-455. Lilyth's puckered tube top was somewhere down around her patched bell-bottoms. Speechless, Mom started to cry. Dad shook his head in disgust as he slowly surveyed the impaled Firebird. The crossbeam of the garage door was wedged into the grille, and a fan belt let out a shrieking whine. Skynyrd's "Free Bird" blared so loud on Kevin's eight-track that he and Lilyth didn't hear Dad coming. Even after Dad yanked open the door, they didn't notice him, so he popped out the eight-track, chucked it on the ground, and stood back away from the pall of marijuana smoke that poured from the car along with whatever perfume Lilyth had marinated herself in that day. Still no reaction.

Then my dad got furious.

Dad dragged Kevin out by the head, cussing over Lilyth's sudden screaming, and threw him facedown on our driveway. Though years later Lilyth claimed she tried to get Kevin to leave before Mom and Dad saw them, I don't believe she ever cared. Then everything got more intense really fast and I was sent into the house, but I sneaked into the garage through the kitchen and peered out through the fresh gap in the garage door.

Lilyth and Mom were still crying, for different reasons. Dad was circling the Firebird, where Kevin had fled back to the safety of his roof and sat with his left leg dangling through the open window, his foot on the steering wheel.

"What the hell is wrong with you, boy? Look what you did to my goddamn garage door," my dad yelled.

Kevin just looked right through my dad and then back to the garage door before replying, "But look at what your door did to my car, man. I think it was a fair fight. I never wanted them to fight, but they just kept getting closer and closer, and I knew I wouldn't be able to stop them." Kevin rambled on, "But I think it's over now, don't you? I think they'll get along great now." Over Dad's shoulder, Kevin saw me peeking out through the gash in the garage door and winked at me. Dad's temper lost its leash. "Hey, be cool, man," Kevin said calmly to my dad, as Dad yanked Kevin off the roof of the car and viciously open-palmed him right across the face.

Then Dad looked Kevin right in the eye, just the way he learned it from Grandaddy. "Now you listen to me, son. You do whatever you want, whenever you want, with whatever drug you want. But the minute I find you doing any of that shit with my daughter, I will walk you quietly down the hall to my bathroom and drown you right there in the goddamn bathtub. Is that clear?"

"Damn."

"Don't you 'DAMN' me, boy! Now you can go wait on the curb, and I'll call you a cab." Dad turned to Lilyth to say, "Your mother and I have trusted you with a considerable amount of freedom with the Pied Piper here behind the wheel." Meanwhile, Kevin leapt back into his sanctuary, smoked the tires backing up, and fishtailed that Firebird the hell down Bentliff Street. Swerving as the splintered two-by-four led the Firebird like a jouster's lance, Kevin accelerated and Lilyth continued to sob long after he disappeared around the corner.

As my dad's car pulled up to the field the next day for my football game, I saw Kevin's car parked just past the end zone, The Plank still stuck in his grille. Although I couldn't explain Kevin to myself, I always wanted to. He was perched on the Firebird roof again, just staring, transfixed at the bench on the opposing sideline. My dad took a PE and let out a *goddamn drug uh-dikt* as I got out of the car and headed over to my team on the sideline.

For each game, we were always to line up on the bench in numerical order according to our jersey number, and mine was the only spot that remained vacant. I was 24. I crossed the field, still looking over at Kevin, wondering what went on in his mind, and wondering what he was staring at so intently. As I arrived at my place on that bench, I finally saw what Kevin was staring at. I took my place and sat directly in his sight line. As if he was expecting me, he pulled a grin so small that I could hardly make it out, and he threw up the peace sign. I looked behind me to see if he was looking at someone or something else, and when I turned back he was pointing right at me and mouthed the word *you*. He held my gaze and after a moment threw both his arms into the air as a referee would to indicate a touchdown. Still unsure who Kevin was gesturing to, I glanced behind me, but there was no one.

"Hey, where the hell you at, boy?" I heard Coach Gasconade yell. "Had a talk with your Grandaddy Charlie, and he tell me he watch you in the neighbor's yard and that you got a hell of an open field run, and that you a lot faster'n even *you* think. That true?"

"Um, I think I'm pretty fast, sir," I said.

"You faster'n my son, Tommy?" he asked.

"Well, no, sir, but I think everybody except him."

"Well, this is one your Grandaddy wanted me to ask you, so why you think you ain't faster'n Tommy?" he asked, a touch of smugness in his voice.

"Because he's the fastest on the team," I replied.

"How you know he's the fastest? 'Cause your Grandaddy don't seem to think so."

This was the first time that I actually thought about how I'd come to this very limiting conclusion. I told Coach Gasconade that I recalled that on the first day of practice starting back when we were in the peewees at age six, Coach Gasconade had told the whole team that Tommy was the fastest, and for us all to do our best to keep up with him when we do laps or sprints. And I had. I had always kept up with Tommy. Up until that moment, it never occurred to me that Tommy might have been going as fast as he possibly could. And if he was, he was a fucking slug.

"I guess I always just did what you said, Coach, and I kept up with him. Never tried to beat him 'cause I figured he had a lot more speed in reserve than even I did. 'Cause you told me he was the fastest on the team."

Coach Gasconade just looked at me in complete dismay, like my Grandaddy's look of disappointment, and I cringed. It seemed like something was sparking in Coach Gasconade's head, like maybe he'd overlooked something, and he pulled out his stopwatch and called Tommy to the fifty-yard line right in front of the bench. He sent Tommy down and back, and then called me to the very same line. Down and back, and then I took my same place on the bench. All the while,

Kevin still kept on staring at me as I heard the coach confer with Lew, nursing his beer on the sidelines.

Coach Gasconade's tongue circled his teeth behind his clenched lips as he stared down at that stopwatch in his hands, slowly shaking his head before slowly looking up at Tommy and casting that god-awful look of disappointment upon his son.

"Okay, new man on kickoff return, and he gonna be joining Tommy in the backfield. 'Tween the two of you, we might just have a shot against these Yellow Jackets."

As the Yellow Jackets assembled on the other side of the field after their warm-up, I saw Kevin still sitting and staring, The Plank from our garage door jutting out of his Firebird. I stared until Jane walked right in front of it, but just as quickly as she appeared, she was gone. She seemed to escape during my blinks. I recalibrated, tracking her every possible move in my peripheral vision. Her next likely resurface at her current speed would be the bleachers. I estimated it would take her fifteen seconds to surface from the crowd and climb the stands into full view. But instead, she appeared in ten seconds on the opposite side of the stands. She tended to warp all my processes that I fell back on to calculate time, speed, arrival, and general physics. All of my best tools and abilities seemed to run and hide in her presence.

I took my first kickoff that day and wound around my pursuers just like I was running into the Milans' front yard. I found my way to the sideline and started pulling away from all the Yellow Jackets, heading straight for the end zone. As they drifted farther behind, I quit looking over my shoulder—and that's when I saw her. Her bright yellow sundress almost stopped me in my tracks; it was the exact same shade as my pursuers. That color should've slowed me down, but it just pulled me faster and faster. She was sitting in an aluminum lawn chair with green and yellow webbing right next to her dad just outside the end zone. In that moment, I wished I had had a quarterback's face mask on my helmet, so she could see clearly who I was. I wanted her to know that *this* was me, and not the kid who nearly hanged himself by his red scarf in class. I wanted her to know *this* me. I wanted her to know that number 24, who was racing toward the end zone, lived right across the ditch flanked by our fences. As I approached the goal line, she slowly stood up from her chair, toppling it over behind her, with her hands clasped as if in prayer. And as I entered the end zone, she was hugging herself and bouncing up and down off her heels. I wanted to stare at her forever as I slowed down to a stop directly under the goalpost, but I also wanted her to see the name on the back of my jersey. I prayed for my prayer to race past hers and get up there first, for her to know everything that I felt about her. I didn't know what she was asking for, but I didn't want it to divert attention away from what I wanted her to know. I gently placed the ball on the ground, just the way my Grandaddy had told me to.

I had never scored a touchdown in a game before, but my Grandaddy had told me exactly what to do when I did. He told me to never spike the ball, or do any goddamn jig in the end zone when you score.

"Nope," he said. "You just politely hand the ball to the ref or gently set it under the uprights and walk away, like you goddamn *expected* that shit to happen. Jigs are for people who surprised themselves. You gonna score, boy. I'm telling you right now, so no need to be surprised when it happens. And when they see that even you ain't surprised, they'll know that you can do it again and again. I ain't surprised by the greatness in you, 'cause me and your daddy the ones that put it in there." He knew more about me than even I did. And I guess it made sense. After all, like my Grandaddy used to say to me, "The only reason you ain't a rattlesnake is that you momma and daddy ain't rattlesnakes."

I took as much time as I could placing the ball on the ground and had a wonderful plan to nonchalantly swing around and jog back to the bench, giving Jane ample time to read my name in bold print across my shoulder blades—but then I got hit by the first wave of my celebrating teammates. The impact took my breath away, *far* away. I went down hard as they all piled on top of me to celebrate. I was underneath our entire team in a complete panic, trying to collect a lungful of air and not lose sight of Jane in her beautiful yellow dress. I don't know if it was the claustrophobia or the fact that my lungs were completely compressed by fifteen teammates, but I lost consciousness. I woke up on the sideline with my Grandaddy staring through my face mask.

I wondered both where Jane had gone, and how Kevin had known. I needed Jane to know things about me—everything, in fact. I wanted her to know that I was the one who scored, but to forget that I was also the one who got knocked unconscious. I wanted to explain to Jane how I was flat-footed and knock-kneed from age three to seven, but that I was still really fast. And that I was dyslexic from kindergarten through third grade, but that I was still smarter than they knew. I wanted her to know that I got put in the slow class and had to wear clunky corrective "dress-style" shoes but that I was still pretty damn good at sports. I wanted her to see that I *had* to wear those shoes and not that I chose to. They weren't the ones with metal braces, but still, they were hideously embarrassing to me. I always wanted Levi's and Converse sneakers, but they didn't sell them at Sears, and you couldn't put them on layaway. I wanted her to know that when I wrote *yekciM*, and my mom got scared and started crying, that I wasn't scared at all. And that I knew the doctor was an idiot when he suggested a special school and to not expect much academically from me. I believed I was fine. I knew it. Shit, I could write everything and anything not only frontwards, but backwards as well. Simultaneous inversion, that was my normal. I wanted so badly to tell Jane that although they placed me with the special needs kids in level four, I was smart. I just needed her to understand, in case she knew about my level four.

In case she'd seen or heard, because the principal insisted on keeping the level four door open all the time—*lest there be an incident*—so you'd see who was "in the dummies," as the kids called it. My comprehension was fine. I just transposed letters. I wanted Jane to know that I scored better than most in everything when it was discussed verbally, and that my eyes were just giving my brain faulty information. My calculator was accurate. I just needed to relabel my keys. I was mortified when I'd have to go to that "special room" with huge windows for thirty minutes every day before lunch to do a mix of body mechanics, visual, and reprogramming exercises. I wanted her to know that I dreaded those thirty minutes, when the entire school would walk by the windows of that fucking room heading for lunch, and see me lying on the floor staring at a ball swinging back and forth from the ceiling to reset my brain while a nurse with a pencil doodled on her paper and I tried to mute out everything around me.

The public display and remarks like, "Oh, Mickey's got dyslexia," petered out, and didn't really bother me because I knew in my gut that I was good and good at stuff. I wanted Jane to know that I may have had a pang of angst about it off and on, but generally I'd ignore most of it. Just like I felt in my gut that I might be faster than Tommy. It hadn't yet occurred to me to beat him because I was only ever told to keep up with him. I was taught to be respectful when adults said *this is how it is*. I was obedient, and so very literal. I didn't actually know for sure if I could beat Tommy, because I hadn't tried to do it. In fact, I accepted his entitlement as faster, since the coaches had always said that Tommy was the fastest on the team. I just figured he wasn't really going as fast as he could truly go when we ran at practice. I figured they knew something I didn't. I figured Tommy was faster than me because Coach Gasconade had said so since I was six years old. And I wanted Jane to know for certain that that was the very last time I would ever let someone else tell me who I was.

Our next game was a rivalry against the Angleton Red Devils. As we did at the start of every game, we were all to stand in a line, helmets off and over our hearts, facing the opposing team about five feet in front of us. I scanned the crowd for Jane, but couldn't find her anywhere. I took my helmet off and covered my heart as every other player had—except one. The Red Devil directly across from me stood there with his helmet still on and his hands on his hips as our national anthem began to play. My dad and my Grandaddy had both served in the military, so not removing a cover for our anthem was not an option that I had ever been made aware of.

"Hey, you gotta take your helmet off," I said.

"Shut up faggit," came back.

I truly couldn't believe what I was hearing, looking to the benches to see if anyone else was as shocked as I was. Not that the Devil had called me a faggit, but that his helmet was still on. I wondered if anyone was going to do something. I wondered if they would stop the national anthem and have him remove it before starting it again. It was how I was raised. Not removing your lid was anathema to my values.

"Hey, take it off right now," I told him.

"Duddn't concern you, fuckin' fag," he shot back.

No one was going to do anything about this kid. I placed my helmet on the ground, approached the Devil, grabbed his helmet, and started to assist him in its removal. Initially, he resisted, and everyone in the stands stood up for what threatened to be a two-team brawl. Both lines started to break up and move around like they were preparing for a fight, when I finally got that helmet off. Coach Gasconade yelled to get back in line, everybody obeyed, and I went right back in line and picked up my helmet as everyone else resumed the proper formation, palms over their hearts.

When the anthem ended, I turned to go on back to my place on the bench, when the Red Devil kid clubbed me in the back of my head with his helmet. I dropped like a stone right there on my ass, dazed. As I was flat out on the ground and still gathering my wits, Grandaddy approached, breathing smoke, and my Mamau was yelling from the bleachers at Grandaddy to sit down, he'd get himself a heart attack, and Grandaddy yelled back that he ain't sitting down ever, woman, in the name of justice.

Then other coaches and parents started yelling, and a brawl ensued. That is to say, all the coaches and parents from the opposing sides came running off the bleachers cursing onto the field, pulling players apart, yelling about what's right and who had offended whom first, all manner of *what-in-hell-about-our-Great-Nation-goddammit.*

I heard Coach Lew keening above the din, "Get her mitts off my goddamn medals!" Lew was gnashing and frothing to shield his Purple Heart and Bronze Star.

My parents reprimanded me, and Grandaddy sent everybody back to the stands when he signaled to James to blast the bullhorn, yelling, "Game on." James's horn was deafening and Lew hit the turf, shielding his head with his arms. When people had gone back to their seats on the bleachers, Grandaddy gave Coach Lew a gentle boot in his side to get with it, and Lew sprang to his feet, looking around to see if anyone had noticed his fit of panic. Then Grandaddy walked to the center of the field where I was finally getting up on all fours and picked me up with one hand by the center of my shoulder pads, nose to nose, dangling me like a whelp for everyone to see. From afar, with his big trigger finger pointing right at my nose, it must've appeared aggressive, like my Grandaddy was reprimanding me. Sometimes there was a difference in what my Grandaddy spoke and what he meant, and sometimes there wasn't. But up close where only I could hear him, my Grandaddy always shared The Law.

"Don't you ever let me see you pick a fight with a little mouse-pussied fucker like that, but goddammit I'm proud of you, son. Ain't the right thing to do, but sometime you gonna see ya Grandaddy being proud of you fer doing the wrong thing. 'Fore you older, you gonna know the difference. I'll see to it. More recipe for my great-granbabbies. This part of the Boudin, so listen to me, boy. Just for today, I'm a let you pick any position you wanna play. So, you tell me...where you wanna be?" I blinked back at my Grandaddy as I saw James slowly making his way toward us, and again I knew what needed to be done...and it was the same thing that I wanted to be done. I told him, "I wanna play directly opposite of whatever position that little mouse-pussied fucker's playin'." My Grandaddy stared into my eyes until I saw the tiniest grin escape his face. He said, "Now don't you tell ya Mamau, but ya Grandaddy gonna give you a PE on that one, 'cause that Devil *is* a little pussy. Okay, you see that piece'a shit on the field, you find him, line up opposite, and you crack him hard. So hard he remember that crack. You follow that little pussy even if he change positions till he leave the field. I love you, son. Now let's show 'em who we are."

Grandaddy set me down, fire in his eyes, and yelled for the game to start just as James arrived. He stopped right in front of me and hacked something huge into his mouth from his lungs, then swished it around in his mouth before finally spitting it onto the field. "Nigger-cock, unnastand?" And I did.

I played a position that I'd never played before just to line up across from that Devil—downs that involved me completely disregarding the action at hand and solely focusing on cracking that little pussy as hard as I could. He was on the field a total of six plays that day, and spent the remainder of the game on the bench.

"Hey, you all right?" Lew Hoagie was extending his hand down to me, flashing a clear prediction of more rain.

Albeit covered in mud, I had padding and a helmet. Back then no one was too concerned about concussions unless you were dead on the football field. I lay down on the bench every time the other side had the ball, and held ice on my head.

The scoreboard read *Angleton Red Devils 35, Braeburn Bears 0*, and parents and spectators were hooting and hollering all around at this possible shutout. Lew dragged me into the huddle around Grandaddy and Coach Gasconade, my Grandaddy sending smoke signals with the cigarette and toothpick, a little bonfire dangling from his lips.

"Listen up, ya little shits! We've got about a minute and a half left in this season, so we ain't gonna win this one, but any you folks thinkin' we gettin' shut out in this game get the hell off this field right now."

My Grandaddy would've kept yelling at us, but Coach Gasconade cut in. "Let's get some touchdowns here!" hollered Coach Gasconade, interrupting my Grandaddy—which, incidentally, no one ever dared do—and attempting to tone down The Language.

But my Grandaddy cut him off before Coach Gasconade could wax eloquent. "Or, get used to bein' where we are, wallowin' in pig shit!" yelled Grandaddy. "But I'll be DAMNED if my BEARS are gonna be shut out like a buncha pussies!"

"Ain't no way!" bellowed Lew taking a drag on his unfiltered Camel.

"Now it's time you men asked yourselves how bad you really want it." Grandaddy's voice got real low. "Life wears a cup, so you kick that fucker straight in the balls, men! Y'hear me? Yeah, that's right, you ARE men, you're not boys, so I'll talk to ya like men!" Coach started to open his mouth but Grandaddy just plowed right through his intentions, and then I saw James give Gasconade a look that was sure to shut him up for good. "It's time to shit or get off the pot! 'Cause otherwise you're gonna regret it your whole life. This is when you decide if you's a winner or a loser. This is when you reach inside yourself and you pull somthin' out that you'll take with you the rest of your lives."

Grandaddy spat out his toothpick and took a long, slow drag on his cigarette before he spoke again. Every one of us teammates hung on his every word. "Let you tinies in on a little secret...tell you how you gonna beat a team that may be bigger, faster, hell, even stronger. Sometime talent gonna get you in trouble, make you fat if you ain't got no heart. Heart gonna beat the shit outta talent every goddamn day. Maybe they capable of playin' at a level ten and you's only capable of a nine. But heart gonna determine how much'a that ten they gonna grab out they pockets every day. Pullin' it all out take heart, desire, discipline; shit my Bears got in spades. Yep, maybe they capable of ten, but I look in they eyes and know they only got the heart to call on eight of they ten, day in and day out. I look in each of you eyes and goddamn if I don't know each and every one'a you gonna demand all nine of your nine...every goddamn day. Sometime the talent you ain't worked for breed pussies, and that what you seein' right now in the eyes of them little shits in them red jerseys 'cross from you. Know it. Today they only grab eight. You squeeze yer nine tight and you go out and you destroy them pussies!! You do this today with your nine, and someday when you finally earned and grew into yer ten, you gonna be able grab it anytime you need it... and ain't nobody gonna stand a good goddamn chance."

"Sing it, Charlie!!" chorused Lew, swigging his Miller.

"Hear it now, 'cause Charlie know!" James's deep, rich baritone reverberated.

"Now there ain't a doubt in my mind that if y'all want to put seven up there on the scoreboard, there ain't one of them corn-fed tub o' shits in them red jerseys gonna stop you! You'll finish the season eight and two, which ain't bad, but you'll be the only little shits that put seven on them pussies! You let them shut you out, and they'll take a piece of you home with them that you ain't never gonna get back. This is a fork-in-the-road moment for all of you tinies. What you do here'll change your path moving forward for better or worse. Up ta each 'n' every one'a you. This is the moment that you got a lot more to lose than any of them fuckers. The crisis of them little shits taking home a piece'a you gonna give you access to the best parts of each one'a you, should you be willing to grab it. They fat right now with thirty-five on the board. This is y'all moment to make them think for a whole fuckin' year about seein' my Bears next season, and wonderin' if y'all gon' play next year like you played the last few seconds of this game. You make them afraid of the Bears they about to see next year, and put seven on those cocksuckers... or you get shut out, and spend the off-season missing a pretty important part of each one of you. You either want it, or you don't. But if you WANT IT, well I know that you all capable of sticking seven on those cocksuckers right here... and RIGHT NOW!!"

Every team member and Coach Gasconade had long since gone silent at Grandaddy's profanity, uncertain if it was okay to appreciate this tactic.

Then from the back of the huddle I heard a rumble, "Seven!"

I glanced back.

"Seven! On the cocksuckers!" Clatterbuck the freckled Bolshevik, with snot running out of his nose and mud everywhere, was yelling at the top of his lungs.

"Don't you never let me hear y'all yellin' like that when they's ladies in earshot, y'hear." Grandaddy glowered. "Not ya momma, not ya sister, not ya girlfriend, 'cause you, Clatterbuck, you gon' have lotsa them, and one's gon' matter to you, so watch ya goddamn tongue." Grandaddy looked long and hard at Clatterbuck.

Clatterbuck's eyes welled and his jaw dropped under the scalding reprimand of Grandaddy's Law. Then with a steely-eyed smirk, my Grandaddy roused the chorus of boys' voices. "Now, 'tween us men, Clatterbuck, and don't you fergit all them women waitin' fer ya in ya future, you tinies say all the cocksuckers you want, but only 'tween us men—'cause that some man talk right there. You ain't failures till you either quit, or you start blamin' somebody else. Now, you tell me right here and right now. Y'all gonna put seven on them cocksuckers?"

Bewildered, Clatterbuck's tears turned to joy, and slowly we all started chiming in, one by one, timid at first, with *seven* and *cocksuckers*, till we had going there a ripping chant. "SEVEN ON THE COCKSUCKERS!"

While the parents were getting over the shock of it, Trent, the quarterback, entered the huddle and issued the play.

"Okay, Mickey, it's you.... Thirty-eight pitchout on two, ready...break!"

"Wait," I said.

"You don't *wait* me, shit head." Trent was pissed, but I continued.

"Well...it's fourth down. If this is gonna be our last play of the year, let's do it like we do it in our backyards."

"What the hell are you talking about, dork?" Firefly burst in.

"Shut up! Firefly!" Trent seemed to understand.

So I explained my plan. "I'll sweep around the end, same as usual, but if I'm gonna go down, let's have someone follow me close...that I can lateral back to."

"We ain't got anybody else that's that fast," Trent objected, and I countered.

"They don't have to be fast, it just has to be someone they can't tackle."

"Yeah, well, who we got on the team that can't be tackled by one'a them huge fuckin' Red Devils?" asked Firefly incredulously, and he and the whole team looked at me like I was completely crazy.

"T. rex the fuckers, Firefly," I whispered across the huddle.

"Holy shit, he's right," exclaimed Trent.

And the team hollered, "Firefly, Firefly, they can't tackle a fuckin' T. rex!"

His eyes lit up with pride that we all thought he could do it.

"Okay, thirty-eight pitchout with a T. rex follow, on—?" Trent looked to me.

"On FOUR! We've never hiked on four," I said.

"Okay...on four, READY...BREAK!"

As the team took to the line of scrimmage, everything seemed to slow down and all the sound around me came to a complete halt. I noticed the red Firebird parked in the adjacent field. Kevin was sitting on the roof as always, watching and grinning at me. Scrawny Clatterbuck, still feeling the power of yelling *cocksuckers*, drew my attention back to the game when he yelled in the face of his opposing lineman, a demonic thug twice Clatterbuck's size.

"Watch out for T. rex, you fuckin' tub of shit!" Clatterbuck screeched.

I looked out at the whole field, and into the faces of each player as the play was called, and Clatterbuck's opponent clearly had heard him, and was seething. A flag went up as Clatterbuck's opponent flattened him, and was drawn offside by our new "hut-four" snap call. Grandaddy smiled his dragon grin, exhaling a lungful of smoke. The next play's snap was called, and Trent pitched out to me as I swept around the eighth hole in between two defenders. I found myself running downfield along the sideline, occasionally looking left as defenders came into view until I outran them all. But one sole Red Devil defender had an angle on me. I kept on going, with widemouthed fans, parents, Mom and Dad yelling nothing, until I turned to see the defender right there. I stopped in my tracks, sending the defender flying right by, and spun completely around to find Firefly approaching fast, but still about ten yards behind. I looked at another looming defender approaching at light speed while I stood still. I waited until Firefly was finally close enough, and I lateraled the ball to him about a millisecond before I got hit, hard! As I went down, I could see Firefly continue to the end zone with two defenders on his back, his cleats churning up earth. Looking at them sideways as I fell, amidst all the sea of helmet grilles that crossed my field of vision, I recognized her. Jane. She was there. She had to be there. And she wasn't watching Firefly tear down the end zone. She kept her eyes on me...until it all went black. When I came to, I tracked the stands for her, but only my parents and James and Mamau and Grandaddy and Lew and a lot of litter remained.

"Sug, let's get you home for a hot shower," murmured Mom, soft palm on my brow.

Jane,

I scored today. I saw you. I was Number 24.

I stole a stamp out of Mom's butcher-block drawer in the kitchen and walked over to The Dancing Mailbox on the corner of Bentliff and Sandpiper. Mailing letters to Jane at a made-up address was like throwing a ball into the stratosphere and waiting for it to come back down. My rationale was that if she was meant to get it, then grace would step in, and the postman would do the right thing and reroute it accordingly. I was hopeful. I never told anyone about my affection for this tempestuous creature. She moved me so much that I kept on going. I learned at an early age that there were seventeen important people in the universe, and that Jane was nine of them. She was more than half...just like my Grandaddy said.

Chapter Four

One, two, three, four, five, let's go!" There was that counting again. Something was always starting on the count of five. And it was something that I was growing accustomed to not being invited to.

I got dressed and picked up yesterday's clothes off the floor, uncovering four of my favorite 45s all stuck together with pink goo. My stomach recognized the substance on the records even before my brain could, and I immediately tried to keep my belly intact, but my sister's chewed, cigarette smoke–infused Bazooka bubble gum had undeniable power. I pinched my lips together as hard as I could and ran for the kitchen sink to remove the sticky glob from my records before her death smell claimed a win. I had my belly fully in control until I rounded the corner into the front hall and saw my mother speaking to the mailman at the front door. Victory was in sight if not for the bundle that the postman was handing to my mom. My heart withered as all the balls of hope I had thrown so high crashed down around me in the form of one brown-wrapped package of letters stamped

RETURN TO SENDER ADDRESSEE UNKNOWN. I don't know if it was my hatred for that postman or my disgust at Lilyth's dirty "smoke" gum on my 45s, but I could no longer combat my belly's urge. I just made it to the kitchen sink as all of my stomach's contents left me.

"Sug, you okay?" I heard my mom yell.

I wiped my mouth, laid my gooped records down, and set out to face my hatred. By the time I got down the hall, Mom was wrapping up the conversation at the front door and holding the bundle. The bundle I did not want to see. The postman stared past Mom at me, foreboding like the Grim Reaper. My eyes widened in gnawing fear. It was too late for me to hide from the postman's inquisition.

"Sug! Sugar? Come say hello. The nice mailman returned eight letters to you that you have addressed to a . . . Jane. Sug?"

My brain imploded on my cottonmouth, and yet from the ether I mustered an answer.

"Oh yeah, we're doing a project thing at school, um . . . about the postal service."

Mom smiled and handed me the bound letters. Before she closed the door, the postman waged a long, sharp look at me, as if a warning to me to convey that neither snow, nor heat, nor gloom of night, nor Lew Hoagie's rain could stay *this* courier from the swift completion of his appointed rounds. Nor even Jane. I stood in the hallway as Mom's words sloshed in my ears where my tears were hiding. The postman turned and disappeared.

"Your dad and I talked about it, and we decided that it's okay if you ride your bike to school, Sug. BUT, the first time I hear that you're late for class . . ." Mom kissed the top of my head as she dashed back to the kitchen. "Here's your lunch and a quarter. The mower gas tank is full, too. You all right, Sug? Lord, have mercy, what's in the sink?" I couldn't answer. "What happened to your records, Sug?"

"Lilyth," I mustered, teetering back into the kitchen as the front door closed on the vanished postman.

"Oh, it's *fine*, Sug, Lilyth duddn't mean it bad. I'm sure it was an accident. She's a *nice* girl. It's fine. I'll wash 'em off for y'Sug." Mom dried my eyes.

My mom was wrong. It wasn't *fine* and Lilyth wasn't *nice*.

I rode my bike to school, cataloguing all I wanted to tell Jane. My homeroom peers were rowdy, jumping around out of their seats, unsupervised because the new homeroom teacher hadn't arrived yet, and so I palmed a stamp from the teacher's desk where they were kept in the top-right drawer for writing to our congressman.

The smell of mothballs sent everyone to their seats. Mr. Totter, our principal, entered with a tall, exquisitely beautiful woman with long, wavy, brown-black hair.

"Lest you forget, children, the sooner y'all start acting like adults when no one is around, the sooner no one will need to be around to remind you that you're not adults." The conundrum of the principal's cyclical reasoning was lost on us.

Smiling amiably, our pretty new homeroom teacher turned her attention to the principal, saying bemusedly, "Mr. Totter, well, if that's not the tree falling in the forest!" He grunted and she continued to smile patiently at him. "I can introduce myself to my new class, thank you."

But Mr. Totter stood his ground.

"Okay, people, as you know, Miss Flinch has gone to teach at the new Quail Valley Elementary School. And this lovely young lady is your new homeroom teacher, whom I'm sure we will all grow to love. I've advised her that any misconduct should be directed to my office immediately, so that her transition will be as seamless as possible. Any questions?" No one in the class responded; they just stared at him. "Good, oh, and lest you've forgotten, tomorrow is Halloween so no one gets into class without a costume, but I don't want to see ONE piece of candy or gum, understood? Don't hesitate to send for me if you need to, Lola." Mr. Totter's unctuous drone pattered to a close while the new lady thanked him and held the door open for him to leave already as he eyeballed her up and down.

I liked her *way* immediately. She was so familiar.

"Well, I will start off by apologizing for Mr. Totter's introduction of me. I usually don't go by 'lovely young lady,' but by my name. Y'all are welcome to call me by my first or my last, whichever makes you feel more comfortable. You can call me Lola or Mrs. Bradford."

After school, I skulked around waiting for Mrs. Bradford until she approached an orange '73 VW Vanagon, climbed in, and sputtered away. Then I pedaled my Sting-Ray as fast as I could, taking every shortcut, even the one past The Hole. I knew that if I was right, she had to make a stop before coming home, and if I was right, I knew where her home was. On Bentliff Street, I ditched my bike just as the orange VW Vanagon pulled into Jane's driveway, and Jane and Mrs. Bradford got out and went into the house. I had known for sure where that van was going before it got there. I knew it. Mrs. Bradford was Jane's mother. From then on, most of the things I learned about Jane came from her mother. Mrs. Bradford spoke of her daughter often, and because she went to the new school in Quail Valley, I was sure I was the only one in home-room who knew who her daughter was.

Through the bushes, I watched the garage light come on and the door come up to reveal Jane placing paintbrushes in a jar of turpentine to soak off the pungent oil paints. She had a small canvas on her easel that was an entire field of green. The blades of grass in the foreground were defined with a tack-sharp clarity. And I wanted to play on a field like that someday—a field like Jane's.

"You need fresh air, Two," said mother to daughter. "The fumes from those oil paints can't be good for you."

"I guess, but there's just something about the smell of tur-pentine that I like," Jane protested a bit too loudly with her headphones on, gazing at her partially completed canvas from her cinder block stool.

"Well, keep the door open so you get fresh air," said Mrs. Bradford before heading back inside the house.

I loved those headphones because they muted my world just a little bit, and at the same time amplified the most beau-tiful being I had ever seen. I knew I had to go home so my mom could fit me for my Halloween costume, but I wanted every possible moment with Jane. Her closed garage door was the only thing that would send me away. I spent hours watching Jane create, and something always happened to me in her presence. Jane was drugs. And she could completely re-organize my chemistry from across the yard. When the door rolled down, I headed home.

I stood stock-still, quilled on a chair as Mom adjusted pins all over Speed Racer.

"Hold your scarf out of the way, darlin'!" instructed Mom, gritting through a mouthful of straight pins.

"Are we too poor to buy him a new costume?" asked Lilyth, chewing the Cocoa Pebbles she kept waving under my nose. "Last bowl, punk." I tried to take a bite and Lilyth pulled it away, causing me to jerk and get stuck by pins.

"His new homeroom teacher hasn't seen this costume yet. Quit fidgeting, Sug." Since last Halloween, I had outgrown the white pants and blue shirt, but Mom had hand-made my costume like she did all my other clothes—with enough seam allowance to give an extra size or two as I grew.

"Come over here, Lilyth, and help me pin your brother's pants."

"No, she'll stick me!"

"Course she won't, Sug. She'll do no such thing."

I recoiled. Yes, she would. I knew she would. To this day, I still have the scar from Lilyth's experimentation with tailor's shears on the thin skin of the inside of my elbow when I was two. When my parents found me bleeding from the fold in my arm and asked Lilyth what had happened, she simply replied, "I wanted to see if he'd bleed."

"Lilyth, give your brother a bite." Mom glowered at Lilyth.

Ignoring Lilyth, Steve McQueen sauntered into the kitchen with a half-chawed eight-track streaming tape and stared at Speed Racer on TV next to me.

"I hope that eight-track wuddn't a good one," said Mom as she rigged up her old Singer sewing machine.

I grabbed the eight-track and chucked it on the table, relieved it wasn't Kevin's "Free Bird" I'd rescued from the driveway the day of The Plank.

"Hope it's good for something," Mom added, looking up from the sewing machine.

It was.

I pulled the tape out in fourteen-inch lengths and cut them off. When I had a good bunch, I wrapped one end in Scotch tape, making a tassel. The smell of tuna casserole baking made my tummy rumble. Then my ears caught on fire as Mom started in again about Mrs. Bradford.

"Sug, your homeroom teacher called all the parents of her new students and gave me her number just in case. She said she lives on Sandpiper Drive, that's right directly behind us across the ditch out back. Or, at least she will for a few more months; they're having a house built in that new subdivision, Quail Valley, out on that new golf course. She said she has a daughter going to Quail Valley Elementary, about your age."

"Hey, Mom, how long does it take to build a house?" I avoided her gaze and kept measuring lengths for the next eight-track tassel.

"Depends, Sug." Mom smiled more to herself, because I was still not looking right at her, for good reason. "Mrs. Bradford said that they hoped to be in their new house by summer."

"So, how far till summer?"

"About forty feet, ya retard." Lilyth could be counted on to bludgeon my quest for knowledge. "It's probably right out back, ten feet down in that gorge of a *ce*ment drainage ditch. Why don't y'all go take a good long look'n' see if you cain't find it underneath a crawdad, you moron."

"That's enough, Lilyth, y'all be kind to each other. Best friends forever, remember that, you two." Mom repinned a section on my costume. "It's still October, Sug, and summer duddn't start till June...so about seven months."

Dad came in with a pair of old flight goggles and handed them over to me proudly.

"Go, Speed! How about these for your Speed Racer costume? They're my old air force flight goggles, virtually fog resistant, except under the most severe weather conditions, but they look like the ones Speed wears on the show, don't they?"

"No, he wears a bubble shield, but these're even better, Dad." I slid out of my iron maiden Speed Racer costume so Mom could have at it on her two-hundred-pound black machine. I noticed the first thing she did was stitch up the *Made with Love by Mom* tag in my collar that had been dangling by a thread since last year when Lilyth tried ripping it out.

"Seedlin', get out here!!" So, out I went.

My Grandaddy had been on the porch with a pencil and a single sheet of paper. I had wondered what he had been writing on it, and why it had taken him so long to fill up a single sheet. Maybe it was the dozen ponies at his feet that slowed him down, but I always knew that the lack of pace was almost always made up for by a willingness to hand over early an insight that I'd take with me for the rest of my life. He sat in his lawn chair right next to James's empty chair, whose webbing looked as if it had had a bowling ball dropped right through it. Grandaddy leaned way back in his chair to ease a hand into his right front pocket and extracted that single sheet that now looked like it had been folded and unfolded and pocketed and unpocketed about a hundred times.

"James's big ass broke the webbin' so you gotta stand, but this only take a second. Mo' ingredients go in the Boudin to feed my great-granbabbies. I wrote 'em down for ya. You gone have ya own, but these is mine, ta give ya idea what I'm talkin' 'bout. That list there is the most important peoples in my life. On the left is what they do. On the right…who do it. You need a goddamn gardener, I don't care, write it down. A momma for ya babies, write it down. Everything that you need for tha' good life that ya either ain't capable give to ya-self or you don't wanna give to yaself. Next to it, ya gon' see tha name o' who I found ta git it from. Now, I got a big list there, but you see you Mamau's name next to th' majority of 'em…That why she a unicorn. That the qualifier for when you ready to wife-up…you don't quit lookin' till you find one that right. List all the important people in ya life on tha left…but ya wife need ta fill more than half of 'em 'fore you chapel her up, hear me, boy? Don't matter how many people on that list you got, so long as the one you plan ta wife-up more than half of 'em. Maybe one or two of them people gonna seem more important to ya early on, but know that some'a the least important peoples on ya list is gonna become tha most important later on. Plan for that shit. Don't neglect today, but plan to please the person you gonna be when you's old like ya Grandaddy. I plan that shit perfect with ya Mamau. Time's right, you gonna know. Any damn mirror'll show ya. Right one's gonna do somethin' with ya face. You gon' try, but cain't hide it. Now, you see that you's tha last one? That why I call these porch meetin's when everybody else inside. I pick you 'cause you ain't the kind ta ever have nobody do his gardenin' for him. I plant this shit in you 'cause I trust you gon' take care of tha sprouts and hand 'em down proper. I

76

ain't gon' be around, so it gotta be someone I trust. Put this in the Boudin and feed it to my great-granbabbies. Now get t'hell inside'n' git t'bed fo' ya Mamau come holler."

———

"Two! Three! Five!" hollering out back somewhere over on Sandpiper Drive woke me up the next morning with a start, and I smelled autumn. I stared at the ceiling where all my World War II model airplanes were perfectly hung in various dogfight positions with fishing line, and I watched them gently sway in the humid Texas breeze. When Dad had time off from work, he and I had painted one of my bedroom walls white, one forest green, one celery, and the ceiling baby blue as a backdrop for a perpetual airstrike. My shelf held my favorite football, and race cars. Having been in the air force himself, my dad had a love of all things airborne and helped me to build squadrons of 1/48th scale World War II model airplanes to hang from my ceiling. Each plane was a piece of art. I knew every fact and spec of everything that flew in World War II. From fishing wire on I-hooks there hung in mid-fight two German Messerschmitts, two Focke-Wulf fighters, a gaggle of Japanese Zeros, Corsairs, a B-17 Flying Fortress, Hellcats, Spitfires, P-38 Lightnings, Thunderbolts, Douglas Dauntless dive-bombers, and others. My dad had used a hot sewing needle of Mom's to strafe some of the airplanes, like machine-gun holes, and made them look like they were on the losing end of a dogfight. He pulled cotton into one-inch strands and blackened it, then added bits of yellow, red, and orange paint to create a fiery smoke that came out of the cowling of a shot and limping fighter. But my absolute favorite, the P-51 Mustang, had come loose and was now dangling by its tail in a sort of death dive, as if it had been shot down by a Messerschmitt, of all things. But the P-51 was the baddest thing in the skies in World War II. That Mustang put fear in the hearts of everything it came into contact with.

After I'd watched my reel of Jane on her trampoline, hidden everything in my Charles Chips can, and prepared her letter about seeing her at the football game, I stood up on my bed and restrung the P-51 Mustang's wings to the ceiling and righted that Mustang's trip of vengeance on its foes. It was Halloween morning, so I raced to school on my bike wearing a perfect Speed Racer costume, complete with helmet and goggles. Leaves were pretty much off the trees by then, but some still fluttered around me, joining the others to crunch under my tires. The eight-track Steve McQueen had mauled had turned into two perfectly constructed streamers on the end of each handle grip. I passed other kids on their bikes all in various costumes that were cool, but I was Speed Racer. I was always Speed Racer, from the earliest Halloween that I can remember.

As I left my bike in the rack outside school, police sirens were splitting my eardrums. Kevin tore past with his plank in the Firebird racing a '70 Chevelle, followed by the cop car. Kids were still hooting and cheering when Mrs. Bradford appeared out of nowhere in front of me, dressed up like an Indian medicine woman.

"SPEED RACER! Did you bring a record?" The only thing I wanted more than to see Kevin race that Chevelle was to talk to Jane's mom.

"Yes, ma'am, I did, ma'am." But that was too many *ma'ams* for her to tell her daughter that I was cool. I had music that

I wondered if Jane had ever heard. I tried to pull my records out of my brown paper lunch bag while holding the door for Jane's mom and just barely missed accidentally letting it go too early. "I got 'You ain't nuthin' but a Hound Dog' by The King and 'Sunshine Superman' by Donovan."

And Mrs. Bradford smiled that lopsided, smirky Jane way as we entered our classroom. "By The King, huh? So, you're an Elvis fan, Mickey?" She plugged in the box record player that sat on a stool by her desk.

The classroom writhed with a monster mash of ghouls, characters, witches, and fairy princesses. Emmalyne was Dorothy from *The Wizard of Oz* and Firefly was the bionic man, with circuits and wires coming out of his arm.

"So Speed Racer is the only one who brought a record today? Mark my words, in a few years you're gonna *wish* your teacher would let you listen to music in class." Emmalyne raised her hand. "Go ahead, *Dorothy*. As long as we are all polite to one another, we won't have to raise our hands."

"Oh, well we don't have any records at my house, Mrs. Bradford. My dad threw them all out when we got our new cassette tape player."

"Shut up, Emmalyne, showin' off yer daddy's got money!" nipped Firefly.

"Don't you see my blue gingham dress and pigtails? I'm *Dorothy*, stupid!"

"Okay, there, *Mr. Austin*. Well, *Dorothy*, let's hope that your father at least gave them away and didn't just throw out the vinyl with the bathwater."

"Huh? Yeah, I think he did."

"Well, class, we have two from Speed, and I brought one. Since we only have three, we can probably get to them all."

Mrs. Bradford turned the lights off and placed one of the records on the turntable, with two of them above it waiting to drop.

"The first one is my daughter's. It's her favorite. It's called 'The Sounds of Silence' by Simon and Garfunkel."

The room got very quiet as we listened intently to the crackle of the needle waiting for the song to start. After a bit, most of the kids were fidgeting with their desks or each other. Except me. I was listening to what Jane heard. I was hearing The Silence Jane loved. I wondered if she had ever heard mine when she was jumping. Though it was barely audible, I could hear Mrs. Bradford singing along.

When I woke up, Donovan's "Sunshine Superman" was finishing as the bell jangled me back into the classroom.

"Mickey? You fell asleep?" I raised my head off my desk to see that Mrs. Bradford and I were the only ones left. "I think your 'Hound Dog' was the big hit, huh, Mickey?"

I didn't even remember it playing.

"Mrs. Bradford, do you think I could trade you my two records for Jane's 'Silence,' just for tonight?"

I already had my own, but I wanted Jane's. I wanted to touch her "Silence."

Mrs. Bradford regarded me thoughtfully for a moment, probably wondering how I knew Jane's name, since Mrs. Bradford had only ever referred to Jane in class as "my daughter." "Certainly, Mickey, I don't think she'd mind at all. As a matter of fact, I think she'd really love 'Sunshine Superman.'"

And as simple as that, I was holding her "Silence" in my hands.

"Thank you, Mrs. Bradford, I'll bring it back."

She smiled again and turned to go.

"Oh, Mickey, I almost forgot. We're having a haunted house in our garage tonight. A haunted pirate ship, actually. The pirate idea was...my daughter's. I thought I'd let you know because your mother said that ya'll lived right behind us on the other side of the ditch. You should stop by."

"Yes, ma'am, I'll try," I said, in full knowledge that absolutely nothing I had experienced up to that point in my tiny little life could possibly block my path to that garage. I was Speed Racer. Propelled down the hallway by rowdy students pushing like cattle in a stampede, all aching to get home and scarf down their dinners so they could go trick-or-treating and egging cars, I was soon ejected by the crowd down the main stairs and found myself close enough to the bike rack to spit on it by the time the tide of costumes subsided. I was still lost in Jane and the record I held in my hand, when I saw it. And it stopped me cold.

The bike rack was empty. My bike was gone. And there was that noise again, that noise that my throat would make so it would be too busy to cry—a little Grunt that came when I called on every one of my personal resources to not burst into tears. I stared in disbelief, as a sharp pang of loss drowned out my thoughts of Jane. On the very first day my parents ever allowed me to ride that Schwinn Sting-Ray to school, I had left the chain and padlock negligently wrapped around the seat post. I would have always preferred anger to come from my dad and Grandaddy, but I knew that it would instead be a devastating dose of disappointment that waited for me.

Walking home, I accepted that I would be late for dinner and Mom would be worried, even if I took the shortcut through the football fields past the baseball diamond and through the stand of trees with The Hole. The Hole scared me terribly. Even on a practice day with my entire football team covering my back, I wanted nothing to do with it. Now it was just me, no bike, no Steve McQueen. It was Halloween and nobody would be at any practices, so I would have to walk alone past The Hole, an inexplicably harrowing crevice in the earth that I was sure was the doorway to the devil. The one time I would eventually try to climb down into The Hole it was breech, while The Pole would be headfirst. Yet, oddly enough, while The Hole took me further into this world, it was the The Pole that would take me away.

When I got past the stand of trees, I sprinted past The Hole, pausing only long enough to glance into that black gash to hell. I finally got past it and came to the baseball diamond only to find The Plank and its red Firebird right there, directly in front of me. It was silent except for the sound of a radio playing "Crimson and Clover" by Tommy James and the Shondells. I never thought Kevin would, but I actually loved that song. I couldn't see him anywhere around, so I cautiously approached his car on the passenger side and looked in. Stretched out on his back across both front seats was Kevin with his mouth wide open and his head propped up on the driver's side armrest. Radio blaring.

I had never seen a dead person before, but this one looked anything but alive. I was both fascinated and shattered with fright at the same time. But at such a tender age, fear inevitably wins. I backed away from the car and ran into the stand of trees by The Hole to find a small tree branch. Nervous, I peered down the dark crevice again and ran back to the car and stuck the branch through the open window and slowly poked at Kevin's cheek. Nothing. I waited a moment and then pressed that stick even harder up his cheek—so hard that his upper lip crept high enough to expose his teeth. I held that stick there and prayed for some movement—any movement. But there was none. I dropped that stick right in Kevin's car and ran for help. I got about twenty feet in ten directions when I heard something coming from the car, so I stopped. I had to go back. When I approached the open window this time, I heard a low, sort of guttural moan coming from inside the car. Slowly and carefully I stuck my head back through the window and picked up that stick to touch again. Suddenly, Kevin's eyes popped open and I immediately jerked myself back, violently cracking my head on the top of the roof before I fell to the ground. I heard another groan as I sat on the ground looking up at that car, so I gathered myself and slowly approached the window until I could see him . . . and he could see me.

"Sorry, I thought you were dead."

Kevin pondered that before asking, "So, wha'd I look like, man? Happy or just sorta peaceful?" And it looked like he really wanted to know.

"Just dead, I guess."

Gradually, Kevin sat up, staring out at the horizon, but not the way Grandaddy stared out at it. I don't know if Kevin was fried out of his mind on something or if he just saw things that no one else saw. Their faces were pointed in the same direction, but what they would extract from the view was completely different. Kevin saw smears of color, not hard specifics, whereas my Grandaddy saw every detail before it even got there and long after it was hidden.

"Where's Trixie?" Kevin demanded and I just stared at him. "If you're Speed Racer, where the hell's Trixie?"

I really had to think about this. "I don't know."

"Speed, she's up above you in a helicopter watchin' your every move, man, that's where she is."

Kevin drew himself up and stretched, climbing on the hood of the car right in front of my curiosity.

"And all we're left with is a monkey in the trunk that likes playin' with this weird-lookin' fat kid. But don't worry, ya know the higher you go, the thinner the air gets up there. She gets too far away, she'll come crashing down faster'n she can handle." It seemed like he was really contemplating this for a while, and even looking for her up in the clouds for me, when he suddenly started chuckling to himself. "Besides, we got a fast car! Hah! She's got a chopper, but we got a *car*, kid! We got us a fuckin' car, Speed!" Kevin patted his car and lay back against the windshield to stare wild-eyed at the sky.

"Uh...do you know what time it is, Kevin?" I think that was the first time I ever called him by his name, and probably about the first time we had ever had any kind of conversation.

"I try not to...Sometimes ya can't help but know, but myself, I try not to." Kevin stared me down for a long time and it felt weird, but then he suddenly focused. "Why, you gotta be somewhere, Speed?"

"Just home. My mom worries."

"Nice to have a mom's worries." His eyes drifted off.

I noticed the stopwatch tied around his car's rearview mirror with a lightning bolt logo on the back, and I pulled my leather thong up to show him my dad's stopwatch. Kevin smiled and closed his eyes.

"It usually takes me fourteen minutes and eight seconds. Well, that's the record. I coulda broke it today. But they stole my bike."

"Who's they?" I had to think about that, too.

"I don't know." Kevin smiled at me this time, not at his horizon.

"Yeah, they're always stealin' shit ain't they, Speed, the fuckers. It's a dog-eat-dog world, man, you can't be sportin' Milk-Bone underwear. Where do you live?"

"Just on the other side of the park, over there." I pointed toward home.

"Wanna ride? I'm thinkin' we can crush fourteen-eight."

"No, my mom won't let me ride with pot smokers." Kevin chuckled, normal this time, and looked me square in the eye.

"Your mom's smart." I nodded my thanks for his approval and waved bye. I got about forty feet from Kevin's Firebird before he yelled after me, "Hey, Speed! Tell yer dad I'm sorry 'bout tha garage door, but I know he duddn't got a bathtub to drown me in."

And Kevin was right; we only had a stand-up shower. He grinned and flashed me the peace sign, then leaned back to rejoin his horizon. I watched him a moment longer, but there was Jane and Halloween, so I ran, faster than Tommy, across the entire field of diamonds to the edge and down the path into the trees that lined the field, farther and farther away from The Hole, from Kevin's radio and that song.

Still sprinting to get through the section of vacant houses and run-down warehouses, I ran across the second intersection before it turned red on me. Just then I heard a distinctive fuzzy thrumming motor right behind me that had run the yellow, too. My goggles blocked my peripheral vision a bit, but I recognized the warm purr. It was a uniquely comforting sound, so I knew it was not the throaty Firebird or Dad's Gran Torino or Mom's Dodge Dart. A VW Vanagon is its own instrument in the concert of road traffic, maybe akin to a syncopated popping, like John Bonham's hi-hat counting down before he plunged into "Moby Dick." But any illusion of Zeppelin faded as the orange VW Vanagon pulled up alongside me.

"Want a ride?" Mrs. Bradford was smiling, calling out her driver's side window. "Why are you walking so far from Bentliff Street, Mickey?"

"Oh, hi, Mrs. Bradford, they stole my bike." I guess Mrs. Bradford somehow understood my loss, or maybe she just smiled at my matter-of-factness.

"Yeah, they'll do that, won't they? Well, shame on them. Can I give you a ride?"

"No, thanks, Mrs. Bradford, it's just a coupla blocks more."

"Nonsense, hop in, I wouldn't want my daughter walking around here alone."

"Yeah, me neither."

"What?"

"Nothing. I like your radio. I mean the song on it."

"Serendipity!" Mrs. Bradford smiled.

"What?"

"Nothing. Hop in."

I would never insult love by claiming that it can be found with a single sense, but I now had three that were conspiring to convince me that it was here. I walked around to the passenger door, and when I opened it up, "Crimson and Clover" welled and I was engulfed in the familiar sweet spice of Jane. I caught my breath. I saw the suede moccasins first, then my eye slid up to her shorts, her tasseled-front suede vest, and then her headdress wrapped around the most beautiful face I ever hoped to see. Jane stared down at me there, rooted to the sidewalk. Far away I thought I heard Mrs. Bradford introducing the two of us. All I could see was Jane, a glittering and perfect unicorn. Dazzling, dressed for Halloween as an American Indian squaw, Jane's face and arms were painted with cobalt blue stripes and a headband with a single blue feather in the back, exactly like her mother from head to toe.

I know we actually drove home so I must've climbed up into the VW Vanagon, but in Jane's presence I was never able to bring space and time into a manageable volume. I only remember spinning completely out of control. Like an unresponsive fighter plane, my ailerons were out of order, and I expected impact at any moment. Jane would distort everything I knew to be true, even the constant of gravity. She moved differently than others. Around her, my senses seemed to be just a touch out of calibration, delayed, but still crystal clear when it mattered. Her gravity was different somehow, and her inexplicable weightlessness swam around in my head. Seeing her in that proximity put me in a state of grace that would completely shut down my frontal cortex, forcing me to use my primitive brain stem as my sole operating system. Jane was everything I had never seen before. She made me worry that she wasn't secured to the ground, that she might just come unattached and drift away. But I wanted nothing more than for her to be secure. She was the polar opposite of my Grandaddy, whose feet were locked and loaded in The Law.

I know we drove home because that's where Jane left me standing, still rooted and gazing up at her at exactly the same angle, but in my own driveway. I had remained hiding the whole time behind my Speed Racer aviator goggles. But Dad was right—I could still see clearly, though my body was steaming. It was as if all of my atoms had locked down at once, and I was in emergency orbit. All I could do was wave my hand and watch Jane's Vanagon drive away with her smile a spotlit bouquet in a florist shop window as she peered out past the flapping back window curtain.

My only real proof that I had ridden in Jane's presence was that I now held in one hand her cobalt blue feather and in my other, her "Silence."

"You got Simon and Garfunkel there, son? Been sittin' here for minutes waiting for you to move, Mickey."

"Sorry, Dad."

"Who was that?" Dad pulled his Gran Torino up to the shattered garage door.

"Oh. My homeroom teacher. They stole my bike."

"You didn't lock it, did you?" I was humiliated, but after my moment with Jane I didn't even need a Grunt to get through his disappointment.

"What'd I tell you?" And then he stopped. "Well, let's go right now to the police station so you can report it."

At the police station, I sat shamefaced in the shadow of the hard-nosed sergeant. My Halloween costume sweltered in the overheated office, and my helmet and goggles were starting to itch.

"Shoulda locked it up, Speed Racer. That's what happens when you don't take care of your things. Did you have a lock?"

"Yes, sir."

"Well, hell, no wonder you lost it if you have a lock and you don't even bother t—"

Dad stopped him.

"You know, sir, if you have the forms, my son will give y'all the necessary information."

Eyeballing me, the sergeant handed a theft report to Dad. "What kind of bike was it?"

"A Schwinn Sting-Ray with a black banana seat and purple handlebar grips with brand-new eight-track streamers. It was a racin' bike."

"A racing bike, huh? If only kids nowadays would memorize their serial numbers, my life would be a lot..."

"4TOE776449," I said.

And with that, I saw the Sergeant's shift in demeanor from irritation to, well, something else. "Okay, can you repeat that again? Slowly, please." He jotted it down, then led us out back to a small fenced-in area filled with stolen bikes of all kinds.

My hope slipped into despair, and I shoved my fist against my mouth to hide my quivering lip. There was not a complete bike to be found, nor one that even looked remotely worth rebuilding. Dad rummaged through the piles and parts.

"We'll give you a call if we find it, but don't hold your breath, Speed."

"This works." Dad lifted a rusted-out frame, with only a rear wheel attached, but it was a Schwinn Sting-Ray. "Sergeant, write this serial number down. If no one claims it in ninety days it's mine, right?"

"Yeah, hell, that mighta been here ninety already. You can probably just take it now if ya want."

"No, just call me when you find out."

With all the delays that Halloween, Dad and I sat down at our little white kitchen table just as Mom was carrying away two plates of blackened hot dogs and beans.

"It's cold. I'll make you fresh." Mom never grumped over stupid stuff.

"We'll eat it, Genie," Dad instructed her, giving her a kiss on the lips, and patted her backside.

And then my mom protested slightly, "Paul, not in front of Mickey," as if I hadn't already grown up my whole life seeing my dad do this.

"Seedlin', get out here!"

Out I went. I found my Grandaddy on the porch in his lawn chair, where he always was, watching Magda wiggle sexily up the sidewalk in her skimpy Halloween costume. He pointed at her shaking ass strolling up our driveway toward the front door and asked me, "What you think o' that one, boy?" I saw him gesture at her ass, and I knew exactly what he was referring to.

"You mean Magda?"

"Yep, that one."

Until that moment I had never thought about Magda, so I hesitated before answering, as I actually found her fucking repellant. "Um, she's pretty, I guess."

He let out an almost undetectable grumble and slowly shook his head back and forth.

"I want you ta take a good look at that one and 'member what you seein'. That one got the VD right there. You need ta know for when you go out huntin' what ta look for. Hunt that breed an' you gon' starve. All treat and no sustenance. Ain't got what ya need, though ya eyes be tellin ya otherwise. That trash right there. Ain't got nothin' ta offer a man she ain't given away free to ten others 'fore him. Ya don't marry on one sense, ya marry on all of 'em, and they more than five you gon' find. A woman you after come inta this world with a lotsa negotiatin' power. That power called 'the virtue.' She lose a little bit o' that power every time she let a fella bother her. She ignore all tha' botherin', then she got lots to negotiate with. She do too much botherin', she use it all up and wonder why no man give a goddamn. You find yourself one that done lotsa ignorin', hear me, boy? Hussy don't make no wifin' momma. A momma fer ya babies need ta be able ta offer ya lots o' things that she ain't never offered no man 'fore ya. If all it is's a child, then move along. Birthin' just take care of the nature, but ain't no quality nurturin' possible if she in the 'Virtue Debt'; you gotta 'member what the VD look like for when you old enough to hunt, it wearin' that same costume... and you sidestep that shit when it come lookin' for my granbabby. A hussy got her place, but the chapel ain't it. Hear me, boy? Now don't tell ya momma I'm learnin' you up early."

Magda let herself into our house like she always did, and hugged my mom and dad as I followed her inside. She turned around to me and wobbled my Speed Racer helmet, steering my eyes right to her cleavage.

"Hey, punk." Magda tried to make her voice seductive even when she talked to a kid. And her trashy streetwalker costume didn't help.

Lilyth ran into the kitchen costumed as a risqué Tinker Bell with a winged bikini top.

"I'm going to Magda's."

"You're not going anywhere dressed like that." Dad frowned.

Lilyth looked to Mom for support. "Mom, tell him."

"Tell him what, Lilyth? I told you y'all gotta put clothes on. You too, Magda."

"I shoulda just snuck out and been Cher!"

"You can go as Cher *now*, as long as she's fully clothed."

"If she can wear it on TV for the whole world to see, how come I can't wear it two doors down to Magda's?"

"She can wear it on TV because she's not fifteen, Lilyth."

Lilyth waited for them to change their minds. Mom and Dad ignored her and Magda's pleading look of innocence.

"Fine!" Lilyth stomped off down the hall to her room to change, followed by Magda making apologetic faces at my parents.

Once the girls were out of earshot, Mom leaned in to kiss Dad and whisper, "Don't you let her leave the house like that. I don't want her endin' up like Magda."

By then, Magda had already had one abortion that got shushed up, but it was a small Texas town, so everybody knew. Too early, Magda and Lilyth had fed off each other to take the maximum amount of risk trying to get what they thought was the maximum amount of reward. To Lilyth's credit, and Magda's, from very early on, they were determined—usually just to randomly get their way without any real goals, but still they were determined. Grandaddy had already taught me that it never worked that way. The thing that bonded them early on was Girl Scouts, which my sister was thrown out of when she got caught in her hiked-up scout skirt with the head of that rotten-toothed scurvy guy from the Texaco station planted underneath. But before that, what bonded Lilyth and Magda happened one day when they were selling Girl Scout cookies. Two men driving a black Gremlin robbed their Girl Scout cookie cash right in front of the Utotem. The men ran to their car with two hundred dollars. Lilyth and Magda ran after the thieves as they climbed into their car. Both girls grabbed the driver by the hair as he drove off with his door not yet fully closed and pulled him completely out of the car as it continued straight into a light pole. I don't know if the driver's face was damaged more by the ground as he fell or the girls beating him after he landed. But his picture in the paper was pretty disturbing. So for Lilyth, sneaking out dressed up like Tinker Bell was nothing.

Lilyth tiptoed back toward the kitchen, out of Mom and Dad's view, as my dad had joined my mom giving candy to trick-or-treaters at the front door. To the back of a frumpy old muumuu sweater, Lilyth had Scotch taped the Tinker Bell wings off her bikini top, and she was stuffing the bikini top in her shorts. She noticed me staring at her and put her finger to her lips with a smile shaped like *I'll kill you if you rat on me.* And I knew she would. She had tried several times before, starting with the time she rolled my favorite red fire truck out into the busy street at our old apartment complex. Of course, I had toddled after it, smack into an oncoming postal truck that landed me in the hospital with my first concussion. If it weren't for Steve McQueen having run interference, I'd be dead.

Magda was whispering, "Hurry up," and I just stared back at Lilyth, but her Tinker Bell bikini was our secret. We heard Dad saying good-bye to the little goblins out front, so Lilyth and Magda made a run for it out the sliding glass door and down the back way. I watched them go, relieved as my eyes rested on Jane's head rhythmically popping over the fence.

I waited. And there it was.

"One, two, three, four, five, let's go!" The familiar yell wafted through the neighborhood like a soft prayer on a wing.

Jane vanished from my view.

That night I must've gone through the haunted ship four times, but I never saw Jane. They even had a dry ice machine making fog in there that made it a little hard to breathe, but walking through her garage was one of the most magical experiences I ever had. I would have gone through it another ten times if my mind hadn't been completely on Jane.

There was a makeshift doorway that led to the garage, where the Bradfords had created a black tented passageway. Before you got into the garage, you had to walk through the passageway lined with a series of horrible tableaux, like bloody skeletons, severed heads that talked out of a tabletop, and a bowl of flesh-eating piranha that really were goldfish. Eerie music was playing, hollow sounding, like it was reverberating off the walls of an abandoned castle. The strobe light disoriented me, and by the time I reached the entry to the garage—the haunted ship, that is—I was bug-eyed. Then a bloody thing popped out at me from a garbage can, and I jumped back. It was a huge glow-in-the-dark gloved hand covered in fake blood, reaching out to grab ahold of people every time they passed. The trash barrel was painted to look like a beer keg with *Cap'n Bolan's Brew* scrawled in red across it.

The garage was so crowded with trick-or-treaters that I couldn't scan feet for Jane's moccasins, so I scrutinized the crowd for a beaded headdress—but her feather, which would have pointed her out, was home safe in my Charles Chips can. The ship was meant to scare, but I absolutely loved being there. I desperately wanted to see Jane in that ship, but after a while even the creepy exhibits were turning a sickly shade of green from all the dirty hands touching them, so I headed out completely disappointed into the chilly night air.

Lilyth didn't show up to walk me home, as she had been instructed. By the time I walked around the corner past The Dancing Mailbox, Mom and Dad were asleep on the couch, holding hands with a melted bowl of ice cream in front of them. They had fallen asleep waiting for Lilyth to come home with me, but she never did. I just listened to "The Sounds of Silence" in my room, with Steve McQueen curled up on the foot of my bed, and tried to towel off the green stain on my hands from one of the grotesque concoctions I had blindly placed my hands into at the Halloween party. My sister ran away that night, but we found her at the Utotem the next day. When he saw us come in, the Utotem manager, Samir, had tipped his hand, bobbling his blinding white smile in the direction of Lilyth's whereabouts. Mom and Dad just had to follow the scent of her latest cheap fragrance down the aisle to where she was playing pinball with a bunch of hippies. Samir had attempted to soften Dad's ire, saying, "Surely she is have go home when she no more quarters, Mr. Micmic Father."

Chapter Five

*J*umped. *Fed Donovan. Saw the mean sister and her friend. Mom said stay away from girls like that. Did the spooky house. I loved. In the morning I waited by the bean tree as long as I could, then mom said it was school, I think he was asleep.*

Jane,

Why only when I do stupid things? I'm a lot cooler than the me you've seen.

The Houston fire hydrants were about head height when I was a kid, set up on a cement slab that gave them more height. They had a bulbous top, larger than nowadays, and two valves protruding from either side like little arms. My dad called them the creatures on the corner. Well, the arms were outstretched and my dream was Jane, so I closed my eyes and imagined. I remember the hydrant being prohibitively cold with our narrow window of winter coming on, so I took off my Cowboys jacket and clothed the little creature. I hugged it and hugged it until Jane and her mother drove right by me in their orange van. I saw Jane staring right at me. I don't know why it was always in those moments that she came, but I was utterly humiliated. I was so lost in thought about hugging Jane that I didn't even register that syncopated thrumming of the VW that I had become so attuned to detecting from blocks away. To this day, it still boggles my mind as to where the audio went hiding as her van approached.

_____

Jane,

I know you saw me on the corner that day. And just so you know, you were The Fire Hydrant. At first you were to cold to really hold. But then I gave you my jacket. And I think that's all you needed, you felt great in my arms.

_____

Calculating my pursuit of Jane, I would sit in the dark in my bedroom for hours watching Jane footage projected on my celery green wall with our blue feather twizzling between my fingers as I hugged my Charles Chips container, a limping German Messerschmitt overhead trying desperately to evade the deadly sights of my most lethal allied fighter, the P-51

Mustang. But the enemy had nowhere to go. Alone under my padded black headphones, I listened over and over to Jane songs.

"Mom, can I do swim team?"

"What're you still doing up?" asked Mom, lighting a cigarette.

"They're having sign-ups tomorrow at homeroom, but we have to have permission."

"I don't like the idea of you going all the way across town alone for practice. Especially nights. And, Sug, that's way the heck out by the golf course."

"The days'll be longer then."

"Not for a while, Sug. We'll talk to your dad at breakfast. Oh, and remember tomorrow your sister will meet you out in front of school to go to the movies. And stay out of the garage. Your father's using dangerous chemicals in there that'll kill you."

I hugged my mother and ran to bed, and thrashed for hours under the covers imagining what it would be like to pull up past the golf course to the swimming pool. I knew Jane's new house was being built somewhere on the golf course, whose eighteenth hole ended at the country club where a horseshoe-shaped parking lot wrapped around that gorgeous new swimming pool. Now I just had to find a buddy for swim practice.

———

I sat down at a table in the school cafeteria, where Firefly slumped across from me fuzzing his red buzz cut with his palm. After he stole and downed half of a bologna sandwich without asking the kid next to him, he said cautiously, "Hey, Mic, I saw your name on the sign-up sheet for swim team."

"Yeah?"

"Can you swim?"

"Not racin' strokes, but I think they'll teach us those anyway."

"My dad told me to sign up. I think he just wants to get me off the couch so I'll stop watching *Gilligan's Island*. Man, I swear to God sometimes you can almost see Ginger's titties! Who you like better? Ginger or Mary Ann?"

"Well, my Grandaddy always says Ginger for an hour, Mary Ann for a lifetime, and I'm gonna live a lot longer than an hour anyway. So, Mary Ann."

"What? Are you stupid? Ginger's a fox!" He waited for me to change my mind. "Mary Ann...that's the most dumb-assed shit I've ever heard. So, Mic, d'you think we can do swim team without putting our head under the water?"

"Um, well, I think we'll hafta do the ones they do on the Olympics."

"What? WHAT? I ain't scared of gettin' my hair wet, I just don't like puttin' my face in the water. And don't eyeball me! You eyeballin' me, fuckhole?" Firefly kept on staring at me for a reaction. I just looked at him, wondering how he went from calm to enraged so fast. Then I reached into my paper lunch bag and pulled out an aluminum foil pouch. I opened my milk carton and poured the pale brown powder into it and shook it up. "Hey, hey, what the hell's that, Mic? Is that Quik? Damn, your mom's cool." I chugged my chocolate milk out of Firefly's reach, but then I handed him the other half of the Quik powder left in the foil pouch. "Really, Mic?" I pulled it back out of his reach.

"Only if you do swim team with me."

"Really? Whoa, I gotta go get a cut." I watched Firefly run straight up to the front of the lunch line and barge right through the crowd to claim a milk.

I hoped and prayed that my future with Jane was sealed with Quik and chlorine, so I floated to the movies that night to meet my sister, completely neglecting that I was supposed to wait for her out in front of school. Had Lilyth actually been outside school waiting for me, like she was supposed to, of course, I would have walked with her to the movies, like my mom had instructed me to. But Lilyth wasn't there. And I doubted she'd be waiting for me at the movies, either. I swept through the heavy glass double doors of the fusty old theater and stared around at the chipping paint and gum-spotted red carpet. Lilyth was not in the lobby, so I went back outside to look for her and glanced down the alley along the theater wall, where I guessed maybe she would be smoking.

"Hey! Are you Mickey?" A tall, skinny teenager in an usher's uniform popped his head out from a cracked theater exit door and gestured enthusiastically for me to come down the alley, and I obeyed without thinking. "Your sister's in the fourth row. Yeah, she's really a fox, wow. C'mon, quick, I'll let you in this way, but stay behind the curtains until the lights go down."

I nodded just to make him leave and went and hid behind the heavy green velvet curtain that smelled like old books at the public library. It was a full house. I spotted Lilyth as the lights went down, and went and sat inside her cloud of fruity perfume.

"Didn't Mom have enough money for my ticket?"

"Yeah, she gave us money, but you want candy or not?" I nodded, hungry from the long walk. "Good, 'cause we ain't got enough for both. All right, you little shit, sit here and don't move. I'll be back."

Lilyth got up to leave and left me sitting there alone to watch the previews. I waited and watched, glad the air was clearing. My stomach rumbled. But Lilyth never came back. At the end of the movie, I left the theater alone in a throng of people all over twenty years of age. I sat on the front steps looking around for my sister and noticed a crowd my age slowly filtering out of the theater on the other side of the building. From the younger crowd, someone was calling to me.

"Hey, Speed, you fall in love with her?" Kevin came up behind me and tipped my head up to look at him upside down, then released me. "Shit, I'd fall in love with her but she's too little for me. Any chick with wings though's gotta be pretty damn close to perfect. Too perfect for Peter, that's for sure."

"Who's Peter?"

"Yeah, who the hell's Peter? And he can't fly without her pixie dust anyway. Kid, where's your sister?"

"I don't know."

"You here by yourself?" I was afraid to answer. "Well, how you getting home?" For a long time I looked out at Kevin's piece of my garage in his grille and then past the thinning parking lot at the horizon, buying myself time to swallow the lump in my throat.

"My mom'll come."

"If you say so, kid." Kevin looked off toward his Firebird.

"Why don't you fix your car?"

"'Cause the same piece that made the hole is keepin' the water in. Some wounds you just gotta live with, ya know?"

"I guess."

"Radiator's stayin' together so far, and a new one's a hundred bucks."

"Is it pretty speedy?"

"Three hundred and seventy-five horsepower without nitrous, and it only weighs thirty-five hundred pounds."

"My dad says handling is more important than horsepower."

"Yeah? Well, neither one's as important as the windshield." Kevin swaggered over to his car and opened the driver's side door. "Come here and listen to this!" Kevin climbed in and opened the passenger door for me. He fired up the engine, and the ground under my feet shook in sync with the four-hundred-cubic-inch engine.

I liked it. So I climbed into the passenger seat to sit for just a second. In awe, I took in the vibe and the scent of the car, which still smelled new mixed with saddle soap, marijuana, and a hint of Lilyth's latest fruity trend. The engine fell back down to a loping idle like a well-fed wolf. The sun visor on my side was down, and I noticed a heart carved in it with *Lilyth* in the middle, and an arrow pointing down. I understood why Lilyth liked him.

"What a punk! Will y'look at that, Speed!" Kevin was staring out his window at a primer-matte '67 Chevy Nova driving by, revving its engine. Suddenly, Kevin's hand dropped down onto the gearshift and the car was in motion. My door was thrown shut as we leapt forward. The car made a U-turn out of the parking lot with the back end stepping out under heavy acceleration. The Firebird came to rest at a stoplight right beside the waiting Nova. "Here, kid!" Kevin leaned over to fasten my lap belt, quickly glancing up at the cross traffic light as the Nova prepared to launch. "Unscrew that red nozzle on that nitrous tank at your feet." I started to unscrew the top nozzle of what looked like an oxygen tank for a deep-sea diver, and I heard the rush of some type of gas filling the lines that left it. "Good, now tell me when that light turns."

"Now!"

Kevin's hands weren't even back on the wheel when the light turned green and the Chevy pulled its front wheels off the ground as it left the line. The Firebird lit up the tires in pursuit. We steadily gained on the Chevy as a grin streaked across my face. The engine screamed as Kevin's hand slapped the Hurst ratchet shifter. The back end broke loose as the car happily found second gear. The rear bumper of the Nova was now racing toward us as second gear approached the red line. I glanced at the speedometer as it flew past eighty miles per hour. We were gaining, creeping steadily past the Nova just as a cop drove by in the opposite direction. The Nova locked up the brakes and turned off on a side road. Kevin looked in his rearview mirror to see the police car whip a U-turn in pursuit. Kevin braked and turned down a street lined with cluster housing. Before the police car rounded the corner, Kevin had doused his lights and coasted with the engine off right up a driveway to a house that had all its lights off.

"Get down!" I hit the floorboard as Kevin ducked down by the steering wheel. Fascinated and exhilarated, I just stared at Kevin as he brought the car to a stop by using the emergency brake, just in front of the garage door. "Emergency brake won't turn on the brake lights, kid," he whispered. We both hunkered there, two statues, staring at each other in silence as the police car drifted slowly by, its radio squawking. "Shh! Make your heart stop beatin' so loud, kid. They're gonna hear us."

I saw his eyes go down to my heart, and then back up to my eyes.

"How do I do that?"

Kevin grinned at me. "I'm just kiddin', man. You can't control your heart. Figures, too, the most important part is outta our control."

As the sound of the police car faded, Kevin slowly sat up and looked around. I wanted to do it all over again, but I didn't want to get caught. Kevin let out the emergency brake, and the car rolled silently back to the street before he fired up the Firebird's engine.

"I should go, Kevin." Kevin smirked at me and punched my shoulder as we crept back to the theater at twenty miles per hour. The parking lot seemed desolate as we approached, then a set of headlights careened into the parking lot. "There's my mom," I said, as the car lights swerved down the alley on the far side of the theater.

"Since when'd you get a station wagon?"

"Yeah, it's her." I knew it was not my mother.

"Hey, if you don't tell anyone I kidnapped you, I won't tell anyone that you rode with a pot smoker."

"I won't. Hey, you hit that mailbox with the bent leg, din't you?"

"Either that, or it hit me. How'd you know we'd met?" Kevin smirked quizzically.

"Just guessed, that's all."

I got out into the brisk night air and closed the Firebird door with reverence, waving to Kevin until he drove off. Then I sat down on the steps of the empty theater, watching as the station wagon drove by slowly. I looked the other way, pretending to be expecting someone to get me. My stomach tightened as I waited for Lilyth. Finally, another car, an El Camino, approached from the other side of the theater and stopped in the alley. I was scared, but I hoped it was Lilyth. With my back to the car, I heard a door slam.

"Hey, ya little brat! Sorry I'm late. Been sittin' here long?" Lilyth walked up from the alley chewing a big wad of gum, taking it out of her mouth to talk, then sticking it back in.

"Just a couple minutes."

"Bullshit, it ended thirty minutes ago! So what'd ya think of the movie, ya retard?"

"Well, it wuddn't a cartoon like on the poster."

"No, but I figured your brain needs a little poisoning. How'd ya like the part where that guy with the eyelash crushes that lady to death using that big white stone dick!?" I must've made a face that she didn't understand. "God! You're such a baby."

"The bad guys had a cool race car, and the music was good."

"Yeah, my friend Max has the soundtrack, it's great. Ludwig van Beethoven on fucking acid! Come on." We walked across the dimly lit parking lot. I glanced back at the two-sided theater marquee. *Peter Pan* on one side, but the farther we walked, the more the second side of the marquee came into view, and I found out the title of the movie I had seen was *A Clockwork Orange*. "And remember, we saw *Peter Pan* together."

"All right. Where're we goin'?"

"To the new Baskin-Robbins. I told Mom to pick us up there at eight, in case I was late."

"Where'd you go?"

"None o' your beeswax, ya little shit! But I had to go over to Magda's 'cause her boyfriend just dumped her."

"Why?"

"'Cause she's gonna have a baby, she's keeping it this time, and if you tell Mom and Dad, I'll kill you. Anyway her boyfriend duddn't love her. It don't matter, he was an asshole anyway." I glanced back at the El Camino as it was pulling away. "He ain't father material, is all."

"Was that him?"

"No, that was Felix, he just gave me a ride. He's a friend of Kevin's. His real name is Oscar, but he loves *The Odd Couple* and he's more Lemmon than Matthau, so I renamed him."

I pondered this. "He let you?"

"I just did it, dumbass, I didn't ask. Like when I started calling you Mickey when you was a baby 'cause you reminded me of that stupid fuckin' mouse Mom'd make me watch when she was dotin' on you."

"Then how does he know you're not just dumb?"

"Why would he think I'm dumb?"

"Maybe he thinks you forgot his name." I kept my hands shoved in my pockets and Lilyth stared down at me, shaking her head.

"You're stupid. You're smart enough to know that, right?"

Lilyth cupped the back of my head just as a shiny new custom Chevy van idled up alongside us. A long-haired guy with a goatee that looked like pipe cleaners stuck his head out of the passenger window.

"Hey sugar-pop, I recognize that perfume from Halloween. I float 'em, Utotem, baby. Want a ride?"

"No, we're fine." We kept walking and Lilyth didn't even look at the car.

"C'mere, baby, lemme show you somethin'."

"I said we're *fine*." Lilyth stopped in her tracks and pulled me behind her to face the man directly. I tried to peek around, but she kept her arms behind her like a corral around me, and I gagged on the smell of her perfume steaming off her jeans, even in the autumn chill. "Drive away, fuckhead! Drive away right now, or I swear to God I will pick up a rock and smash it through your fucking car window!" Lilyth reached down to grab a piece of rubble. She wound up her arm like a viper ready to strike.

"Bitch!" the hippie yelled as they shoved off. "Why y'ain't *nice* no more?"

Lilyth gently drew my hand out of my pocket and held it, and we crossed the boulevard just like that, hand in hand. I was powerless to refuse her. And I wondered how long this was going to last before she cuffed me or pinched me or came up with a new hateful remark. Once we got to the other side, Lilyth kneeled down and hugged me tight. I stiffened, holding my breath against her caustic perfume.

"Come here, Mickey." She leaned back to give me space but stayed kneeling right in front of me, looking at me compassionately. "And hey, don't tell Mom and Dad about that hippie van, either, or we won't get to come here anymore."

For the first time, I felt oddly safe with my sister. Hostage and jailer: I guess I was hers to abuse. I let Lilyth continue to hold my hand until we reached the ice cream place, where we stood in silence under the fluorescent lights waiting for Mom.

I had been to this spot a million times with my Grandaddy for a delicious breakfast when it was still The Piccadilly Cafeteria. My stomach grumbled loud enough for Lilyth to hear it, but she gave no reaction. I didn't dare break the peace asking if there was any money left for food at the fancy-looking Baskin-Robbins that had replaced The Piccadilly.

"Anyway, you wanna know why Mom and Dad wanted me to take you to the movies?"

"Why?"

"'Cause they're at home in the garage fixin' a surprise for you, not that you deserve it, ya little shit bag." I stared at my sister.

"They can't be. Dad's using poisonous chemicals in the garage. Mom said."

"GOD! You kill me. Those chemicals are the paint for your surprise, dumbass."

To my astonishment, Lilyth was pushing me inside the Baskin-Robbins, cutting in line past kids younger than her but older than me, and pointing at a million flavors as she pulled out a wad of cash. I could not understand why she had so much money or why there were so many choices in ice cream flavors.

"Chocolate, please," I said. Andy and his nerd friends were already at the register paying, and Andy was licking a pink ice cream cone. I raised my hand by my chest, and he raised his palm back at me in mutual, respectful, indifferent recognition. Since Andy bailed after the first day of football season way back, I only ever saw him in passing. "They've got chocolate, Andy, they ain't out of it," I said earnestly. I meant it.

"I like strawberry," Andy said softly between licks, like I

would have said I like football, or race cars, or most especially Jane, had I ever told anyone about her. Andy's strawberry ice cream made no sense to me at the time. Why strawberry, when chocolate was what mattered?

I nodded politely to the alien savoring strawberry ice cream and turned away to watch the lady scoop my chocolate chilled heaven into a waffle cone.

"Don't you wanna know what it is?" asked Lilyth.

"What?"

"Your surprise, dipshit."

Andy's friends eyeballed Lilyth as they crowded toward the door.

"It's a surprise. I'll see it when we get home." I remained cool, but inside, of course, I was getting flutters of curiosity. Anytime something amazing was about to come into my life, I wouldn't discuss with anyone the possibility of it arriving, not even with my Grandaddy. I've always felt in the back of my mind that acknowledging something good's close proximity to me would somehow slow its approach or make it turn around and go away altogether. Conversely, if I was afraid of something, I had to look it in the eye, address it out loud. Acknowledging something bad seemed to always make it just a bit smaller, a bit more tolerable. I could quantify its danger and develop a game plan or escape. But now, Lilyth was popping her seams wanting to be the one to tell me what I was getting and spoil my surprise.

"Bullshit, it's a bike. Dad got one of the stolen ones from the police station, and he's rebuildin' it and paintin' it in the garage, so people won't know that we're poor and have to have used stuff. But I'm not supposed to tell you. So don't tell them you know, or I'll tell 'em you bit me." Lilyth opened her mouth and started biting her own hand. A horn honked. Lilyth stopped and turned her back on me. I watched as she walked off toward the door and out to Mom's Dodge Dart, leaving me standing there to nurse my cone. "Well, hurry up, shit head!"

Inside, I smiled.

Mom was so happy when Lilyth and I got in her car, saying how *nice* to see you two smilin' like the best friends that you are.

⸻

"Ready?" asked Dad, standing next to the garage door like he was about to show me the wizard behind the curtain.

"Yeah."

My dad slowly opened the garage door, and right next to his British racing green '58 MGA sat a completely redone and gleaming British racing green Schwinn Sting-Ray with all new components. Brand-new green handle grips with black streamers, a brand-new black banana seat with a silver stripe, a new chrome sissy bar, polished chrome handlebars, and two new tires, the rear being a slick. I just stood there silent and frozen, with my hands over my mouth trying not to cry.

"I couldn't wait for Christmas," admitted Dad. "But don't touch it yet."

A newspaper beneath the bike with green spray paint splotches slowed my advance. Mom held Steve McQueen so his thumping Weimaraner tail could wag and not get stuck in the paint. I didn't dare even sniff the bike up close.

My throat closed on a lump and I could hardly breathe. The Grunt came, and I buried my face in Mom and Dad, hugging them to hide my emotions. I could hear my sister screaming from inside the house, "Oh my God, I love it!" before joining us back in the driveway.

"Well, what do you think? I put a lower gear on it so it'll accelerate out of the corners like a bat outta hell."

Crying over a bike was only something that pussies do, and I was calling upon all of my resources to not be a pussy. But the Schwinn Sting-Ray that my dad built and painted for me in that garage was the best gift I have ever received in my life ... and my sister got a new shag carpet.

"I love it." I hid my eyes. My dad gingerly tapped the crossbar, testing the paint.

"Hmmm, feels like it might be dry enough." Dad looked at me expectantly. "Wanna take it for a spin?"

"Yeah!" I exclaimed, my grumbling tummy long forgotten.

"It's dark out, y'all," my mom called.

"Let's live dangerously." Dad jerked his head toward the street mischievously.

I handed over the leather thong from around my neck dangling his silver stopwatch. Dad followed me in his car with the stopwatch around his neck as I rode furiously around the block. That first night, the Bentliff block lap record fell by almost four full seconds. As I sped past Jane's on Sandpiper Drive, I prayed she saw me from her window. The lights were on there, so I guessed they were still in the process of moving, even though I had not seen her. The temperature had dropped and the air was fresh and crisp, but I was sweating so much I did not mind it.

"Okay one more lap, Sug. Time for bed," hollered Mom, shivering under the big bean tree at the foot of the driveway as I sped by again.

I parked the Schwinn right in my bedroom that night, and I don't remember sleeping at all, even with Steve McQueen curled up as a foot warmer. Steve's slobber and Mom's perfume woke me early when she kissed my brow. I had gone to bed in my clothes so I would not have to take time to dress. My prize gleamed in the morning light, and I sprang out of bed to ride it. I angled the Schwinn past the projector on the floor where I had left Jane pointing at the wall. I took the film from the projector and stowed the reel back in my Charles Chips can, and stuck the can in my closet. As I wheeled my new bike out to the kitchen for a spin around the block, a pop and whoosh followed by a waft of Folger's coffee grounds overtook the smell of peanut butter on burnt pancakes.

Lilyth had left early, so I felt safe and happy and very, very hungry.

"Zat you, Sug? Eat! Breakfast's on the table." In the kitchen, Mom handed me a stack of more returned letters and my lunch bag. "You got ready quick, Sug. Oh, take your milk money, and here are some more postal experiments. In lieu of that broken box on the corner, we're gonna have to mail them from another part of town. Seems the mailman thinks we're wastin' tax dollars."

"Are we?"

"Are we what?"

"Wastin' tax dollars?"

"Absolutely not! You can mail as many as you want, from any postbox you want. Now, git!" Mom hugged me hard and shoved me off gently toward my plate of food.

On the way to school I timed myself around Bentliff Street, past Jane's on Sandpiper Drive, then flew across the baseball diamonds straight for the other side of the park followed by Steve McQueen at full gallop.

"Go on home, boy!"

As I approached the stand of trees where The Hole hid, I saw The Plank with its red Firebird parked alongside the gash in the world. I coasted over to the car, but no one was in it. I looked around and still saw no one. As I was getting back on my bike, I heard the groan of someone in pain, so I stopped. The moaning continued and I followed it into the stand of trees and then right up to the mouth of The Hole. Blackness disappeared into eternal blackness, and the moaning persisted.

Lilyth had been the first one who had ever told me about The Hole in the world right on the edge of the diamonds, and that you could go there and hide if you wanted to and no one would ever find you. But the groans worried me because if someone had gone to hide, they must have accidentally gotten hurt and needed help. The opening into The Hole was hardly big enough to squeeze into if you were an adult. I kneeled down and peered in. I dropped my feet down into the narrow chasm and I tried to wedge myself into it. I got about four feet down before the gap got a bit tighter and the floor seemed to disappear, and my head was stuck at a bad angle between two slabs of compressed earth. Unable to feel a path for my feet, with four feet of stone and dirt above me, I started to panic. Clearly there was a path that zigzagged downward, and someone down there was hurting. The moaning below me echoed up at me, wedged in there between the rock surfaces, my breathing quickened, and I had to climb back out or hyperventilate myself into a coma. I could not imagine how anyone bigger than me could even fit through the tiny slivers of twisted space to get in there. Steve McQueen whined, staring down at me. But I was relieved he had disobeyed me and waited. As I pulled myself up out of the rock crevice, Steve licked my face and bounded around, and then I noticed a bra lying in the dirt next to Kevin's car.

"Go on home, Mr. McQueen. I'm fine." I patted Steve to send him off, then I walked over and picked up the bra and backtracked to look down The Hole again, reaching it just as words arose from below.

"Oh my God, Kevin! You're SO deep!"

I ran for my bike and pedaled as fast as I could straight for school. I had never thought for a second that Kevin was a guy who would go hiding himself in The Hole, but if he was, at least someone had found him. At school, Steve McQueen lumbered around after squirrels as I parked my Schwinn at the rack under Mrs. Bradford's classroom so I could keep a close eye on it. They were already somewhere between attendance and the Pledge of Allegiance.

"Go home, Steve!" I shooed off my dog.

Before I could lock my bike, Mr. Totter's shadow arose behind me and he slammed his wooden paddle on my banana seat. Steve McQueen barked.

"Mickey!"

I turned around to face Mr. Totter just as he reached for my sissy bar and removed the bra that had somehow got caught as I was fleeing The Hole. He held up the bra accusingly, sniffing it as if he could identify the owner solely with his nose. Like he was a sommelier of lingerie. Totter's shadow of suspicion solidified to a lump of char.

"March! To the principal's office!" He stared at me like a

field commander willing a soldier to go AWOL so he could unleash even more of his misappropriated authority. But I knew that he had probably ridden at the front of the bus his entire life and dodged spitballs shot at the back of his head. And I bet he deserved each and every one of them.

"Yes, sir, I'll just lock my bike up first."

With bra and paddle Mr. Totter threw me toward the school door two-handed, and I stumbled, but caught my balance before smashing my face into the door handle. There was no way in hell I would let someone like Totter upset my balance enough to put me on all fours.

"Is this your idea of a joke, boy? I think you'll leave your bike right where it is, and come with me for a little chat." I turned around away from the school steps and walked right back past Mr. Totter to the rack by Mrs. Bradford's window. "Where are you going?" But I just kept walking. I had to. "Damn it boy, you'll listen to me when I talk to you!" Steve McQueen barked again. "Lest you forget, I am an adult!"

"Don't holler at him, Steve, go home." I patted my dog, who stood on point to protect me. "I'm *fine*, Steve. Go on." But I was not about to tell Steve this was a *nice* man. Mr. Totter's shouting had drawn Mrs. Bradford and a crowd of students to the window. Firefly was tapping on the glass, but I did not dare make eye contact. I just locked up my bike.

"Do you wanna get a *pop* right here, boy? Who in the hell raised you to think that you can just ignore an adult!" When I finished locking my bike, I turned to face the principal and I looked him square in his cold rat eyes.

"The same adult that told me to lock up my bike...unless you wanna tell my daddy why it wuddn't locked? Now, you wanna talk about the bra, sir?"

"In my office! I'm calling your father."

I glanced up at my homeroom window. Mrs. Bradford tipped her head compassionately, and Firefly was doing his fat dance and mouthing the words *lest you forget.*

———

I was instructed to sit outside the principal's office, where his secretary could watch me. As if I might go stealing another bra if left unguarded. Behind the frosted glass I could hear the muffled argument going on inside Totter's lair. His assistant Claire was pretty and young and seemed uncomfortable with the whole business seeping through the door. She kept staring at me as if she was sizing me up for a special mission that she wasn't sure if she could tell me about just yet. She even stuck her finger into her ear and swirled it around a few times before pulling it out and looking at it. I thought it strange for her to so unself-consciously do that without taking her eyes off of me. And I wondered if any other girls did things like this. I knew Jane didn't. But, I guess I wasn't in the age range of guys that Claire would feel embarrassed in front of. The two of us just stared at each other while the yelling swelled. She then leaned all the way across her desk and held her wrist out—upturned to me.

"Do you think this smells nice?" Claire didn't even wait for me to answer. "It's Charlie by Revlon. *Vogue* says Charles Revson's got a nephew who's a Formula One race car driver..." Claire stopped when the din within increased, and I really wished her to stay stopped so I could hear what was being said, unless she added more things about Formula One.

"The next time you approach my boy and threaten him

with that goddamn paddle in your hand, I swear to God I'll come up here and shove it straight up your fuckin' ass!"

"Paul, I think..."

"So, ya ever heard of Led Zeppelin?" Claire asked me.

I nodded, not wanting to miss the argument.

"Don't *Paul* me! Every parent knows about you. You drag me away from work for something as ridiculous as this shit? Oughta fuckin' be ashamed of yourself, Totter! Is this about that fuckin' cannon?"

"Well, the renegade efforts of the cavalier men in your family to impress the fairer sex..."

"Fairer sex, Totter? You need ta fuckin' watch it right now. Her name is Genie, and she's *my* wife. It was never gonna be you, ya little turd! And she didn't marry me because I rolled a goddamn cannon into an intersection! It was high school, another part of your life you musta slept through."

"Well, I just thought Mickey..."

"You thought!? Just find out next time before you go pointing your goddamn finger at everyone you *think* has done something wrong! But you have to ask him. Do it calmly, and in private. He'll answer any questions you've got. But you've got to go about it in the way that you'd eventually like him to go about it."

"I think Robert Plant is God," murmured Claire.

Suddenly the door opened, startling Claire, and Mr. Totter came out behind a fake smile, attempting to glad-hand my dad.

"Well, Claire, balance is restored at our school. You're safe." Dad rolled his eyes, as if Claire had been at risk. "It seems Mickey was just helping his mom with some laundry before school, and it must've just...gotten stuck. I'm sorry, Mickey, you can go to class now. Paul, always a pleasure."

"Likewise, Mr. Totter, and don't hesitate to call me if that boy gives you any trouble." Dad winked at me, and I headed to class.

My dad didn't even ask me about the bra until that night. When I told him, he just laughed, but he told me to stay away from The Hole.

"Mickey!" Mr. Totter speed-walked down the hall at me once he checked that my dad was out of sight. At that moment, Andy was arriving late to school and walking toward us. "Uh, you might return this, uh, brassiere to your mother." Mr. Totter handed me a brown paper lunch bag stapled shut just as Andy walked past, pretending politely to have overheard nothing about a brassiere. "Now, I've double-bagged the brassiere, lest you forget, I don't want to see or hear of that bag being opened until you get home, understood?"

"Yes, sir."

"Very well, then." Mr. Totter tilted and spun on his heel and sped back to his office.

I opened the door to my homeroom just as Andy was entering his homeroom down the hall. We nodded to each other, acknowledging each other's existence, and mostly, politely and simply acknowledging that neither one of us cared that we had absolutely nothing in common with each other, from sports to ice cream. As I entered Mrs. Bradford's homeroom, everyone turned away from the three paintings leaning on the chalkboard and stared at me.

"Everything okay, Mickey?" Mrs. Bradford smiled.

"Yes, ma'am."

"Okay, well, we were just talking about inventions." She retrieved something from her satchel while I passed the three paintings slowly. All three paintings were small and all were signed at the bottom-right corner: *Jane Two*. I felt a surge of joy, like seeing old friends.

Firefly was shooting me thumbs-up from the back of the group. As I walked down the aisle to my seat, I noticed that everyone looked at me just a little bit differently.

"A bra?" Emmalyne asked, hushed. I glanced at her, but kept walking to my seat. Others ran with it.

"I heard she had big boobs, too."

"I heard she was in high school!"

"And he smacked Mr. Totter or somethin' like that."

"Cool bike!" whispered Firefly.

"All right, I'd like everyone to write down an idea for an invention and bring it to class tomorrow." Mrs. Bradford handed one paper to the first desk on the left row, then another to the first desk on the far row. "Here are a couple of examples to look at. It can be absolutely anything." One of the papers that finally got to me smelled of that sweet spice I loved. I read it and inhaled her, and all the silence in the world came screaming into the room. I remember the example I read was for an antigravity machine that utilized two objects that wielded the same attraction and would thus cancel each other out. I didn't have to see *Two* in the corner to know it was Jane's creation. One of the objects was a cat, citing the fact that no matter how you held a cat and dropped it, it would always land on its feet. The other was a slice of peanut butter toast, which, with ten years of breakfasts to the inventor's credit, had been proven to always land peanut-butter-side down, if dropped. The inventor Suggested that if the toast were strapped to the back of the cat peanut-butter-side up, then the cat would just hover if dropped—in defiance of gravity—with each side insisting on hitting the ground, when only one could be allowed.

Jane's parents were Woodstockers who actually numbered their children. Two had become Jane's middle name by the time I discovered her. Jane Two. And that's when it dawned on me what I had been overhearing in my neighborhood, "One, Two, Three, Four, Five, let's go!" It had been Mrs. Bradford calling each of her children to come inside and eat. Jane was a true flower child, and the more I learned about her, the more I fell in love with her. And because she was the only daughter of Mr. and Mrs. Bradford, and she went to a different school across town, I was reasonably confident that I was the only person who understood this secret reference to Jane.

John Lennon once said to me, while my ears were wrapped in headphones, that he thought no one was in his tree. And that's too bad, because as my Grandaddy used to say, loneliness is an eyesore. But I had definitely found someone in mine. Jane's nonsense suited my nonsense. To say I was smitten would qualify for the understatement-of-the-year award. Jane was the most perfect person in the history of perfect people or in the history of ever, for that matter. Jane was the answer.

I charged home after school as fast as I could pedal, passing The Plank with its Firebird right where I had seen it that morning. I felt like a superhero. As I flew past, I believed Kevin's car stereo when it told me that once I made my mind up, neither Superman nor the Green Lantern had anything on me. Kevin was on that Firebird's roof again, holding court to the other heads and druggies, with Lilyth, his queen, cuddled up right next to him shivering in the cold under a football blanket—my football blanket! She had skipped school again. Kevin shot me a sly grin. I always liked when he did that, but I just kept on pedaling.

I could usually tell pretty accurately what radio station a person would listen to by the type of car they drove and the look of the driver. And because it was usually a searing heat in Texas, and rarely so cold to require a sealed and heated car, almost everyone had their windows rolled down regardless of the time of year. So, if I heard something good, my route home could become somewhat erratic trying to continue the song on the radio of passing cars. At the first intersection after the park, I headed for a Mustang with some high school kids in it backing out of a driveway, swerving around it to Donovan reminding us what happens to a mind when it surrenders to a forever love, and I pedaled away. I rounded The Dancing Mailbox at the corner on Bentliff Street as I blazed down Sandpiper Drive, straight for Jane's house, cross-referencing which most important thing I should say to her first. When I reached the line of tall bushes that lined the Bradfords' driveway, I set my bike down behind it, parted the hedge, and poked my head through just enough to see that their garage door was open. It smelled of spilled turpentine, even from where I stood, and Jane's spice. On a cinder block bundled up in a poufy purple down vest, painting under her headphones, sat Jane. Her voice was soft, filling the air with "Sunshine Superman" and the rewards of giving love time. I'd already heard the song end as I rode past a Camaro, so I knew that she was singing along to my 45 . . . *my* 45!

I had so many things that I wanted to tell her, and I just didn't want them to all overlap. I wanted her to hear every one of my thoughts alone, so she could understand, but I also wanted her to have the feeling of them all combined. I had all of my love for her categorized alphabetically and damn near subdivided by category, and I wanted to give it to her in a delicately wrapped box. I straightened my hair, took a deep breath, and stepped through the ficus bushes just as AMERICAN VANLINES obliterated Jane from my line of sight. As the movers backed up the driveway, I heard Mrs. Bradford greeting the driver, so I ducked back behind the bushes and listened to her give the driver directions to a storage facility as the new house was still under construction.

Truck doors slammed and I waited while the movers followed Mrs. Bradford into the house, then I strode around to the garage, where Jane had been just moments earlier. I could still smell her there, but my eyes could no longer find her. I wanted to continue on to the front door and ring that goddamn bell, but my legs stopped working when my window of confidence slammed shut with that orange VW door. The snickering engine propelled the VW Vanagon forward, and I watched it drive off with Jane lightly perched in the front passenger seat.

As my Schwinn careened around the corner a few houses up from mine, I waved to the Milans, out bundled up in wool Cowboys blankets nested in their lawn chairs drinking beers and holding hands. Even from afar they recognized me, and Mr. Milan hollered, "There's my soldier!" Then I saw The Plank. Lilyth was getting out and blocked my path as she saw me approaching, so I skidded to a stop beside the Firebird.

"Hey! Listen, Mickey, don't tell Dad that Kevin gave me a ride home, okay?" Kevin flashed me a grin. "I'll give you a dollar, ya lil' brat! Kevin, give me a buck." Lilyth snatched my brown paper bag hostage to prevent me from tearing off before she could hand me my bribe money. "What's in yer lunch bag?"

"Give it back, Lilyth!"

She tore open Totter's staples. "Where the hell did you get this? Kevin, Mic's got my bra!" I tried to put everything together, and even looked to Kevin for explanation, but he was too high to clue in. "Answer me, y'little retard!"

"From, um...Mr. Totter...he..."

As Lilyth looked to Kevin for support, I took off pedaling for home.

"MICKEY! Damn it, get back here!" Winded, I dragged my Schwinn inside the house and leaned against the front door to catch my breath, trying to process one of life's little revelations now aggregating in my head.

"Wanna eat somethin', Sug?" I just stood at the door processing my sister and The Hole. "You fine, darlin'?"

"Yeah, Mom." I gasped for air as I walked to the fridge to grab the bottle of Gatorade. I gulped green, stopping only to catch my breath. Mom kept on charring fish sticks and stirring grits.

For a long time, I hung on the refrigerator door and chugged.

"Shut that door and use a glass!" I sat down at the kitchen table. I needed to after that. "Lawrence and his mother came by today. Seems you and Lawrence will be on the swim team together. And she and I think it'll be okay to ride bikes if y'all go together."

"Who's Lawrence?"

"Y'all played football together. Big ole thing for a young fella. I think y'all call him Fireball? Or, Fireplug, maybe?"

"He's actually gonna swim?"

"I s'pose so. And as long as y'all stay together, bikes are okay. But stay together and be careful, that pool ain't just around the block."

I hugged my mom and thanked her, and as soon as I got my wits about me, I opened the sliding glass door and thumped out just in time to hear, "One, Three, Five!" So I came right back inside to the kitchen just as Lilyth stormed in, eyes aflame, breathless.

"Mom! I just thought you should know, I'm really concerned, I saw Mickey smoking."

From the stove, Mom turned to me and took a long drag of her cigarette. I knew she was thinking what to say. For a time she regarded me, standing there dumbfounded by Lilyth's bold-faced lie constructed to get attention off her bra, in case I had already told on her. I didn't tell on her and I didn't smoke. I had never smoked. Smoking fucking disgusted me. It still does. But I didn't know any words to protect myself outside of *that's not true*, so I left the room without saying anything else.

"Mom, I'm telling you!" persisted Lilyth.

Mom called after me, "We ain't done discussin' this till your father's home, Sug." I went straight to my room—to my Charles Chip can. I lost myself in her, and I didn't hear another lying word about smoking for quite a while.

On Saturday morning, I met Firefly by The Ditch about an hour earlier than swim practice and we set out across town. We didn't really know how long it would take us to ride to the pool, so we gave ourselves a healthy margin. Down the golf cart path lined by huge houses under construction, we gaped at the fancy neighborhood. Eventually, I had to stop and wait for Firefly because he lagged so far behind.

As he caught up, I heard him yelling, "What the hell you stoppin' for, Mic? You can't hack it? I mean, if you need to, it's fine with me! We can stop if you need to. Do you?" Sweating profusely, Firefly coasted to a stop alongside me. "Damn, what is this place?" From under the trees near hole eighteen, we looked out at the landscape, and we both had to sit our asses down, taking it all in. There were huge houses everywhere like giant empires growing out of the verdant sod. Across the groomed green, I saw a giant butter yellow house still under construction that looked like something out of the movies. Firefly rolled on the golf turf that looked just like the fake grass at the Putt-Putt, only it was real. "Jeezus, how they git it like this?"

"It's like velvet." I joined Firefly and rolled, too.

"What the fuck's velvet?" asked Firefly.

"My Mamau has some. It's really nice. Expensive, too."

And then out of Firefly's mouth emerged James's gold standard. "Man, these houses are fuckin' NIGGER-COCK!" I asked Firefly where he had heard that term before and what he thought it meant. He said he had heard some cool black man on my porch say it when he and his mother had dropped by to talk about swim team, and that while his mom was inside, Firefly had sat next to him in a rickety lawn chair and coaxed the meaning out of him. And sure enough, James had told him the same thing that he told me that day that I was getting red-necked by Eddy.

"Nigger-cock, it just a little bit bigga, an a little bit betta'n anything like it. Now hush it, boy'n ya don't say it front a tha ladies." I guess, until I heard Firefly say it, I had just never heard it used to describe anything besides ability.

"Hey, that yellow one ain't got no door yet; let's go check it out," said Firefly. We rode our bikes across the exquisite expanse of emerald toward the inviting yellow clapboard structure. "It ain't got stairs, Mic." Firefly followed me as I clambered up about five feet of stacked building materials and crawled into a gaping entryway where a new door leaned against the wall. It looked like the workers had just suddenly got up and left. Big black thermoses and lunch boxes remained in the middle of a polished hardwood floor in what seemed like it would become an auditorium. "You think they got giraffes, Mic?" asked Firefly panning up wide-eyed to the ceiling of the living room. It smelled of new wood, Formica, and factory chemicals. "Mic, it's like inside a fuckin' whale's stomach!" The Moby Dick ceiling vaulted to heaven. Trimming the room's circumference halfway up the walls was a balcony whose dark, lustrous wood matched the crossbeams ribbing the high ceiling. "How the fuck you get up there? Must be stairs, right?" Firefly then grabbed a cedar roof shingle from a neat pile by a closet without doors, set it between two sawhorses, and karate chopped it in half with a loud Bruce Lee wail. "Hey, how many families do you think live in these things?" Firefly bit a shingle splinter from the butt of his hand.

"I'm pretty sure just one family each."

"Damn! Let's check out the bedrooms."

Down a wide hall past a huge, modern kitchen, I found what should have been stairs, but, like outside the house, there were just two flanking zigzag supports. I grabbed some planks that leaned against the wall and set them across the zigzag frame and climbed up to find two more floors, counting the attic, and five bedrooms each the size of my living room. The largest bedroom on the second floor overlooked the golf course at the back of the house. On the third floor, the back bedroom was in the process of being painted bright violet with apple green trim. I noticed another sawhorse, measuring tape, carpenter's pencils, and raw wood shelves. Across the room, two shutter-style doors hung ajar. A single poster was curling off the back wall of the walk-in closet. A large can of primer sat empty beside the closet door. I crossed the large room and opened the two doors all the way and stuck my head inside a walk-in closet that was the size of my bedroom. It looked like someone had abandoned a tea party in the closet with five purple toy cups and saucers and purple napkins and a guttered candle. A Farrah Fawcett T-shirt lay rumpled as the tea mat. I pulled down the curled corners of the poster to see that it was a classic shot of Marc Bolan from his T. Rex tour. I thought about stealing that poster until I saw a small, unfinished painting leaning against the wall in the corner. It was the painting of the field of green that I had observed Jane laboring over in her garage, with those detailed blades of grass. It now had a giant white *H* goalpost right in the foreground. And I knew exactly where I was. It was Jane's room, and I was standing in it. I grabbed one of the wide-angle carpenter's pencils from the toolbox and quickly scribbled *I liken us to two balloons* across the bottom of her Bolan poster. And again, I prayed that she would remember that first day in the classroom.

"Jeezus, mother of Christ, Mic, where do they get the money?" I had no idea. "Oh shit, Mic, we better get the fuck outta here, I hear a motor." In a fit of panic, Firefly's red crew cut disappeared as he ran clomping back down so fast he knocked off most of the stair planks we had laid in place, forcing me to jump from the third floor to the second and then climb down a window frame all the way to the ground. My fear of going to jail superseded my desire to stay in her room forever...so I ran.

As I met Firefly out back behind the Leviathan past giant rolls of lawn sod, I noticed the pipes of the in-lawn sprinkler system and realized that even their dirt was "designed." And then a golf ball rolled right up to our toes. Gasping for air, Firefly reached down and started laughing uncontrollably, reading the ball.

"Fuck does zat mean, Mic? *Tit-lee-ist*? Like the biggest tits? I'm titly-est! Balls fer boobies." He held it up to his chest like a nipple then popped it in his pocket. "Check out that fuckin' golf cart goin' in circles. Buncha faggits, look at 'em wearin' them pink and bright green pants! Hey Mic, how far to the pool?"

"At the end of this path, there's another velvety putting green thing. Right next to that."

"You've been here before?"

"Only with my mom to sign up and get a suit."

"I ain't wearin' no faggit's underwear, showin' off the baloney pony! I ain't no goddamn figure skater!"

"Maybe you can ask to wear something else? But my dad says you won't go as fast."

"Shit! We gonna hafta start doing this trip five times a week!"

"It'll get easier."

"No it won't, I'm gon' die!"

The golf cart cruised up with two older men dressed to a T, one in starch-pressed pink trousers and the other in creased Kelly green trousers, and matching alligator shirts. The pink pants had a fabric belt with little blue-and-white whales on it. And the green pants had a matching green belt with little white sailboats around his gut. The older golfer in pink pants, who was around forty, came up to us with this swagger that looked like he might even fall over. You could tell that he was trying to be stealthy like a shark, but he just looked like a fat, overfed goldfish. Firefly and I got on our bikes.

"Say, have you boys seen a Titleist Three around here?" We looked at each other and shrugged before Firefly turned around to talk to the man.

"The hell's a Titus Three?"

"*Title-ist*. It's the brand name of a ball, a golf ball. Have you seen anything roll through here?" We shook our heads and started to pedal off. It was funny, I thought at the time, how the man had rolled out the word roll like he was putting on a south-of-the-border migrant Mexicano *rrrrrr*, yet he was talking like Mr. Howell from *Gilligan's Island*.

"Kid, if you should see it on your way, do grab it and I'll give you a buck for it."

"A whole buck? For a little piece a plastic shit?" yelled Firefly over his shoulder. Then Firefly locked up his brakes and tore a slash in the velvet green beneath his tires and turned to face the man. We both looked at him in disbelief. Then Firefly yells out, "I can find it for a buck. I mean, probly. I can probly find just about anything for a buck."

"All right, let's see you do it!" said Green Pants, the younger of the two.

I followed Firefly around the hedgerow where we huddled. Then we turned around and headed back toward the golfers.

"Hey, mister, found your Titly-est!" yelled Firefly.

"So, kid, how do I know you didn't have it all along?"

"Well, I guess ya don't."

"Well then, I guess I don't know if we'll give you two little thieves a dime!" snarled Pink Pants, but he wasn't very convincing.

"Then I guess I'll run and chunk it in that lake over there for the gators to chomp on, sir!" Firefly looked to me and grinned. "Can you believe these queer baits wearin' these weird-ass colored clothes? Fuckin' pink!"

"Boy, I'll run your fat ass down before you get ten feet away," boasted Green Pants. "And it is *Nantucket red*, you nitwit, not pink."

The provenance of pink trousers was lost on us, but Firefly, whose eyes sparked piss and vinegar, and smiling wide, threw the ball to me. "Yeah, well both of you together cain't catch Mickey. Gimme the buck and it's yours... or Mic runs, Mr. Pinkie, sir!"

Pinkie and Green Pants finally agreed to pay us, and I realized that our golf course currency was more valuable to them than the thick wad of cash they had in their pockets. Our economic glory led to ice cream from the Snack Shack at the pool, and to Firefly shaming himself in front of the young lady behind the counter.

"How much is a Fudgsicle?" Firefly ogled the waitress's chest. "Do you see them titties, Mic? She's the Titly-est right there, man!"

"Thirty-five cents. Hurry up, there's a line behind y'all."

"DAMN! What a rip-off. Okay, gimme one of those, and a Coke. How much is a Coke?"

"Twenty-five." The girl got his ice cream and drink from the cooler. "Anything else?"

"You sure, Mic? There's forty-five cents left. But if you get something, you're just as big'a crim'nal as me."

"It's forty cents, dumbass! And I'll have an ice cream san'wich, please, ma'am."

Firefly choked down the last of his Fudgsicle, disfiguring his mouth with brown glop, just as a sun-straw blond California surfer-type guy reeking of body odor approached us in nothing but a Speedo and flip-flops. Ominous like a giant praying mantis behind his mirrored aviator shades, he was very fit and very tan, and seemed very intent on us.

"Nice shades. Jeezus, this beach bum smells like he bathes with a crystal. Or shit, right?"

The man had stopped directly in front of us with his hands on his hips.

"Okay, which one of you is Mickey, and which one is the Food Flea?" He growled when he spoke.

"Who the hell wants to know, Leif Garrett? You eye-ballin' my friend here? Mic, will y'look at this faggit, he's nekked!"

"I can hear you, you little shit. You do know you're standing right in front of me, don't you? I'm Coach Randall, and I need you to watch that tongue." As our new swim coach's eyes seared a laser burn around Firefly's slack-jawed and chocolate-ice-cream-slathered mouth, he reached over and removed my ice cream sandwich from my hold and threw it in the trash without taking his gaze off Firefly.

In awe, Firefly finally conceded, "Fuck, I'm sorry about them cuss words. That last one, too, even."

"I'm guessin' you must be the flea. So you must be Mickey. Your principal told me all about you." I wasn't sure what Coach Randall had heard, so I kept silent. "But I think Mr. Totter's an asshole, so, you two should be all right with me. C'mon. Let's warm up. Oh yeah, and there's only one rule. You can't eat for an hour before practice. If ya do, well, you'll see." Then Coach Randall looked at me and softened a bit. "After practice, I'll buy you another ice cream sandwich."

Right then and there, as we walked together from the Snack Shack to the pool, Coach Randall started making us learn his oath he had picked up on Maui as a surfer. *I pledge allegiance to the health of this wondrous jewel that is my body. One instrument, under God, that every positive act I intend to contribute to this world is necessary for, and without which, the provisions of love, knowledge, and goodwill*—on and on it went, but by the end of our first practice, Coach Randall had succeeded in beating the oath into us.

And sure enough, right off the bat Coach Randall exhausted us both, traversing that pool more times than I could count. By the end of practice, Firefly was puking up his Fudgsicle and wailing about the loss of our extorted funds. Our teammates fled the pool as I grabbed two skimmers and helped Firely clean the water, since I did not want to swim in his vomit, either. There were two Olympic-size pools right next to each other, and the twelve- to sixteen-year-olds' team in the other pool kept ragging on Firefly about the puke.

"I couldn't help it. Hey, can I have a bite, Mic?"

As promised, Coach Randall handed me a new ice cream sandwich and then headed over to the other pool, shouting instructions to each lane, mostly kids with kickboards doing laps. I savored the first bite slowly and then handed the remainder to Firefly, who wolfed it and immediately wailed, "Brain freeze!" and threw himself into a poolside conniption, banging himself in the head with the skimmer lid, then wrapping the skimmer net around his head as he rolled around by the edge of the pool.

"Okay, I'm fine." Calmly, he stood and looked around. "Is there more ice cream?"

In the parking lot just past the fence, I noticed the red Firebird, so I moved closer with the skimmer, still pretending to scrape the surface of the water. At the adjacent pool, Coach Randall talked through the wrought iron fence to Kevin, leaning on the hood of his car.

"Oh, he's a fuckin' pothead. Coach'll get him arrested."

"Shhhh." I sidled closer to the wrought iron gate to eavesdrop.

"What the fuck's wrong with his car? Fuck, I want that car."

"Shut up Firefly, I wanna listen."

"Kevin, don't let the others see you smoking!" Coach Randall snatched Kevin's cigarette and doused it in a puddle poolside. "I don't care how good you are, if you don't put in during practice, you're not swimming in the meets." Grinning, Kevin was looking right at me once again. "Hey, are you hearing me? Kevin, eye contact, right here!" Coach Randall was gesturing big to get Kevin to look at him. Kevin never responded. "Kevin, you gotta show up for practice!"

"You ain't the boss of me," Kevin bit off.

"Kevin, Jesus! Hey!" Frustrated, Coach Randall glanced around and waved the swimmers to focus on practice.

Kevin grinned and gave me the peace sign, then fired up his plank and drove off.

On our way home, Firefly and I biked by Sandpiper Drive past Jane's house, where the movers were in the truck. The house looked empty, as if this was maybe the last load.

"Ya know, Mic, it's quicker to take Bentliff the whole way."

"This is the way you gotta go, so I might as well just go with you then go around."

"But we could drop by your house and eat somethin'."

"We're nearly to your turnoff."

"God, I don't know how you don't get tired ridin' this far. I'm fuckin starved."

We reached the end of Sandpiper, where Firefly had to go straight to reach his house, and I turned onto Bentliff.

"All right, see ya tomorrow, man."

"Yeah, meet you at The Ditch first thing."

I waited till Firefly was out of sight, then turned right around, riding back by Jane's. From the ficus hedgerow, I sat on my bike and observed the movers loading furniture. After a while, I set my bike down and pushed past the branches to the other side, and peered around the corner. After Jane's couch got loaded onto the truck, the movers glanced over at me and went back into the house. I crept around the side of the garage and looked in the backyard, where her trampoline was rusting. I was appalled—*her* trampoline was rusting. I headed back around to the front. One of the movers was strapping in a chifforobe against the inside wall of the truck, so I ventured closer.

"Hi, sir."

"Hey, kid!"

The mover went back into the house, and I took a step into

the garage, where Jane's paints remained on a table. Her canvases were stacked up against the wall. Another mover came walking out with a taped-up box.

"Hi, sir." The mover ignored me and mounted the ramp into the truck. So, I got a bit closer and tried again, looking up at him. "Hi, sir."

"Hi, there!"

"Do you know if the Bradfords are home?"

"They've been gone most of the day."

"Do you know if they're gone for good?"

"Electricity ain't even on in the new place yet; guessin' they'll be back if ya wanna wait."

The mover jumped off the truck, and when I was sure he was all the way inside the house, I approached Jane's workbench with her brushes and paints like I was approaching a shale precipice. I picked up an old brush encrusted with dried paint and inhaled the pungent chemical scent Jane breathed every day. I put on Jane's headphones and felt the foam that had wrapped her ears wrap mine.

"Hey, kid, you a friend'a the little girl?" I jumped and yanked off the headphones.

"Um, I don't know ... maybe ..."

Chuckling, the man continued on into the truck to set down his boxes, smiling to himself.

"Well, when are you gonna know for sure?" It took a second for me to figure out if he was still talking to me or not, but there was no one else there.

"I thought maybe today."

The man nodded knowingly and went back into the house. I looked at the paintbrush in my hand and then back to the door to see if anyone was looking. I ran through the bushes to my bike. Struggling with my bike that was caught up in ficus, I dropped the brush but caught it before it hit the ground, and rode off. As I rode past, I waved at Mr. and Mrs. Milan parked out on their supreme green lawn and realized I was waving Jane's paintbrush. Without disentangling their clasped hands from each other's, they waved back at me as one.

Lined up on aluminum lawn chairs in my yard, I found Mom, Dad, Lew Hoagie, and his can of Miller High Life and a cigarette surrounded by remnants of the garage sale they had had out front. As I was riding up the drive, Lilyth was finishing selling her black velvet wall tapestry of a tiger to one of Magda's grimy new boyfriends.

"Yes, I'm sure she loves it. Just buy it for her, stupid."

"Hey, Touchdown, what do you say, Mic?"

Lew raised his beer and cigarette to me in greeting.

"Um, I don't know, Mr. Hoagie."

He was already pretty drunk, and his short shorts were riding up his chicken legs toward his gut.

"You want to go to Shakey's tonight, Sug?" I hugged Mom and remained attached to her hip. "Your dad and I made a hundred and eight dollars today."

"Wow, yeah! How'd ya do that?"

"Garage sale, Sug."

"Whole neighborhood came over and bought all the junk your mom's been keepin' for a rainy day, and Lew sold his Purple Heart from Vietnam."

"And his Bronze Star. Them medals was so *nice*."

"Fuckin' meant nothin' t'me," slurred Lew.

"Mickey, go put your bike away so we can eat, 'cause we gotta stop by the Piggly Wiggly, too. Lew?"

"Bring me back one of them hamburger pizzas, Genie.

And a six-pack, if you're goin' by the grocery. I only got four left."

I ran my bike toward the house, while my parents and Lilyth gathered up to get in the car. Molded to his chair on our lawn, Lew stayed.

"You sure, Lew? Don't taste so good out of a box."

"Tastes better if it ain't burnt, Genie," Lew slurred aggressively.

"Watch yourself, Lew, she cooks things exactly how I like 'em." Staring Lew down, Dad put his hand on Mom's shoulder.

"Sorry, Paul, I meant no disres...," quailed Lew, completely stewed.

My dad watched him sternly. "Lew."

"Yeah, Paul?" My dad just kept watching Lew, but Lew was past giving a shit. "What the fuck does Genie know about nice medals?"

"Lew, that's enough!" Dad shot back.

"It's *fine*, Paul, Lew's just drunk. I don't take it personal. He's a *nice* man, I know that."

"Let's go." My dad kept an eye on Lew while holding the car door for my mom and kissed her as she stepped in. "I'm sorry, Genie."

"It's *fine*, really. Paul, he's one of your oldest friends, I know he don't mean it."

We piled into the Gran Torino, and when I turned around to look back, Lew was already passed out.

At Shakey's we feasted on pizza and Coke. Mine tasted like Lilyth's perfume and I felt nauseated. Lilyth had on cutoffs and kept wiggling her shoulders to Little Eva's "Loco-Motion" on the jukebox, readjusting her button-down shirt that was not buttoned, but tied. Mom kept scowling at her and they started bickering, so Dad rolled up his Shakey's placemat, I guess to tune them out, and tapped me on the head. I wanted to roll mine up, too, and have a sword fight with him, but I needed it for something else.

"So, how's swim team, son?"

"It's good, I think Firefly might drown, though."

"That ain't *nice*, Sug! Lawrence is a *fine* boy." Mom broke off her wrangle with Lilyth to admonish me.

"Well, I do," I said.

My dad leaned down and stuck me in the ribs saying, "That's all right, son, so do I."

"Paul, you hush up! That ain't kind."

"When's first meet? I'll be there."

"Last week in June, Paul, you're . . ."

"I work for myself now, Genie, I'll give myself that day off. Let's hope Firefly gets in shape by then, 'cause I ain't jumpin' in after him!"

We laughed, even Lilyth, and I curled the edge of that Shakey's placemat with my fingers. I liked the woven texture of the paper it was printed on. The waiter brought over Lew's to-go order, and handed it to Lilyth, looking down her shirt as she reached up for it.

"Medium hamburger pizza y'all ordered. I put extra cheese on it, too, but I didn't charge you." The waiter smiled eagerly at Lilyth locomoting her cleavage rhythmically at him. He completely ignored the rest of us sitting there like we were the curtains. Dad grabbed the box from Lilyth and stared at the waiter.

"Charge us! Go back to your goddamn cash register and charge us!"

"Yes, sir. Y'all ain't gon' tell my boss, sir, please?"

"And why shouldn't I?" My dad stared him down for a good long time, then whispered, "Get the hell out of here."

The waiter disappeared.

"Dad! Mom, tell him." Lilyth looked humiliated.

"Tell him what, Lilyth?"

"That *hormone* was lookin' at you like you's a T-bone steak. He can damn well charge us."

Lilyth burst into tears, and reminded my parents, "And yet you don't do nothing about Mickey smoking!?"

I couldn't duck, so I prepared to take my punishment for something I had not done.

"Oh, Lilyth, stop it! Mickey, have you ever smoked?" my dad asked, as he looked right into my eyes.

"No, sir," I said.

"Well there you go, then," Dad concluded.

"You're just gonna believe him? Why don't you ever just believe ME?" hissed Lilyth.

"Different people require different methods."

"That is bullshit!" Lilyth stormed out.

"That was fun." Dad sighed.

"But, Paul, why would she say that if he hadn't done it? Paul! Go talk to her! And Mickey, this iddn't over."

Dad got up, obeying Mom's request, and when they weren't looking I slid my Shakey's placemat off the table and folded it in half, tucking it inside my shirt. At the Piggly Wiggly I ran straight in so I could go frost-whiffing. I loved the freezer section—the smell and sound when you open the big glass doors, and the weird thing the sudden cold does to your nostrils. Crinkling them up inside. But mostly, right then I wanted to get the dirty scent of Lilyth's perfume out of my nose. And frost-whiffing did the trick. It was a cool spring night, but I rolled down my window anyway and hung my head out till we got home. My dad pulled the Gran Torino into the driveway as T. Rex's "Cosmic Dancer" was finishing on the car stereo. It was dark and Lew was right where we left him, passed out and tilted off to one side in the lawn chair, cigarette in his lips burned down to the filter. I helped Dad unload groceries from the car as Mom and Lilyth approached Lew.

"Let him sleep. I'll wake him up after we empty the car."

"He's drunk and he reeks." Lilyth leaned over Lew, she of all people fanning her nose.

"Y'all go inside. Mic, take this bag and get ready for bed. I gotta get Lew off the lawn anyway." I carried a bag of groceries and unloaded it on the kitchen counter and headed for my room. I stopped when I thought I might have heard something. I put my ear to Lilyth's bedroom door to confirm, then slowly opened it and peered in to find Kevin, alone, sitting yoga-style on Lilyth's shag carpet and leaning against the wall with his eyes closed. I don't know how he could sit in there when the curdled stench of Lilyth's army of perfumes was enough to gag a maggot.

"You come through the window, don't you?"

Kevin opened his eyes and smiled big at me. "Shut the door, Speed."

I hesitated and took a deep breath, then committed myself to the sugary haze probably intended to mask the fog of Kevin's smoke.

"Why don't you just knock on the door?"

"I think it's easier to get forgiveness than permission, don't you?" I wondered for a moment if forgiveness and permission could ever be granted for the same thing.

"I don't know. I guess."

"You can tell yer dad if y'want, but say I broke in, don't say she leaves it open for me."

"Are y'all gonna have a baby? You and Lilyth?"

"I'd smile if we did. Someday, maybe. Oh...The Hole?"

"I wuddn't spyin' on y'all."

"I know you wuddn't. I love your sister, you know that, right?"

"I know."

I was about to leave when Kevin stopped me in my tracks. "You should talk to her."

"What? To...*her*?"

"Yeah, man, you'll never understand her if ya don't."

"What do you mean?"

"Ya'll seem so far apart, ya know? But you ain't."

"Well, we're about to be."

"Nah, ya'll come from the same place. You wanna understand her, don't you?"

"I think I already do, and that's what I wanna tell her."

"Well, what are you wait'n' for? I know she'd like to hear it."

"Well, I mean, what if she...?"

"She won't! Look, you're young and you've got dreams to live, right?"

"Yeah, I guess."

"Well, I bet you don't remember her absence being in any of them, do you?"

"Nope, she's in every single one of 'em."

I marveled at how Kevin knew all this. It was clear to me that Jane's unicorn power had spread even to him.

"I'll leave, you know, if you wanna do it now."

"Well, YOU don't hafta go, I mean it's too late tonight anyway."

"Well, don't wait too long, Speed."

"I won't, I'll do it in the morning. I tried already. Twice. But..."

"She's a mythical creature, Speed."

"I know, she's a unicorn." I turned to leave.

"Hey, Speed." I held on to the doorknob, looking back. "You're a cool kid."

"You're a cool *big* kid."

I smiled and left. And I knew that Kevin totally understood. So, I went right to my room to plot my ship's course to navigate straight to Jane the next morning and tell her all the things that I wanted her to know. In preparation, I rattled around inside my closet looking for my can, when blistering panic suddenly streamed through my whole body.

"Mom?!" I ran out of my room and outside. "Mom!" She, Dad, and Lilyth were still trying to prop up Lew's amorphous mass. "Mom, have you seen my Charles Chips can? It was in my closet under my football blanket that Lilyth borrowed."

"The one you painted on the inside, y'little retard?"

"Lilyth! You gotta stop callin' him that! Zat the one, Sug?" I nodded. "Well, Sug, I think we sold it. I know it was on the sale table."

"Yeah, it got sold. I sold it." Lilyth knew that my Charles Chips tin meant a lot to me, and she avoided eye contact. "What? It's not my fault."

"Why, Sug, did you want to keep it?" I don't know why

my emotions affected my body so much, but once again The Grunt came, and I could neither move nor block the gaping holes in my eyes.

"No, no, I was just wonderin'..." I did my best to hide the fact that everything was ruined in that very instant. I don't know how long I stood in the driveway and stared at stewed Lew, whose balls were once again peeking out, but it was longer than a moment. And I could see the imprint that the lawn chair's webbing had left on his backside as he was hunched over to one side about to fall onto the grass. It looked painful and red, and was an exact detailed embossing of the intricate plastic webbing underneath him, but I knew it would be gone long before he ever woke up. "Better roll the windows up," I said.

My sister just looked at me as I stared at Lew's balls until my body came back and I turned and went inside.

"What'd he say?" asked Mom.

"Dunno, he's weird," countered Lilyth.

The house door closed behind me and Steve. I went straight to my room and watched the rain slowly start to trickle onto the window until I could no longer see lights from Jane's house at all. Never again did I hear another word about Lilyth's smoking accusation.

Chapter Six

Even after my talk with Kevin, I figured that losing my film of Jane was a sign for me to just forget about her. Summer was fast approaching, she was moving, and so was life. But Kevin was right. I had to at least try before she was gone. One more try. For the longest time, I stared at my reflection in the mirror as I combed my hair to the side. I put on my nice green, short-sleeved button-down shirt with the newest pair of Toughskins I owned. Steve McQueen and I crept as quietly as possible to the front door with my bike and two records in my hand. I reached the front door and slowly opened it.

"Bye, Mom, I'm heading to swim practice."

"Aren't you going to be hot? It's so muggy out today." Mom peeked around the corner from the kitchen.

"Oh, well, sometimes it's cold when we first get out of the pool."

"Well, Sug, why don't you..." She stopped herself and just smiled at me. "Okay, well, try not to get that shirt too dirty."

"Okay, bye!"

I biked down Bentliff, my world glossy and sparkling as the

sun burned off the clouds. The Milans weren't out yet, maybe on account of the early rain. Funny, usually you could bounce a quarter off the Milans' green velvet lawn, almost like at the golf course. But riding past it, it looked as shitty as all the other neighbors' on my street, fringed partway up the legs of the Milans' two vacant aluminum lawn chairs. I reached Sandpiper Drive, and the closer I got to Jane's, the less I could remember of what exactly I was going to say to her.

Her home felt like a haunted house for real now. Jane's garage was completely empty, except for a trace of Jane's lingering scent. I put my bike down and proceeded to the front door with the two records in my hand. I got about halfway up the lawn when I stopped and ran back to my bike, picked it up, and positioned it just right against her mailbox. I took a deep breath and strode up to the door, knocked real loud, and took a step back. Steve McQueen loped across the lawn to join me at the door. Then I remembered the doorbell. What if they didn't hear me knock? I fretted over whether I should have rung it or if it would be rude if I rang and knocked. What if they preferred you to use the doorbell? I mean, after all, that's why they had a doorbell. Terror finally resigned, and a certain calm came over my mind and body. I waited. Steve pressed himself against my leg. Like magic, the door sprang open to me. My mind was a blank slate, I had no idea what to say to the mustached man at the door, and all I could think was that he looked exactly like Sonny Bono. But I was young, and I didn't know.

"Hey there, little man!"

"I, um, I gave her my 'Hound Dog' and 'Sunshine Superman' for her 'Sounds of Silence' but she can keep mine 'cause my sister has an eight-track machine that records, but I don't know if ya'll have one so I wanted to give her this one, called 'Cosmic Dancer.' It's a different song 'cause they sold her 'Sounds of Silence,' so I'm returning, I mean it's one of my favorites, and it duddn't skip or anything, and I'm giving her my 'Silence' 'cause I already had one, and sorry I wrote 'Mine' on it, but she can have it 'cause I lost hers, um . . . but it's almost summer and school's out soon so I probably can't give it to Miss Bradford, I mean Mrs. Bradford, for her to give her, and I . . . um, um."

Mr. Bradford stared down at me and his smile kept stretching his face wider than I knew it was possible to stretch a mustache.

"Um, is Jane home?"

"Let's see what you've got there." I handed over the records and he read the labels, mirth in his eyes.

"'Cosmic Dancer' . . . well you got her pegged, she'll love it."

"I'm replacin' her 'Silence' there, too, sir." I pointed awkwardly.

"But they won't be home for another hour."

"Oh." I was devastated. "I have to go to swim team practice."

"I can give it to her for you." I nodded. "And I'll tell her you came by. What's your name, son?"

"Mickey, sir." I reached out to shake hands.

"Well, Mickey, I'm Troy Bradford, Jane's dad." He shook my hand and held up the records, smiling all the while. "And I will make sure Jane gets these."

"Thank you, Mr. Bradford, sir."

"I thank you, son, Mr. Sunshine Superman."

Jane's father closed the door between us, leaving me deflated on the slate stoop, staring at the door. It felt so good to be on her doorstep, I didn't really want to leave. Steve McQueen gave a little bark and I knew it was time to go. Straight off, my dog led, and I sped faster than I had ever pedaled over to The Ditch on Carvel Lane to meet up with Firefly. Steve McQueen kept up alongside me, sniffing everything in the gutters ripe after the rain. Up Carvel Lane I headed toward the bridge that crosses over the tiny stream surrounded by concrete that snaked slow and thin through the city and into Braes Bayou. Sun was searing off everything, including my good button-down shirt that I stripped and stuffed in my waistband for safekeeping as I rode.

The water was a little higher in the creek below, and Steve McQueen ran down the cement steps that flanked the angled concrete walls of The Ditch, whose walls sloped twenty feet down to the water. I dropped my bike and removed my good britches down to my Speedo, and barefoot I followed Steve McQueen down to hunt crawdads while I waited for Firefly and swim practice. The cement steps were littered in broken liquor bottles and used-up old *Playboy* magazines rumpled in heaps in the corners along the slanted walls of our descent. On the bottom step closest to the water, I found a small battered suitcase containing playing cards, poker chips, used shell casings, syringes, a pistol's breech, and a cylinder of WD-40. I never thought anything of the illicit paraphernalia. I had found worse there before, but I seized on the WD-40. I gave the little can a shake, and since it felt pretty full, I took it, knowing it would save me a trip home for Dad's can. Then I kept on, wading down the creek at Steve's urging for me to hunt with him. Like furry stilts, Steve McQueen's long, gray legs poked along the filthy stream as he snouted at crawdaddies and floating trash. The place was a dump heap. I followed behind him and caught a struggling lizard washing by in the sleepy current and set it against the angled cement wall, where it clambered up to safety.

There was no sign of Firefly. Looking back down the creek, on the bridge I now saw the red Firebird with The Plank in its grille, way up above the concrete vertical, parked next to the guardrail. I couldn't climb up from the water as the concrete vertical was too tall, so I waded back to the stairs and got my bike, leaving Steve McQueen, not yet satisfied with a day's kill. At the bridge I parked in front of Kevin's Plank and looked over the edge way down and saw only the lazy brown liquid lolling on toward Braes Bayou and my dog shaking the life out of a water snake by its head. I lay down on my naked belly and Speedo to hang my head over the edge and look under the bridge. Upside down, my eyes adjusted, and the crinkled *Playboy* centerfolds that stuck to the wall became apparent. I read the white-paint graffiti claiming who was an easy fuck and saw Lilyth's name had been covered partially with the words, painted in black, *Fuck you! Lilyth is a Mythical Creature!* Then I spotted him.

Tucked up in the crevice between the bottom of the street and the concrete slope sat Kevin like a Buddha, eyes shut, smoking something. Finally he looked right at me as if he had known I was there the whole time.

"What happened to your head, Speed?" Kevin chuckled. "You should try to turn it over, or ever'one's gon' look at you funny." He toked deeply. "You should think about get'n a car, too, 'cause it'll be harda ta get around with just a head. Or maybe not. It's all in the shine anyway, you know? And it'll be here till tomorrow."

"I forgot to tell you, your 'Free Bird' fell out in my drive-way."

"That's 'cause it *is*, Speed." Kevin just stared at the water. Occasionally the hollow sound of a car rumbling over the bridge caused me to glance up. Still no Firefly.

"It is what?"

"Exactly, and it'll never change."

"Want it back? Your eight-track?"

"How old you think this is, Speed?" I looked around, I didn't remember The Ditch ever *not* being there, and I wondered about it.

"I don't know. It's been here since I have."

"Six thousand years old...or four-point-six million?" Kevin took another drag.

"Um, that seems like too much."

"What's enough?"

Even before his head dropped beside me, I smelled peanut butter and burnt pancakes, and I knew Firefly had mooched breakfast off my mother again, surely pretending to have forgotten he was supposed to meet me at The Ditch. Wide-eyed, Firefly gawked at Kevin, who did not look up.

"Uh, we gotta go, Mic." Firefly withdrew. Next he tried to jerk me to my feet by my Speedo and thumped my bundled britches at me. "Dumbass, you know who that is?"

"Yeah, Kevin."

"Exactly! That's KEVIN! He's been *arrested*! He worships the *devil*!"

"Shut up! He duddn't!"

"Let's just go! And c'mon, dipshit, you can't go ridin' through town in that damn weenie bikini, showin' your helmet all over Houston."

I threw my head over the edge one last time. "See ya, Kevin!" I got back up and pulled on my trousers.

"Water at your hairline, Speed Racer!" Kevin's voice arose from below my feet. I looked to Firefly to see if he knew what Kevin had said, but he just raised his shoulders at me.

"Uh . . . what?"

"When you swim! Keep the water at your hairline. I've been watchin' you, Mickey. Trust me, you'll go a lot faster." I was stunned that Kevin even knew I swam, much less that he had been watching me.

"Oh yeah, okay. I will. Hey, thanks, Kevin." I looked at Firefly solemnly, like, yeah, this cat gives me pointers all the time.

"Sure. Later, man."

"Yeah, later . . . man."

"Damn, Mic! I can't believe he even knows your name!" Firefly paused and backed up his bike a stride and yelled down over the edge, "Later, man!"

Firefly waited, but Kevin didn't respond.

As we rattled across the bridge toward swim practice, Firefly belted out Pilot's "Magic" and kept right on yelling it clear across the golf course, down past the country club and the new homes, and Jane's at hole eighteen. He never gasped once, just kept belting out his tune, cocooned and fledging as he was now by swim practice. Firefly and I rode past the Halfway Food Hut at the ninth hole, where golfers could stop and snack to a familiar mix of smells: chlorophyll as the wide-blade mowers snickered past us, and the sulfurous stench of greasy egg-and-cheese breakfast burritos as golfers fattened up.

"I wonder if there's anything I can eat that'll make me float better."

"Ask Coach Randall. I don't think so, though."

"I can't even go a whole length without sinkin'!"

"Yeah you can, you can go a lot further than you could when we started."

"Shit, you think anyone else'll have to stop during their leg?"

"I don't think so, 'cause it's slower if you touch anyway."

"I still wish we had more time. How come you gotta start the relay last? I'd'a thought Coach would put you first."

"I don't know, I guess..." But suddenly there was something more important than what I was saying, and I had to shut up. It was the hi-hat sound of that wonderful VW Vanagon gradually increasing nearby. I looked straight ahead and came to a stop right there on the crest of the green.

"What, Mic?"

"Kid, outta the way!" A golfer in bright, crisp-pressed attire was pitching a fit.

"And put on a goddamn shirt, y'little street urchin. This is a golf course, fer Christ sakes," his partner railed on me.

The "Moby Dick" intro became louder and louder, and then like a sunrise, Mrs. Bradford's orange VW Vanagon pulled into the driveway of the butter yellow house whose backyard flowed into the golf course. The one that now had a trampoline. I studied specks on the horizon. And there they were, Mrs. Bradford and Jane getting out of the orange van.

"Earth t'Mic, what the fuck's with you?"

"Nuthin'." I felt my mouth stretch across my face as wide as the Texas horizon, but I buttoned it up sharp and tight like my Grandaddy's smile. My more than half was right across that course.

"You're weird." Firefly left me there, rode off down toward

the pool, stopped, and looked back at me. "What? C'mon, Mic, I still gotta get into my faggit suit."

"I'll meet you at the pool, okay?"

"What do you mean? Wait, where are you going?"

"I'm just . . . I just gotta go do somthin' real quick."

Perplexed, Firefly frowned at me, and I pedaled off across the golf course toward Jane's new house on the other side of the fairway. As I rode, I put my shirt back on and buttoned it with one hand. On the far side of the Bradfords' new garage beyond the VW van, I set down my bike and peered around the corner as I tucked in my shirt, watching Jane and Mrs. Bradford unloading the orange van into the house. I waited around the corner of the garage until they came back out for another load. Jane was barefoot, her red and blue 95s dangling around her neck. She and her mother were at the van, and I stepped out around the corner, opening my mouth to speak and fully prepared to say I had found just the thing Jane needed, when a voice pounced on us from the street.

"Hi there, neighbors! We're from two doors down. We brought y'all some macadamia nuts from our trip."

I stopped before Mrs. Bradford saw me. She looked over at the street and went around the van to greet the intruders. Standing curbside by Jane's new forest green mailbox stood an over-tanned young mother with far too much makeup and a tanned adolescent boy who was not exactly obese, but chunky-fat with a double chin, looking like he ate for sport and was allergic to dirt, dressed nicer than most kids I had ever seen. I stayed back and watched him shake Mrs. Bradford's hand with his fingertips, like a girl.

"Y'all must be new! I'm Christina Parsifal, and this is

my baby boy, Baxter. We saw the two of you drive up and just wanted to come on over and welcome you to the neighborhood. Invite y'all to dahn with us at the country club, or bingo, and we got them sportin' events right here to watch anytime, polo and swimmin'. Y'all gon' love it here."

"Well thank you very much, that's so sweet; I'm Lola. My daughter, Jane, is around here somewhere. JANE!" From the corner of the garage I watched Jane inside the VW van through its opened sliding side door gathering up her record collection to take into the house. She heard her mother and parted the curtains inside the van to peer out at the street. "JANE!" Jane ducked down below the window as if she'd rather not be social. "JANE, please come!" From my vantage point, the street was partially blocked to my view by the van. Finally, Jane resigned herself to come out, and with an armful of records she hopped down from the van. When her feet hit the cobblestone driveway, her gaze landed on my bare feet. She straightened up slowly until her eyes found me, frozen in place. But Jane didn't move; the two of us stared at each other intently with her name rolling in the air. Her eyes finally left mine as her mom came around the van and approached her. I didn't know if she was scared or intrigued. I certainly wondered about her stare, but I only knew about mine. "There you are, honey. Come and meet our new neighbors."

Jane looked down at her record collection and hesitated a moment, before glancing back up at me, then reluctantly followed her mother around the van. She got about halfway down the driveway when she stopped and turned around, looking right at me again. I waved, before turning and heading off to swim team practice. Then I remembered. I removed the cylinder from my back pocket. Between the shiny chrome-plated springs of Jane's trampoline, I tucked the cylinder of WD-40. It was a brand-new trampoline, which blew my mind, but I left her the can just the same, knowing that without it, the shine would eventually fade to rust.

Something inside me woke up that summer, like up until then I had almost been asleep. I thought about that look in Jane's eyes as I rode back across the golf course, slowly unbuttoning my shirt. At the cart path where I had left Firefly, a golf cart was approaching, and its driver was waving at me. Then I noticed Firefly hiding in a stand of trees grinning up a storm. His pockets bulged with golf balls.

"Who was that chick eyeballin' you, Mic? When you was by the trampoline."

I looked back, but Jane was gone.

"Hey, kid!" I froze, staring at Firefly with his pointer finger to his lips. "Seen any balls layin' around this area?"

For a long moment, I stared at this golfer and more carts behind him circling: So many men also searching for their balls. A smile crept through my soul as the entrepreneur inside me recognized opportunity in our most abundant natural resource on that golf course: lazy people.

"No, sir, but I might be able to help you find 'em."

"Well, that'd be great, kid!"

"Buck a ball, sir." I heard myself state it like it was God's honest truth.

"Seventy-five cents."

"Buck a ball, sir, five for $4.50, if ya go bulk."

"Huh, impressive, well, hell, that seems reasonable."

From that day on until our first swim meet, Firefly and I cleaned up on golf balls and fueled ourselves with garbage from the Snack Shack after each swim practice. All on account of having finagled a way to be nearer to Jane, my world changed, and I witnessed what financial independence could provide.

"Firefly, you know rich people got lawn mowers that push themselves." We stood in awe and wonder. Self-propelled, guys would keep walking behind to steer. They were all the rage till some kids got their toes cut off because the mower was too heavy to pull backwards without leaning so much that your toes went under the spinning blades. Or, guys just kept walking, not paying attention under their headphones plugged into radios, and then lost toes trying to pull it to a stop. To be even closer to Jane, I mowed lawns near the golf course. I was a little marketer. I even had flyers. In contrast to the big eight-foot-wide mowers on the golf course and baseball fields, mine was a simple push mower. But that was okay, because I always preferred the safety of my own momentum.

I loved the Great State of Texas. Year-round it still got hot enough for grass to need cutting, though on rare occasions in the winter, folks would have to leave their faucets dripping so pipes would not freeze. The smell of Texas was the smell of progress. My nose was intoxicated by the scent of newly imported Formica, and brand-new swimming pool liners, still empty, and fresh-cut chlorophyll rinsed away each time a wall of water passed through. I would hide with my push mower under the lush trees and wait. Seventeen minutes later the torrent of rain would move on with its cloud bank to wash someplace else. The heat would come back up, and with it came aromatic success. So by the time of our first swim meet I had earned a grand total of $223 on golf balls and cutting grass, and Firefly and I were good and sugared up. *Two hundred twenty-three dollars.* Man, it seemed so much at the time.

Swimmers took their positions with pink and purple index fingers from dipping them in boxes of fruit-flavored Jell-O and licking off the powder that reeked of chlorine and fake fruit. Smiling proudly as the large crowd cheered and burst into applause, the bleachers were chock-full with friends and family and kids in Speedos cheering on teammates. As our relay race was under way, Coach Randall, Firefly, and I were behind the starting block in lane five as our teammate swam ferociously toward us. Firefly prepared to take his mark and turned back to us, all nervous.

"Aw shit, I think I'm gonna pee my pants, Coach."

"As long as you do it once you're in the pool, Lawrence, no one'll notice."

"I've never even made a whole length before; I mean, what if I can't make it, Coach?"

Coach Randall leaned in, right up close to Firefly's face. "Listen to me, Firefly, if you have to touch, go ahead, there's nothing to be ashamed of, but I don't think you'll have to. I've got faith in you!"

Firefly looked anxiously at me, and I pointed over at the kid on the block in the next lane whose teammate was neck and neck with ours.

"T. rex 'em! And hey, water at your hairline, man."

"Yeah, water at your hairline, man."

Trimmer now, Firefly's fat was well on its way to becoming muscle bulk. He climbed onto the block and tucked down, waiting for our teammate to touch.

"You gotta want it, Lawrence! Want it, man!" Coach Randall watched and waited as he murmured to me, real quiet, "He ain't never *had* to make a whole length."

"He can't touch from this lane anyway, can he?"

"Not even if he grew a foot. I'm a second away from him the whole way, though." Never taking his eyes off Firefly, Coach Randall kicked off his flip-flops and dropped his shorts with the lightning bolt logo, so he was wearing only his Speedo. He held his hand above Firefly's back. "Okay now, Firefly, just like in practice." The two swimmers touched almost at exactly the same time. Randall slapped Firefly on the back. "GO!"

Firefly's mass splashed into the water, displacing his opponent in his wake and causing the kid to lose a whole second. Immediately Coach Randall ran around to the side of the pool to follow Firefly's trajectory, all the while shouting encouragement. Firefly attacked the water with passion, but going nowhere fast he lost ground quickly to his opponent. He was halfway down the pool dropping us now to third place, but he was still paddling. As he neared the edge, Trent, our former quarterback, stepped up. Coach Randall was leaning over the edge in front of Trent cheering Firefly on. "Okay, Trent, it's your race, baby! Just get us close!" Finally, Firefly touched. "GO! Trent, go!"

Coach Randall scooped Firefly out of the pool and hugged him, while Trent plunged in hot pursuit, closing us to second place. Coach raced around the pool to me on the block already stretching. Ever louder, the crowd cheered and chanted. I looked out across the pool, tracking Trent's every stroke. I was tucked and ready for a launch when I saw it. The volume continued to mount to a deafening blur as I recognized the blossom of yellow at the far end over at the wrought iron gate, and everything became clear and silent. It was Jane, dressed up for supper in my favorite dress of hers, the one from my first touchdown, the bright yellow one with white piping, sleeveless and baggy, leaning, looking at me with her head through the iron bars. Her tan fingers gripped the bars like an inmate. Her naked feet stood on the lower horizontal connector, her 95s dangling around her neck. And then, through the silence, she slowly waved. I was paralyzed on that starting block, as I wanted to look behind me to see if that wave was for me, but my lips gave a smile anyway.

"*Be here now*, Mic!" barked Coach Randall, snapping me back to the block. "On your mark!" Trent approached the wall, tied for second place, and about two seconds behind the leader. Exhilarated, I crouched on the block perfectly still and turned to my competition in the next lane, who looked nervously at me coiled there grinning. I glanced back at Jane, and she was bouncing once again, with her hands clasped in that little silent prayer. I was completely lost in her when I felt the sting of Coach Randall's hand impact my back with a "GO!"

So I plunged. My competitor was about a body length and a half ahead of me by the time I hit the water, and I started closing the gap immediately. I remember my body tingling during that race, the vision of Jane in her yellow dress smiling right back at me all the while. And the tingle just got stronger and stronger the closer I got. My opponent and I were about halfway across the pool as I advanced on him, even closer. I glided down lane five, with every breath glancing up at Coach Randall cheering me on. With the water at my hairline, occasionally I thought I saw Jane, like a starburst, walking right beside him and staring at me. I know I was guided by some sort of sonar that day, because I was not even there. I felt like I was with Jane the whole time, engulfed in her sort of velvet unicorn magic. It seemed like we had touched the wall at exactly the same time, but once I picked my head up out of the water, my competition was still about a foot away. The entire crowd was on their feet cheering. Coach Randall plucked me out of the pool, with Firefly screaming, "fuckin'-A that was so nigger-cock!" and Trent smacking me on the back like in football.

This was it. She had seen me do something really cool…and absolutely nothing embarrassing. My eyes went straight to the wrought iron fence, but there were too many people crowded around to see through. In the mayhem, I broke away and made for the fence, with Firefly calling for me to wait up. I pressed through the crowd, dripping wet, and reached the iron bars—but Jane was gone.

At the wrought iron fence I saw Jane headed off barefoot across the parking lot with her parents, her little wiener dog Donovan puddling after her on a leash. Sticking my head through the bars, I watched Jane walk away, unsure of what to do, until my heart made my throat just belt out, "Jane!" It was the first time I had ever voiced Jane's name to her. Her family hesitated a bit when Jane stopped as if she might have heard something. She turned around just as a car slowly drifted by between us, looking for a parking spot, separating us for what felt like forever. As soon as the car had passed, I saw them continue on toward the country club on the other side of the parking lot by the putting green. Like a contortionist, I slid my head through, then twisted the rest of my body through the bars and yelled again. "Miss Bradford!"

Firefly tried to squeeze through two rungs down, but got stuck.

"Mic, wait up!"

Jane and her parents stopped and turned to see me, still dripping wet and out of breath, just as my foot caught on the bottom horizontal bar and I tripped flat onto the concrete. Quickly, I picked myself up and ran up to them, with blood drizzling down my knee.

"Whoa! Mickey, hello! Are you okay? Troy, this is my best student I told you about."

"Why, of course, it's Mr. Sunshine Superman!" exclaimed Jane's dad.

Jane and I stared at each other, me only occasionally glancing up at her parents.

"Hi, Mrs. Bradford, I'm okay. Hi, Mr. Troy Bradford, I just wanted to say hi, because I met Mr. Troy Bradford, and I said she can keep my 'Sunshine Superman.' Jane, I mean."

"Are y'all coming?!" The macadamia nut intruders descended on my precious moment again, the chunky kid in the alligator shirt and that woman that was his mother. I stopped short. Jane's parents turned to the approaching family and introduced me, as Jane and I kept right on staring at each other. The neighbors sauntered over, stiff-collared and pressed, looking a bit over the top in stark contrast to the Bradfords' unassuming manner. Jane's family was originally from Lubbock, friendly people, though compared to me Jane seemed unfathomably rich. As their new neighbors got closer, something familiar about the macadamia boy struck me but I could not yet place it. I wondered if we had fought ever, and I hoped we hadn't. When they got close enough, Steve McQueen growled at the boy, then lost interest and sniffed around Jane's little dachshund on its leash. Jane knelt down and petted Steve, and he licked her face. I felt barbaric with no leash for my Viking Steve McQueen, who towered over Jane's Donovan before plopping down to relax right next to him on the concrete. Dogs know shit.

"Oh yes, but come here a minute, Christina this is one of my favorite students. Mickey, meet Mrs. Parsifal and her son, Baxter. Mickey, Baxter and his mom just got back from vacation in Hawaii." I had never been to Hawaii—in fact, I had never been anywhere except Grandaddy's and Mamau's and Galveston Island in Texas.

"And where d'y'all summer, *Best Student of Mrs. Bradford*?" Baxter's mother drilled in on me, sizing me up as she extended a red-taloned hand. I truly had no idea what she meant.

"Um, I guess we just let it come to us."

"Well, if *that* ain't the quaintest, y'all let it come to you." She pressed on, "So, where do y'all go for your vacation, boy?"

"Well, so, here I guess. Or the beach. Sometimes we get to go to the beach."

Some kids in my school went to fancy places that I could not pronounce for Christmas, but those were the kids whose dads worked at Texas Instruments or had married into old oil money families. My family was not old rich or new rich or any kind of rich, or at least not any kind of rich that required money. We were regular people grateful to Sears's layaway plan for school clothes. A couple times we did go camping on the beach at Galveston Island, when Dad could get time off from work. He was innovative and he rigged up a flatbed U-Haul trailer on which he would place our own homemade pop-up tent so no bugs or rattlesnakes could get at us, and we would park it right on the sands of the Gulf and fall asleep to the waves. I could never imagine anything being better than the Galveston that my mom and dad showed me.

"Which beach?" Mrs. Parsifal was relentless. But, I just wanted her to shut up. I only wanted Jane. I thought of all the different pronunciations I could give to Galveston to make it sound better, but it didn't need any. My beach would always be better than Mrs. Parsifal's beach.

"Galveston Island." And before Mrs. Parsifal could probe further for which side of the island or what hotel, Mrs. Bradford diplomatically redirected the conversation.

"Mickey, are you sure you're all right? That knee looks bad." I hadn't even noticed my knee was scuffed and bleeding all the way down my shin and foot, until I took that brief moment to look down.

"Oh yes, ma'am, I guess I should prolly go fix it, Mrs. Bradford. It's okay, though. I just wanted to say hi, really..." I wanted to be cool and look at other things, but it was impossible to pry my eyes off Jane.

Chunky Baxter walked around the side of the group and stood right next to Jane and looked down at her bare feet and then over at mine, disdainfully.

"She'll need shoes or they won't let her into the country club for dinner."

"Baxter, hush up, baby boy! That's for her momma to take care of, my lovey sweetheart."

I remember wondering how Baxter could not see those glorious 95s dangling around her neck. But then I remembered that he and I shared not one human similarity.

"Got 'em right here." Mrs. Bradford smiled. "Well, how's the swim team going, Mickey?"

"Mickey won, Mommy," said Jane softly staring at me.

Mrs. Bradford smiled at me, and Jane beamed even brighter. "Did ya?"

Mrs. Parsifal examined me more closely. Up close, I was getting a better look at Baxter and it was starting to dawn on me where I knew this kid from. It had been a competition. But I had not beaten him up, or even beaten him at anything. I could see it was just dawning on Baxter, too, that he knew me from before—the very first track meet I had ever run in, I got second place and this kid had placed first, only to be disqualified about a month later for being two years older than my division allowed. I remember getting a gold medal in the mail with an explanation. The fat sloth who now stood too close to Jane had stolen first, and I had earned second. But now he was just a lard-ass slacker who would never do anything important.

"Baxter! This boy just won his swim race! Din't y'all hear?"

"He'll need to win something," muttered Baxter.

I never understood people who spoke like that without expecting to get punched in the face, but I could not operate correctly around Jane. And I certainly did not want her to think of me as a hoodlum. In that moment it was okay, because something about her stopped my river of humiliation from decanting into a tidal wave of rage. I nearly puked, listening to the cloying prattle that flowed from Mrs. Parsifal's lips, like, "So what, baby boy, not everyone's as fortunate as you are, Baxter, honey pop, now c'mon y'all, the country club awaits us." But I knew that there was nothing fortunate about her kid at all, and I also knew that years later *fortune* would have had nothing to do with my alarm clock ringing fifteen minutes earlier than his my whole life. I knew that fortune was not just something you could pull out of your pocket, and that *fat* did not just describe his body. And I suspected that one day I would blow by him on life's straightaway like he was standing still. I could see it in his eyes. His mother used words like *kitten fluff* and other nonsense to communicate with that useless coaster. But no sweet terminology would ever make that little shirker a man or even a reasonable human being, even with his mother's incorrect definition of fortune. Baxter's mother straightened his collar, patting out the curl in his purple alligator knit. I presumed he chose purple because it was no secret that that was Jane's favorite color.

It was only at that moment I realized that I was still dripping wet and standing in the parking lot in nothing but my Speedo, trying to separate two violently conflicting emotions. I loved this girl. I loved everything about her. But I wanted to hurt this kid who was in her space. Badly. I loathed Baxter and the fact that he was getting to have supper with Jane, instead of me being the one at her table. It wasn't just jealousy that added an extra level of loathing to my regard for Baxter, or that he was a cheater. Sure I resented snooty people who flaunted the country club, but I embraced success on all levels, whether it was mowing lawns or selling golf balls back to lazy people, or tapping into a Texas oil field. Even at that age, I adored prosperity and those with the work ethic who create it, but I knew enough to loathe the generation that the work ethic skips because of financial obesity. At first I wrote off Baxter, assuming he was just a fat, lazy waste whose family money siphoned off all his drive to succeed. But I hated him even more because he allowed himself to accept average, to stop trying. Stop competing. His personal best was lazy. Baxter reeked of defeat and failure, and I could smell it right there in that parking lot.

"I tried to get Baxter to sign up for the team," his mother whined. I was itching to tell Baxter that I had a fat friend who could swim and had not sunk yet, but Baxter cut me off just as I opened my mouth.

"I'm not wearin' one of those things!"

"Yeah, that's prolly a good idea," I mumbled, and he and I both knew exactly what I would do to him if I ever found him on my side of the fence.

"I have a Band-Aid," murmured Jane, reaching into her matching yellow purse. I remember wondering if she would walk that Band-Aid over to me herself or if she would pass it to her mother to hand to me. But when Jane found it and looked up at me, she stepped forward and placed her palm on mine . . . and I was holding Jane's hand. "For your knee."

I tried not to wait too long before giving her a quiet, "Thank you."

And I immediately tried to calculate whether or not I was squeezing her hand too hard, but it felt too good in mine for math, and I wondered if I could get away with just a few more moments, when Baxter *eh-hem*'d, "I'm hungry!"

I was glad that I managed to keep the *of course you are, you fat fuck* inside my head that time, and just let the "Oh . . . yeah" escape with "Well, I guess I should get back to the pool."

And as I let go of Jane's hand and slowly backed away, I wondered if she would have let me hold it longer. And when she did not immediately turn to rejoin her family, I wished I had stayed just a moment more. I did not even bother to look at Baxter, he had already chosen to lose.

"All right, but make sure you take good care of that knee! And give your mother my best."

"Yes, ma'am," I said, as I approached and hugged Mrs. Bradford briefly, then extended my hand to Jane's father. "Mr. Troy Bradford."

"Very good to see you again, Sunshine Superman!" Mr. Bradford shook my hand like he truly meant it. Just then Baxter muttered another remark about my Speedo that hung in the air awkwardly. Jane's dad rerouted to good cheer. "Don't worry, son, I think you look like Mark Spitz! Take care, y'hear?"

The group strolled off toward the country club with Jane the last one to turn away, her yellow sundress catching the fading rays as another day of Jane was setting. Jane walked beside her mother, who was untying her 95s. Baxter pulled in right next to her. I watched.

"BYE, JANE!" I blurted out.

Jane stopped and turned while the others waited. She smiled and waved at me while she stood there wrangling her feet into her 95s. Finally she ran to rejoin the group, aiming at first between her mother and Baxter. But just when she came up even with the group, she deviated and squeezed in on the other side of her mother, away from Baxter. As they entered the country club Jane turned back again. I was still standing right where she left me in the middle of the parking lot like a drowned rat, blood running down my knee.

We just kept smiling at each other till that country club swallowed her.

Suddenly, a car horn blared at me and I heard tires screeching to a halt.

"Hey! HEY KID! WATCH OUT!" A man's voice bellowed through the open sunroof of a sedan with dark tinted windows. Slowly, I turned toward the car, its bumper a few inches away from my leg as Firefly ran up.

"Hey, lard-ass!! You eyeballin' Mic? What the fuck's wrong with yer brakes?"

"Sorry," I said vaguely to the driver, who continued to rant through his sunroof. In a stupor, I headed back to the pool with Firefly.

"Don't apologize, that maniac nearly hit you with his fucking car, Mic! Who the hell was that fat purple fuckhole with Mrs. Bradford? Was he eyeballin' you, too? 'Cause I'll . . ."

"Nah, I think he's just cross-eyed or somethin'."

"Yeah, well he better not be. Hurry up, now, they's havin' the serious racers, the big kids. And Mic, your mom's got peanut butter and jelly, but she won't open the cooler till you get there." Firefly jogged around the far end of the fence to get back in and, as I squeezed through the bars, I overheard two young mothers carrying on ecstatically about the next race.

"Yes, he's in the next race. Trust me, you want to see this!"

"Is this the one with the . . . ?" The first lady nodded excitedly as they pushed their way to the front.

Wondering whom the women were going on about, I found my family in the stands and sat down. Firefly had already rifled through Mom's cooler and was helping himself. Dad scruffed up my hair and said good job. Grandaddy settled in next to Mamau, and Mom hugged me a long time and said how proud she was, then handed me a napkin for my bloody knee.

"I'm fine," I said. But I wasn't about to waste Jane's Band-Aid on a stupid bloody knee. "Got somethin' on ya face, boy. Makin' the corners of ya mouth go ta God," Grandaddy said with the tiniest of grins. "Maybe came from that parkin' lot."

My mom saw my knee, my Grandaddy saw me, and my dad saw my race.

"I didn't think you could catch that kid, but you're a hell of a swimmer. Like your ol' dad! You too, Lawrence. Great teamwork!"

We quieted down as the announcer introduced the next race. "Well, if that wasn't enough for everyone, this should give you plenty! The sixteen-and-over, one-hundred-yard free." Everyone got real quiet.

"Mom! You gotta see this!" Even Lilyth whispered as she took Mom's hand and dragged her over to the edge of the pool to watch. Several fancy ladies over at the putting green looked up and stared as a lithe young man walked past them.

"In lane one swimming for the Hornets is James Pillar!" The crowd applauded politely. "And alongside him is his teammate Glen Ward! And in lane three swimming for the Braeburn Bears..." A lot more women than men clustered poolside. "Come on, I know he's here somewhere?" Down the length of the pool, the starting blocks were almost all filled. The boys shook their arms to loosen up. One block in the center remained vacant. "There he is, ladies and gentlemen!" Kevin climbed up onto the block to gasps and applause from the crowd. "In lane four, we have Willy Scott...and in lane five, Mark Simpson..." Kevin stood on the block with his back to the audience, his wild blond hair doing what it did. Finally he turned around to face the crowd and wave.

"Oh my!" gasped the woman seated in front of Dad.

Kevin stood there with his manhood stuffed into that tiny Speedo, looking as if it must hurt to keep it restrained. He shook out his arms to get ready. An older man in front of us shook his head in disgust. Kevin spotted me and gave me the number one sign, and I did it right back and smiled. The woman glanced back at me. Her older husband was not looking too happy.

Never once had I seen Kevin practice. But I had always heard that he was gifted, that swimming was in his blood. Kevin plunged and flutter kicked twice, ballet-like, then broke the surface and accelerated. He clearly and consistently pulled away from his competitors. I was astonished. At the far end, Kevin did a perfect flip turn and headed for home. Kevin touched the wall and did not even look to the side, or behind him to see how close second place was coming up. Seconds before the gun, Kevin had shown up, climbed onto the block, beaten everyone by half a length, and then just walked away like he had somewhere else to be.

"Pity that boy's gonna piss his gift away," I heard my dad say.

"What a disgrace, I've heard about this kid! He shouldn't be allowed to swim," came bitter grapes from the man in front of us whose wife had been gaping and gasping over Kevin's physique. I wanted to punch this guy's eye, but inside I knew he was a pathetic Baxter.

"Kevin won fair and square, Dad, right?"

"That he did, son."

Just then Kevin waved at me with his towel and gave me

the peace sign on his way out. The guy in front of me turned around to stare at me, but I just ignored him and waved right back at Kevin.

Kevin never practiced and he never lost all summer—no one ever even came close to him. He waved, he won, and then he left.

"Next swimmers, on your marks!" The announcer's voice boomed for the beginning of another race, and the sudden crack that sounded its start rang in my ears, not like a starter's pistol but like a shotgun.

Kevin was the coolest kid I knew . . . and he was my friend.

Summer didn't wait for me or Jane or anyone—it just kept on going. Burbling along, Jane sightings poolside, swim meets, more Jane sightings with her Frisbee, with 95s and without, catching critters in The Ditch with Steve McQueen and Firefly, concerts, family, and making money on balls and mowing lawns with my push mower. Mr. Milan's grass hadn't been cut in quite a while, so when I saw him out there the next time sitting beside his wife's empty chair, I stopped and offered to cut his grass. He didn't respond. I guessed he was drunk like Lew Hoagie, what for all the Miller cans piled up in the grass. So I went home feeling I should tell my mom, but I didn't say anything and instead just fueled the mower.

Chapter Seven

Summer ended when Kevin blew his head off. They said he climbed down into The Hole, stuck the barrel of a shotgun in his mouth, propped the butt against the wall, and hooked his big toe in the trigger loop. And pushed.

Kevin had never asked for it back, so I was listening to his "Free Bird" under headphones in my bedroom waiting for Grandaddy and Mamau to come by for supper. Still, I could hear a girl crying out in our kitchen. At first I thought my parents were reprimanding Lilyth for some shit she had pulled. They weren't. My door was open a crack and I saw Magda hugging Lilyth, and both were sobbing, and Lilyth was hyperventilating. Mom and Dad were huddled around them. I heard everything, even the stuff I didn't want to hear. I remember every sound and smell from that night, not like it was yesterday, but like it's today. I could not stop my ears from hearing, but I found that I could move farther away. I withdrew from the crack in my door and slowly pushed myself back into the corner of my bed against the wall, still looking out the crack. Behind me, my P-51 Mustang's thread gave way suddenly, and the baddest of all propeller planes crashed to my floor. My eyes were already filled up as I picked up its broken wing and carried it over to my bed, where I sat with my back against the wall rolling its landing gear against my leg. Occasionally I glanced back up through the crack trying to square up with an emotion that had never introduced itself before. Steve McQueen never left my side. He always knew. He followed me the next day when I rode my Schwinn straight to The Hole.

The fog draped thin gossamer across the playing fields as I approached, and morning dew shimmered on the grass, giving it a fairy-tale quality in the morning sunshine. The crack in the earth was cordoned off as a crime scene, and cop cars and investigators were everywhere. Kevin's Plank and the Firebird remained right where he had left it. Steve McQueen ran to The Hole and peered down and barked, but I could not get too close. I didn't understand. I couldn't. Magda's new boyfriend had gone in planning to smoke dope down inside the cavern deep beneath the opening of The Hole. He said he had found parts of Kevin spattered all over *Hustler* centerfolds that were stuck to the walls. He said it was impossible to tell who it was. I always wondered what that must have been like, barely squeezing your body down that long, dark crevice that zigzagged, sometimes even having to exhale and compress your lungs just to squeeze through a space too tiny for yourself, until you finally came out in a small, pitch-black, dirt room . . . and then you light a match. It took the forensics team the entire next day to get all the pieces of Kevin out of The Hole. Then the authorities flooded it with truckloads of piped-in cement and The Hole was no longer a bottomless threat.

Kevin had left a message on the hood of his Firebird in white spray paint: *I was based on a true story.*

As the funeral procession passed with all their headlights on, I hid up in my giant bean tree in the front yard long after my mom had called me to come down and eat something. The branches were so wide I could even sleep up there without falling out. Mortality stymied me, and I just did not know how or why death existed at all. I valued life so strongly. What he did made no sense to me, and it still doesn't. Kevin was contemplative, morose, on drugs, somewhat mad, maybe sad, more scary than sad. Maybe he'd had bad parents. I didn't know. But the fact that you can just decide to take your own life, it didn't compute. The realization that we are temporary horrified me, and fear engulfed me as my young mind tried to extrapolate the possibility of death to my own parents and Grandaddy and Mamau and Steve McQueen. And all the while I remained up in that bean tree watching the cortege pass, Steve McQueen sat below me, waiting. My sister later said they played "Free Bird" at the funeral and that it was a "happy" service "on account a'the fact that that's the way Kevin was...HAPPY." Though, I kept thinking, well, he killed himself for a reason, and I had to wonder if it was on account of some shitty thing Lilyth said to him. Maybe he found out about her going with different guys, or she told him he was a retard one time too many. I just sat up there pondering in that bean tree perfectly still watching the cars go by and watching Mr. Milan's two aluminum lawn chairs nestle into the weeds, and I could not stop those fucking tears.

Kevin was a cerebral dreamer who spoke in metaphors, high a lot, pot-speak, THC vernacular, too-long pauses, but he thought about what he was going to say before he opened his mouth, unlike most people. He loved the music I loved. He picked my sister—why, I could never comprehend—and called her The Mythical Creature.

I stayed up in that tree for two full days. I finally came down when Mom said Steve McQueen could not sleep without me. Lilyth was in the shower taking forever, so I left Kevin's "Free Bird" eight-track on her mattress. That's when I saw Kevin's obituary peeking out from under Lilyth's pillow with a brochure about a birth clinic and another about an orphanage in a convent. I tried to read fast, but Lilyth turned off the water before I could get far.

The obituary read, *...the late Mr. and Mrs. R. K. G. were professional swimmers who trained the deceased...* Since it said that his parents were late, I guessed Kevin's parents were just delayed, not able to get there fast enough to help him not kill himself. I wondered if he had nice parents. The obit included a quote that had been the family motto: *I know of no pain so great that I would exchange even existence for its removal. Training hurts but it prolongs life, so bring on the pain.* I guessed Kevin did not agree with his family on that. Obviously something was hurting him and he wanted it to stop. The last thing I read before I heard the sink running and Lilyth gargling was that Kevin *is survived...* I thought maybe someone had made a mistake, maybe Kevin was not dead and it was someone else's brains that spattered the pages of *Hustler* in The Hole. Until I got to the next line, and my heart twisted. It read, *...by an elder stepbrother and swim coach, from a first marriage, Randall...* The sink faucet squeaked off, and I stuffed the papers back under Lilyth's pillow. As I shut her door behind me out in the hall, Lilyth exited the bathroom with a towel on her head.

"Get away from my door, shit head."

I pointed at my bedroom door and followed my finger. In my room, I stared blankly at the dogfight on my ceiling as my fighter planes swayed gently in the warm morning breeze wafting in, without a Mustang to ensure victory. Now I understood why Coach Randall was so cool. Kevin was his little brother.

I woke up to my mom yelling that peanut butter pancakes were on the table. I sat up slowly, knowing that I would be excited about those pancakes on any other day. But then it didn't matter anymore when I realized that Firefly had probably already eaten most of my breakfast anyway. I was pulling up my drawers when Lilyth knocked before she stuck her head around the corner of my door, first time ever without barging in when I was in my underwear. I didn't know what to expect. She had been so weird since Kevin's suicide. I almost missed her being mean to me, just so she wouldn't be so sad anymore. Lilyth held up the eight-track of Lynyrd Skynyrd, with *Kevin* scratched on it.

"Did you leave this on my bed?" I nodded. Lilyth looked like she might break down, then finally she thanked me and turned to leave. She was different somehow. Sort of radiant.

"Hey, Lilyth?"

She stuck her head back around the door. "What?"

"If you told Kevin you were gonna have a baby, he woulda

smiled, 'cause I know he loved you. You can borrow my records if you want."

For once Lilyth was silent, walking inside my bedroom and closing the door quietly. I was afraid she might come back to her old self and smack me. Instead, she sat on my bed.

"Thanks, ya little butt-hole, how'd you know?" And there it was. She was pregnant with Kevin's baby. I smiled, but I was scared for her. I was scared for the baby. She could not even manage her own life, much less an infant's. I told her that she could name him after Grandaddy. Charlie. But that she'd have to find a girl name if it was a girl.

"Charlotte," Lilyth said plainly, accepting her situation. "And, shit head. Don't tell Mom and Dad." She stood up, then sat right back down. "You'll always be right here, you promise?" I nodded, yet unaware that promises are like babies, easy to make and harder to deliver. "Thanks, Mickey." And that was our truce. Though it was only the beginning of the school year, Lilyth and I were, for the first time in our lives, well prepared for the holiday season of thanks and peace and *nice* and *fine*. "Peace," she said, and flashed me a Kevin peace sign as she closed my door behind her.

My sister was a heartless mystery to me, who now had two beating inside of her. She was more or less nice to me through the holidays, and I started to trust that she would stay nice. Our truce was monumental. But the day after Christmas, its tinsel magic ebbing away, Lilyth deliberately cut the tassels off my Sting-Ray. Our truce ended. Life as I had known it continued, on guard, looking over my shoulder, except when Lilyth went away.

When I walked into the kitchen, Firefly was holding up his bowl to my mom for another serving of Cream of Wheat. He devoured it before the gob of Nutley margarine melted and he did not even mix in the brown sugar heaped on top.

"Mywan nolettuce foot moogar abuttarina reena weep," he said.

"Lawrence, you need to breathe between bites, darlin'. I have no idea what you just said!"

"His mom don't let him put sugar or butter on his Cream o' Wheat."

"Oh, okay, well, ya'll better git for school before the rain starts!"

Firefly and I biked past the Milans' two empty aluminum lawn chairs that remained in tall grass. There was still no sign of either Mr. or Mrs. Milan. I raced Firefly to school past Jane's old house. The new people didn't keep it so nice, and I couldn't wait to tell Mrs. Bradford in homeroom. Before we got to the first intersection, Firefly stopped and threw up just as the sky started to open, then parked his butt on the sidewalk for a spell with his chin propped up in his hands right there in the rain.

"We're gonna be late, man. C'mon, it's first day."

Finally he looked up at me. "Summer should go till Christmas," said Firefly, spitting out a piece of something disgusting.

"The heat, or the no-school?"

"Probly just the no-school." Firefly wiped his mouth with his clean pressed shirt. "You wanna stop at the Utotem, and get a Coke?"

"You just threw up."

"Belly's empty now. Please, I'll never make it till lunch." At the Utotem, Samir gave us two Cokes even though we offered our leftover golf ball money.

"Don't tell the man my boss I give you free. Now, I play you very, very, very new song, Mic-mic!" While we drained our Cokes, Samir played us Melanie's song, about what I'm sure were someone else's roller skates, but I could only see Jane's. Jane had a pair that she had painted psychedelic patterns in purple, green, and yellow. "What is means, Mic-mic? You have new key? I have new skate?"

I promised Samir I would come back by real soon 'cause we were nearly late for school. The Coke's sugar high prevented me from slowing my pedals, and I left Firefly in the dust that was turning to mud in the fresh rain. But I waited for him out in front of the school as I stared at The Pole. Up that flagpole was my conflagration, and her hung 95s. As we locked our bikes to the rack by our new homeroom window I peeked in, planning to wave to Mrs. Bradford, but instead, a dour woman was talking to Emmalyne. I asked Firefly if he knew who the lady was, and he peeked in to see.

"Dunno. Substitute teacher, I guess." Firefly scratched his fresh blood-orange buzz cut.

Dread grew as I hovered by my homeroom door. There was no sign of Mrs. Bradford, and the new woman was not leaving my homeroom. Everyone sat in their rows, quietly inhaling nothing but dread. Firefly and I sat closest to the bike racks, and Trent and Clatterbuck sat next to us. A sheet of paper on every desk except mine added to the gloom. The bell rang. I glanced under my desk for a matching paper, but nothing.

"Good morning, children. My name is Maude Totter. Yes, I am your principal's wife." Her tone was like we were doomed heathens. Heads turned as we asked each other if she could possibly be the same person we knew a year ago before Mrs. Bradford became our new homeroom teacher. There was no way, I thought, no way in hell this was Miss Flinch.

"She's eyeballin' you, Mic."

I shushed Firefly and studied the plump, grumpy woman's face. Her voice was like a violin played with untrained hands, just wrong, ripped and ragged.

"Some of you may remember me as Miss Flinch. Well, children, now you may address me as Mrs. Totter." What had happened to her? She was so nice before, and pretty. Now she was just angry and washed out. "You will find a written code of conduct on your desk from your principal, which y'all should have read by now, unless you've already neglected to follow the rules."

The new Mrs. Totter pointed to the blackboard behind her, which read: *There is a sheet of paper on your desk. READ IT!*

"Please take this time to read and reread the rules. These rules are given to every student, and posted on every hallway bulletin board, *lest you forget.*"

God, I hated that term. Again, I looked around on the floor for my sheet of paper. The new Mrs. Totter busied herself while everyone but me was pretending to read, bowed in silent prayer against The New Dread. I raised my hand, but the new Mrs. Totter was not looking, so I put my hand back down.

"Miss Flinch, er—Mrs. Totter, sorry, I didn't get . . ."

"Young man, what was your name?" I could not believe she had forgotten my name. I was her best student.

"Um . . . Mickey, ma'am."

"Of course," Mrs. Totter intoned as if she had been brainwashed by Mr. Totter's account of the men in my family. "Well, Mickey, we raise our hands to speak in this class. What is it?"

"Could I be excused to go to the restroom, please?"

"Is it an emergency?" Her pedantic probing made me sad. What had marriage to Mr. Totter done to her soul?

"Um, yes, ma'am..."

"Hurry up, then." She looked at me hard. I picked up my paper lunch bag, and headed toward the door. "I know about you and brown bags, Mickey. Leave that behind, please."

"Yes, ma'am." I stalled returning to my desk trying to figure out how to smuggle the bag out of class with me. I sat back down in my seat pretending to place my lunch inside my desk and stuffed it in under my shirt instead. I wanted to devise a sentence that would tell her how I hated everything that she had become, but it came out as, "I'll be right back, ma'am."

And then I walked out. When I got out into the hall, I passed a bulletin board and noticed the rules paper, and read it. Then I walked down the hall the same way I came, ducking below the window of my homeroom door. I continued combing the halls, peeking in every homeroom window. Finally I found her. I knocked. Mrs. Bradford opened the door.

"Mickey! Hello, what a wonderful surprise. Did you have a good summer?"

"Oh yes, ma'am." Jane's mother seemed really happy to see me.

"Class, this is Mickey, he was my student last year." Some class members waved and said hi to me and I waved back.

Andy raised his hand alongside his chest, and I did the same, as was our unspoken custom. I spotted Jane's old box record player sitting on the stool, open. "Okay, don't go anywhere, class, I'll be right back." Jane's mother closed the classroom door behind us and we stood in the hall facing each other.

"Um, Mrs. Bradford, I didn't know that I wouldn't have you this year, and I brought these." I reached under my shirt and removed three 45s from my lunch bag. "I think she ... I think Jane ..." I looked up at Mrs. Bradford. "... and your class will like the 'Drift Away' one. We can't play 'em in our class anyway. Miss Flinch is Mrs. Totter this year and she's ... different." Jane's mother nodded knowingly.

"Mickey, that's very sweet of you."

"Well, I better get back to class."

"*Lest* you get in trouble." Jane's mother grinned like Jane and winked conspiratorially at me. I was determined to see Jane again, and those dangling 95s were keeping that determination alive.

"Bye, Mrs. Bradford." I took a step back, and hesitated, then forward, and hugged her. Jane's mother looked at me, then smiled actually more to herself than to me, and returned to her class. I watched through the window for a short time, wondering if she knew about her daughter's shoes way up in the sky, just a hundred or so feet away. She did not. I could tell. It was just me.

"Well, well, it looks like we have some new music!" As I walked slowly down the hall I heard the needle drop and crackle and Dobie Gray sang "Drift Away." And I heard him sing about doing exactly what I wanted to do every single day of my life with Jane.

It was mid-September, soon after The Pole and my ankle was still hurting, when Andy accidentally knocked over my chocolate milk at lunch. I am ashamed of what I did next. But it is because of that that I believe now. In everything. I want you to know that I have never had a problem with Andy. He knocked over my chocolate milk, and I honestly could not have cared less. But everyone else cared. And I did not care enough about my not caring to contest their caring. Or maybe I was just a pussy. The latter, I think.

"Mic's Quik was gonna be mine, you fuck wad!" Firefly roasted Andy, and set the whole fight in motion.

I should have stopped it all right there, and even now, I kick myself for not having done so. Firefly and I were sitting with some "cooler kids" who were all a year or so older than us, and Andy was sitting with the nerds at the other end of the rectangular lunch table. The nerds consisted of the one who chose never to return to football, way back in grade school, and five who never even tried out. The upshot was, though I felt not a trace of enmity toward any one of them, Andy and I just never really bonded. I knew who had my back, and that was the guys I had pushed myself to my limits with on the sports field.

Trash talk and immature negotiations flew around in between Andy and me with neither one of our mouths moving. We just sort of blankly stared at each other, and before either of us knew it, we were to meet. And fight. At school everyone knew Mr. Totter forbade fighters to wash the blood off their hands so parents would see and know they had been in another fight, so the fight location was declared: the Utotem.

After school that day we would settle everything. Neither one of us even uttered a word, but our respective sides said things like, "You better apologize to Mickey!" and "Andy ain't gonna apologize for shit!" Our silence not only spoke volumes, but had confirmed our agreement to meet after school at the designated location, right behind the store's yellow Dumpster, and settle this *huge* problem once and for all.

Everyone knew I would win. That is because typically in junior high and elementary school I'd secretly get scared and react behind my tears before my opponent would. I'd strike harder before the other guy had a chance to do worse damage to me. In that way, I'd be the one to control the situation. And maybe Lilyth did this, too, but in her case I guess it was not a rush to finish a fight but rush into bed with guys, to be the first one to wrap things up, get it over with before they could do worse damage and control her. I guess in that way she controlled the situation.

But fighting Andy, I wasn't scared. It wasn't a match. I knew I'd win. And it nauseated me. I had always found Andy to be pleasant. Quiet, but pleasant. But because I was too much of a big girl's blouse to stand up for what I believed in, I was now going to fight someone whom I had absolutely nothing against. To this day, I am nauseated by this admission. Tommy Gasconade was the oldest kid in our group, and he somehow puppeteered me that whole day. So, after school, we all marched to the Utotem with definitive purpose. There were four of us. Walking there I tried to rationalize this fight in my head and came up with a whopping nothing, but strode on like a pugnacious, warring creature that charges into battle without reason. A rabid badger, perhaps. I know I was a vicious little guy when there was a reason for viciousness, but in this case there was not a reason at all, outside of looking cool to the cooler kids. For this, I am also sorry, but the fact is that the lessons I learned while at some of the lowest points in my life have always paid dividends in achieving my highest.

Firefly, Eddy, Tommy, and I arrived at the Utotem and waited impatiently around back until about four o'clock when we all realized that Andy was not going to show up. On the inside, all my molecules relaxed at once and I almost passed out from the sheer pleasantness of the moment. On the outside, I was incandescent with rage. I hid that my ankle ached from The Pole. I took the opportunity to rest my limp and pop into the Utotem and say hello to Samir, hoping Tommy would get off his high horse and forget about his justice league. Inside the Utotem, Melanie's "Candles in the Rain" was playing on Samir's turntable set up behind the counter. Two of our band of four boys had followed me inside and listened in purposefully while I struck up a pointed conversation with the Hindu guy—as they knew Samir—behind the counter. As usual, Samir played the latest music, as he said, "for the Utotem customers to *live and let live*," so I had enjoyed dropping by to share my collection with him as it had grown.

"Ah, Mic-mic!" I liked that Samir called me Mic-mic with his accent from *Injah*. "Question for you, Mic-mic. You are knowing this lyric? Why you must *lay down*? Song says you must *lay down*!" His accent sent Eddy and Firefly into a giggle fit. If I am honest, it made me laugh, too, but I always managed to keep the giggles inside out of respect for Samir. I had often wondered the same thing about her lyrics, and that is probably why I liked Samir so much. I wanted to answer him, but I didn't understand Melanie's lyrics all that well, either. But answers or no answers, my two friends thought I was an even cooler kid when Samir was asking me stuff.

"I don't know, Samir, and I'm not sure I know how to let my white birds smile, either. But I'd like to."

I shot Samir a peace sign like Kevin might have only weeks before, when Tommy marched inside gnashing.

"Bullshit, come on, guys, I know where Andy lives."

The feebleness that I displayed that day still haunts me, because I followed them straight into the beautiful subdivision of Quail Valley that I had come to know so well and onto the dense velvet golf course heading straight for the trampoline at hole eighteen and the intended bludgeoning of Andy. I prayed that his house was nowhere near hers. I was deeply mortified at the chance that a unicorn might witness my senseless beating of one of her neighbors.

I suffered this point of contrast, and later it would drive home a mission to live consistently with my convictions and refuse to compromise them for any reason. But in those drawn-out minutes as I approached hole eighteen, I accepted that I was going to hell. Most people haven't a clue as to what to do with their lives, but they all want another that will last forever. I, however, just wanted to die and be done with it.

How Tommy knew exactly where Andy's house was, I have no idea, but he strode straight down the golf cart path. As we followed, I saw a fire engine red golf cart that was made to look like a Rolls-Royce. It was parked at the Halfway Food Hut in between the ninth and tenth holes. Seated in it was an obese man just resting like a giant tumor behind the wheel of that golf cart as he chatted up another Titly-est waitress. He had on a blue alligator shirt with bright orange stains smeared all over the front. As we neared, I saw that he was eating Cheetos, and after every bite, he would wipe his hands down the front of the pale blue fabric. I don't know why, but in that very moment, just briefly, I hated that man. Then, just as we passed him, he stopped talking to the waitress, looked right at me like he knew what I was up to, and turned up the volume of his little in-dash stereo as if he were trying to drown out the inevitability of my callow attack on Andy. His eyes made tiny pinpricks in my chest and I found it hard to breathe. I knew he knew, and disapproved of what I was about to do. Donovan's "Hurdy Gurdy Man" blazed louder and louder on the fat man's radio as my leaden legs took me closer and closer to the residence of Andy and his family, and slowly out of that fat man's gaze.

We arrived at Andy's house and Tommy rang the front doorbell. Impatient, he rang it again. Nothing. Inside, I rejoiced. No Andy!

"Come on, let's go around the back." Tommy strode onward. My heart sank. We walked all the way around to the other side of his house, right on the golf course with no fence to impede the view. I could see the trampoline a few houses down, and that is the first and only time I have ever prayed to not see Jane since she had bounced into my life. The back of Andy's house had a big sliding glass door that hid nothing of the kitchen and living room. Tommy knocked on the glass. Then he knocked harder. It reverberated. Finally, Andy's mother came down the stairs and upon seeing us, broke into a grin whose image burned itself onto the back side of my eyelids.

She flung open the sliding glass door and graciously said, "Hello!" Tommy rudely cut to the chase and immediately asked if Andy was home, without even a *hi, how are you today, ma'am*. And then, the impossible happened. Andy's mother's grin turned into a full-on smile. It was a smile that I recognized from my own parents. It was the smile of pride. Pride at the realization that "cool" kids were finally coming to visit her son. My heart shriveled up to the size of a small, sun-dried raisin, and I accepted as fact that I was probably never going to make it to heaven. The residue of the dried raisin left a stinking picture, and some stinking pictures you just cannot unboil. Andy came walking down the stairs as his mother kept smiling and talking to us. My tunnel vision was on Andy: Our eyes finally met as he finished his descent.

"I'll be back in a minute, Mom." He crossed right past us into their backyard as if he was just going out to mow the lawn or lead us off to play a round of golf. We all walked resolutely out toward the seventeenth green, away from the trampoline, for which I was grateful.

"Come on back when you're done and I'll serve y'all some sandwiches and cupcakes." His mother's voice tapered off.

"Yes, thank you, ma'am, we'll be right back. We won't be long," hollered Firefly.

Neither Andy nor I spoke the entire walk out to the green, but Tommy, Eddy, and Firefly were like three Caesars in a coliseum. When we arrived at what felt like the right spot, Tommy took out the seventeenth hole flag just like they do for the final putt. I dropped my books on the ground as Andy and I turned to face each other. The only thing I wanted at that moment was for Andy to apologize so we could all go home. I heard Tommy start to say something right before I felt Andy's fist impact the side of my head right by my left ear. I stumbled to the right and immediately tackled him before he could swing again. Straddling him, I grabbed Andy's head in a tight vise and asked him if he gave up. Led by Tommy, Eddy and Firefly yelled, "Punch him in the face!" and "Kick his ass!" I held him down with all my weight and switched my grip on him to a conventional headlock to free up my right hand. I raised my fist up over Andy's face and yelled at him to *please give up goddammit*. He would not, I promise you, he would not give up. It is always good to strive to be like people whom you respect. Conversely, I also feel that there are not many things more depressing than finding out that you have things in common with people you detest. I punched Andy on the forehead and asked him again to give up. Nothing. I punched again. Nothing. I threw again for his forehead, but he squirmed and I caught his nose. It opened up, and blood flew everywhere.

"Say you give up and I'll stop hitting you, Andy!"

But he just wriggled and stared up at me. I threw a couple loose-knuckled shots right above his eyes and tried my best to make them look vicious, but I barely connected. Then I asked Andy again. Nothing.

And that's when I got mad. I got *really* mad. His silence was forcing me to kick his ass. And no, the irony is not lost on me. It infuriated and frustrated me so much that he would not utter the three simple words that would allow me to stop bludgeoning him. I got so irrationally pissed off that I tightened up my fist, and I cracked him right in the nose. I cracked him hard. There was blood all over his face and my hand, and I smashed my face right against his.

"That's it, stay down!" I whispered, then I screamed, "Don't make me hit you again!"

I felt his body relax, and I knew it was over. I got up and

grabbed my three-ring binder and social studies book off the ground and stalked off to the other side of the golf course and did not look back. I got about ten yards and all I could hear was "The Hurdy Gurdy Man" and the putter of the red Rolls-Royce golf cart as those Cheetos stains drew closer. Then Tommy, Eddy, and Firefly ran up to me with praise, asking me where the hell I was going. I couldn't even turn to look at them, because I did not want them to see me crying.

I started running and shouting that I was late, that I had to take a shortcut back to my neighborhood. I just ran. I ran the hell away from the seventeenth hole, even hole eighteen, away from Jane, from myself, in between two houses directly across the golf course opposite Andy's house. There, I slid down between a Tudor-style turret and a big AC unit on the side of what looked like a palace to me. Andy was still sprawled out on the green as the guys' voices drifted off toward the cart path. The music was still there. And I cried until empty. I tore a leaf off a banana plant beside the house that I was leaning against and wiped the blood that had now mixed with tears off my face and hands. When I looked up, I saw Andy watching me from across the fairway as he struggled back into his yard. I have no idea how long he had been watching me cry. He stared, then glanced down and picked a few leaves from his mother's garden and began wiping his face off in the same manner that I had. When he was finished, he buried the bloody leaves in the dirt and looked up at me again. Andy raised his hand about chest height. I raised mine by my ear where he had punched me. And then he turned and walked inside. My Grandaddy used to tell me, "It ain't okay just to right a wrong. It ain't okay just to correct it. No, you gotta correct it ten times over."

As I got up to brush myself off, I heard the music approaching. But the song had changed. It was immediately familiar feeling. I looked up and saw that the obese man was driving straight up to the seventeenth hole in his red Rolls-Royce cart. He stopped directly on the green where Tommy had removed the marker pole, and stepped out and looked around, scrutinizing our impact on the fabric of dense velvet green. Finally, he spotted the flag, waddled over to pick it up, and gently placed it back in its cup embedded in the turf. He walked back to his cart, but before he climbed in, he scanned the horizon in all directions until he spun completely around and landed his laser eyes right on mine. Laying a finger aside of his nose, the fat man blew snot out of one nostril in my direction. I wanted for him to look away, but he would not. And then his head slowly started to shake in disapprobation, almost imperceptibly, and then he tapped his ear, without ever taking his eyes off me. He took a moment, then climbed in the red Rolls, turned up the volume of that song—that song that crept into every one of my pores, and puttered off down the cart path. I could not get that song out of my head, or take my eyes off that man until he disappeared into a tiny blotch of color on the Texas horizon. The words to that song looped over and over again in my mind all the way to Samir's, where I wanted desperately to sing it to him to find out its name and author. I had to know. But Samir had closed early, so my legs never stopped. I just wanted home.

That night after swim practice, when I got home, Steve McQueen turned his back on me and wandered off under my bean tree to nap. Steve knew. If your own dog can't look at you, then you have done something wrong. I felt like everyone knew.

I sat out on the front stairs of my house completely alone, my ankle aching, my butt freezing against my cold cement handprints. An entire knuckle longer now, I traced a scarred finger along my three-year-old impressions in the top step. There was still no sign of the Milans except their two chairs, steadfast in the tall grass. I thought Grandaddy and Mamau would be here already for fried chicken but they were late, and Mom and Dad were not home. Lilyth was home—I could tell from the moaning coming from her bedroom window—but she would not unlock the front door for me. After Kevin's death, Lilyth's way of dealing with her grief was to do a lot of sleeping . . . with everyone. It was dark outside, and the cold night air had rooted its brittle fingers into my bones by the time Mom got home. The house was still locked, and Lilyth did not even try to hide anything from our parents. Maybe a half-assed try. She got attention, all right. It's no wonder the jocks had nothing to do with Lilyth. The "heads," "freaks," and dope smokers all went for Lilyth like scoring a free nickel bag of Maui Gold. I gathered my sister was the gold in their eyes.

When Mom finally got home and let the two of us in, I heard the theme song from *Doctor Zhivago* playing. It could only mean one thing, and it made an already appalling situation even worse. Mom's black lacquer jewelry box, which never left her bedroom dresser, was open and in the clutches of this greasy-haired blond guy slumping out of Lilyth's bedroom. He pawed through my mom's personal jewelry collection, not bothering to zip his fly or look up at us. He sat down at our little white wooden kitchen table and lit up a smoke as he continued to dig through my mom's private treasures, sometimes putting an especially sparkly brooch or ring on the table to get a better look as he picked and itched at his scalp and private parts. No shoes, few teeth, grimy. And the stench. I was ashamed of Lilyth. I saw the look on Mom's face as her lip trembled. I immediately heard myself shouting at him exactly where I wanted to see him go, laced with far too much profanity for my mother's presence and ending with "NOW!" Without a word, the dirtbag got up and shut the lid of Mom's jewelry box. Silence pierced the frozen air between us as he scratched and slouched across the carpet to the front door. I struggled against my desire to pull that piece of shit's hair out by the roots.

"You're mean, man." His bloodshot blue eyes shot me a dejected look, and he kept picking and scratching and itching himself all over.

"No, you're dirty. Leave my house now." I followed him to the door and slammed the door on his back.

"It's *fine*, Sug, be *nice*." Mom's *F* word and *N* word rankled. That dirtbag did not deserve Mom's *fine* and *nice*. He had no respect. He had nothing but self-pity.

"No, it ain't *fine*, Mom! And that dirtbag ain't *nice*." Mom did not reprimand me for losing my temper, or even for the profanity, instead sending me to the shower, and quietly telling Lilyth to put her bedsheets straight out in the trash behind the garage. My mom was her mom, and my dad was her dad, so I believed that Lilyth should be the same... but she was not.

Later I could hear through my bedroom door as Mom and Dad disciplined Lilyth, but she had never understood them. I don't know where she learned it, but I knew by then that she only spoke rattlesnake.

"Your mother and I didn't raise you t'be a heller, goddammit. You hang around nine losers and I guarantee you this: your ass will be the tenth."

"He ain't a loser, he's misunderstood."

"Oh, for Christ sakes, Lilyth! That boy is shit, plain and simple shit. If you can't see that, then I got no hope for you. And I don't give a rat's ass about him, Lilyth, it's you we care about. Can't you get that?"

"Paul, be nice, Lilyth's a fine and thoughtful girl. That boy ain't had proper care, is all."

"Our daughter ain't carin' for a loser, hear me?"

It was all fine and nice, and then it wasn't. I know the truth was somewhere in the middle, but the middle was a no-man's-land that I was completely unaware of at that age.

Out the front window I caught a glimpse of my Grandaddy with his giant index finger in that loser's face before he sent him on his way. Then Grandaddy, James, and Mamau came inside, Mamau singing George Harrison's "My Sweet Lord" like she always did, stopping short of the Hare Krishna part she didn't care for, and she reached to crush me into her great bosoms. The night was getting on and everyone was tired. Grandaddy took one look at the scene in the kitchen and turned right around saying, "Woman, we gonna need some ponies out on the porch."

Mamau fetched the tiny beers out of the fridge for him and James, and then set to making fried chicken. Dad and Lilyth continued to argue, and Mom continued to cry. Lilyth tried to hide herself under Mamau's big flabby wing disguised in a gauzy gold-sleeved dress, looking so fancy and pretty, but Mamau shooed Lilyth away on account of spitting grease on the hot stove. Lilyth kept blaming everyone but herself, so Dad finally got up to say he was washing his hands of Lilyth.

That's when Mamau stopped singing. That golden puff of femininity set down the cover on the fried chicken so quietly everyone turned to look. Hellfire seared away the kindness in Mamau's eyes as she turned to face her own son.

"Boy," Mamau said to my dad, real soft and quiet like a crooning dove, a dove whose olive branch had been charred clear off by the coal of brimstone in its beak. "Boy, Lilyth is yo' own blood. You don't *never* let me hear you say you's gon' wash yo' hands of yo' own blood." My Mamau whispered that *never* so soft. And the quieter Mamau spoke, the more my dad heard every word. Then she said what should have been obvious to everyone in the room. "Besides, Paul, you cain't up'n dispose of a child with two hearts beatin' inside her."

My mom choked on a sob, and my dad went ashen. Lilyth kept her eyes on Mamau for safety. Mamau, having arrived at our house mid-argument, had made some assumptions about the cause of the argument. Having seen a few things over the years, Mamau had observed Lilyth's changes in the past few months and she had clearly assumed everyone else saw it, too. From a sickly gray, Dad's face turned a new shade of purple I had never seen before—not even on Jane's paint palette.

"Good thing that drug uh-dikt is already dead, 'cause I'd kill 'em," raged Dad. "Or do you even know who the father is? Or are you gon' sneak off t'get another goddamn abortion?"

As shitty as Lilyth was to me, I had always believed it was Magda who was the bad influence on Lilyth. While Mom wept, Mamau had an idea for a plan: a special school for *special* girls, as she put it in her own sweet way.

"I ain't goin'," sobbed Lilyth, but Mamau just kept right on embracing Lilyth in her ancient cloud of golden candy floss and love, like a fat old magic fairy princess in whose arms no bad could ever happen to you, ever. Turns out, the special school for *special* girls was an orphanage where Mamau had begun her childhood. And even my dad had not known till now.

"Seedlin', get the hell out here!" So I limped out onto the porch, but I kept an ear turned on my Mamau through the opened window screen.

"The nuns were so kind and beautiful like you, Lilyth darlin', and they gave me the name Mary, like Mother Mary, who was from a good family, I'll have you know. She come from money, Jesus's momma did. She was a rich Jewish girl. It's yo' Grandaddy changed my name to Goldie. You din't know that did'y, Paul, baby, 'cause I never tol' ya. Life's too complicated already, boy, I din' wanna make yours any more complicated with your own daddy shot dead in the line's duty, and that's the truth, that is. You were too young to 'splain it all. And Grandaddy Charlie love you like he' own."

My dad just stood up and stared out the back sliding glass door like he was me looking for Jane, but I knew he was looking for something else. I knew that in that moment, he was putting his life together. And in turn, mine. Mamau ignored him and started singing "My Sweet Lord" again and draining the chicken. Suddenly, she looked around. "Oh Lord! Where is Charlie?" Mamau clucked and bustled finding James and Grandaddy with me out on the porch with the ponies that she had given him. She set down a little plate of Bull-Yawns for Grandaddy that I knew would only sit there for a tiny space before I would pick 'em up and return them right back to her.

"Good woman, yer Grandaddy got," said James. And it was at that point that Lilyth broke the profound moment with my Grandaddy and his best friend, shrieking out the front door, racing down the steps crying, and then disappeared, heading off toward Magda's. Mom in tears, Dad yelling, and Mamau and Grandaddy each shaking their heads in dismay and disgust, respectively. James just sat there silent, taking it all in, then he cuffed my Grandaddy on the head and said, "Charlie, y'all get the hell over it y'hear? Y'done all you can do, for that girl. Goddamn drugs these kids're takin' nowadays."

My Grandaddy pointed to Lilyth as she ran off, and I knew something was coming. "Know why that one biting the hands that feed her? 'Cause them same hands is the hands that preventin' her from feedin' her damn self. That one ain't never had t'earn nothin'. Important you keep ya babies hungry, hear me? Not so hungry they starve, but goddamn hungry enough that they gonna least learn how ta hunt. More Boudin, boy." Grandaddy nodded at the plate of Bull-Yawns, and I knew what I had to do.

I don't think Lilyth even knew what was on the plate that my Mamau always brought out to my Grandaddy, much less that they were always meant for someone else. My sister hardly ever spoke to him, and I had never even seen her on our glorious porch—except to go storm raging through it—the porch that shaped more of my life than my bedroom had. But I knew I wanted someone to give mine to, and that Jane was that someone. And that a pair of rescued 95s was no match for a plate of Bull-Yawns.

Chapter Eight

And that was it. Jane was sequestered in her new world over in the rich subdivision of Quail Valley. Lilyth disappeared from home off and on for a while. Mom and Dad never mentioned Lilyth's condition to me, and years would pass before the topic of a little girl named Charlotte would resurface. Without Lilyth, home felt safe for a good long time. I relaxed. But high school was a wasteland; without Jane, life was difficult to breathe in.

Jane,

I can't imagine a time in which disappointing you will be okay.

I got my first high school lungful one day at the roller-skating rink, although I despised our new football coach for buying into the current trend of using shit like ballet and roller-skating and ice-skating to increase the balance and agility of an athlete. He actually had us in full pads and helmets with roller skates on doing wind sprints across the rink like a bunch of nancies. There were trails of sweat thrown across the hardwood floors beneath our feet, and he had even duct-taped the arms of us running backs to our bodies to make balancing even harder as we raced from wall to wall looking like idiots. I wanted nothing more than to skip this ridiculous practice—until my lungs sent me a message. Breathing her in always felt like I had shoved my head into the deep freeze at the supermarket and inhaled like I had just resurfaced from a deep dive. And there she was. So my lungs and nostrils stood at attention and I almost passed out from the over-oxygenation.

I saw her skates before I even saw her face when she and about six other girls were sectioned off in the rink's corner taking what I imagined was some sort of disco skating class. Through my helmet's facemask, I couldn't take my eyes off a pair of psychedelic purple, yellow, and green high-top roller skates from which silver and gold bells dangled on iridescent cellophane threads that only Jane could have produced, spinning around until the skates slowly came to a stop. I spat out my mouthpiece as I saw the only face that had ever given me a nearly paralytic physical reaction and yelled, "JANE" just before I impacted the wall. I got the wind knocked out of me and I collapsed on the ground, finding it harder to breathe in that moment than it had ever been in her absence. I saw her searching each of our helmets for recognition. Now, getting the wind knocked out of you usually creates a panic to regain the necessary lung function to prevent suffocation. But in that instant, I only needed it to find my voice. I just needed to scream her name one last time before our new age coach ended his count and sent us on our final lap and then to the changing room. I didn't even care if she had seen me slamming into the wall like a kamikaze pilot. I vaguely heard Firefly interrupting Leo Sayer, who was singing about needing something, and touching something, until he finally drowned out Leo altogether. My breath came back to me too late for consciousness.

"Man, you had to crack a rib as hard as you hit that wall," was the first thing I heard when I woke up in that stupid, boys' roller-skating changing room. I would have preferred to hear Leo. And Jane was gone.

My Jane moments seemed to be even more fleeting after that. High school happened around me, and sports, and jobs, and saving money for a car. Nowadays, Mr. Milan sat out alone, grass up around the arms of his chair again. I still mowed the grass around him and he still looked right through me. He kept his right hand on the arm of Mrs. Milan's empty aluminum chair and a beer in his left. I kept mowing the high patch at night after he went in. We never spoke. A number of things changed at that point in my life, but Jane was the constant. She always was. I'd read a lot about love in books. And it was always made out to be a wonderfully entrancing experience, available to only those beyond a certain age. But I knew I had already fallen in it. They were wrong. They were all wrong. Love was different. It was different from everything. Sports were always logical, a lot like mathematical equations. What I had fallen in far earlier than they said I could was something that I just could not navigate the same way I could when eleven people were trying desperately to slam me violently to the ground before I could find an end zone. And I was petrified of that level of helplessness. But I had my dancing mailbox. And I had hope.

Jane,

Sometimes they're not just ships passing in the night. Sometimes they're lifeboats.

Time had flown by, but they were wrong about it being a healer. Hell, time healed nothing—nothing real at least. "It heals all" . . . what a load of crap. The years had numbed nothing. And an emotional and musically fueled ride brought absolutely nothing to the surface, because the important things never leave the surface. That's just where they live.

Some things are meant to be shared with lovers. And music was always one of those things to me. I never wanted that magical journey to be interrupted by trivial conversation. I just wanted to know that someone had experienced it, too . . . but only someone important. A concert, for example, was always something I had to take a minute to recover from. So I always went alone. And so did she. But we were not just passing in the night. Toward the end of my senior year in high school, I sat on the side of the downtown Houston auditorium after spending about an hour and a half with Gary Numan and three thousand screaming idiots that had been trying to sonically bastardize my experience. I watched all the people walking to the parking lot with concert shirts in their hands and cars driving by pumping his hit song. And I felt it a bit weird. If they loved his music enough to attend his concert, why did they leave early? Most of the audience had already started to file out after he played "Cars" for the first song of his encore. But there were about ten to twenty people left still in their seats just staring at the empty stage by the time I finally drifted out. Those were the people who saw the same show that I did. I wondered if they, too, had been waiting for "Down in the Park." I know I certainly was. And after hearing it, I just needed another minute alone on that brick wall to watch the people already going home who didn't.

Standing up from that wall, strangely winded, I finally decided to walk back to the '67 Beetle that Firefly and I had put together with junkyard parts and rusted panels. We called that car "The Toaster" because it had no firewall between the engine compartment and the seats. That, combined with the Texas heat, made it almost unbearable to drive. In fact, the rubber would actually melt off of your sneakers if you drove it too long.

You know, it's usually only with a reflection on the collected moments of my life that I can truly pick out commonalities—never in the moment. But with her I always saw it immediately. And standing up from that wall, just like at the skating rink, I understood what that tiny bit of exertion affecting my lungs was trying to tell me. It was an indicator when something quickly took me from not enough oxygen to too much. For some reason, I just did not want to leave yet. I wanted to wait, to put off the long walk to the free street parking where I had left The Toaster.

After thirty more minutes of waiting for nothing, I finally trudged back to The Toaster. Hell, I was starving anyway and desperately needed to get something in my belly before my attitude went to crap. It's really bizarre to me how my brain has decided to retain some random, very specific details about my adolescence, but I remember that I had exactly $6.50 in my pocket that night, and that three chili cheese dogs, french fries, and a drink cost $5.49 at James Coney Island, one of my favorite spots in Houston. That was going to be the second half of my date with myself. But first I decided to circle The Toaster back around to the front of the auditorium just to get one last look. I never should have doubted my lungs, because as I rounded the corner I saw a girl standing right in front of the theater in a short purple sundress—and I knew. I parked The Toaster on the curb about fifty feet from the front and got out just to make sure. But without her even facing me, I could tell. No one was that beautiful but Jane. No one moved like Jane. No one stood still like her. Just Jane. Only Jane.

She had stayed for "Down in the Park," just like me. And now she was slowly rocking back and forth from her toes to her heels on that curb long after everyone else had gone home. Seeing her on that curb brought absolutely nothing back, because it had never left. I did not want her any more or any less at that moment than I did when I was eight. Puppy love is a story told by idiots, about idiots, for idiots. Through the years I've accumulated a number of ideas, secrets, and dreams. Jane's been in every single one of them. I watched her on that curb and wondered if Jane had been at any of the other concerts I had gone to alone. And just how many lifeboats we had missed. My Jane dreams from growing up are all identical today, but dreams are never complicated by social status. In that perfect instant, I wanted so dearly to offer her a ride in something better than that shit box Toaster. And I craved to be able to buy her something, *anything* more than just a few goddamn chili cheese dogs. To this day, there has never been a time in which I have had less and desired more than that night with only six dollars and fifty fucking cents in my hollow pocket. I now know that I was embarrassed about all the things that had nothing to do with who I was.

All of those pathetically insecure thoughts raced through my mind, but I just wanted the car horn that was interrupting my mind to *shut the fuck up*! But then she turned around, and even though she wasn't looking at me, her face gave me enough peace and security to offer her a ride on a goddamn bicycle if that was all I had. My God, she was lovely. But that horn was a wakeup call that came just a hair too late, and it drifted right past me up to the curb in front of her looking a lot like a brand-new red Porsche 911SC. She smiled as someone flung the passenger door open from within, and that tiny little familiar Grunt was there, but it didn't leave my lips. Instead it clicked, a painful snap inside the roots of my sinuses, and then it left my soul. I watched Jane climb in, and I watched that car take her away. I had never grown out of crying and fighting, and I wanted nothing more right then and there than to have five minutes alone with the entitled jackass who would not at least get out and walk around to open a car door for my Jane. I wanted to hurt him badly . . . even though I could not control my eyes.

K7, K8, K9, and K0 were the four Elvis songs on the jukebox at James Coney Island. Those songs were important to me, and they were free, which left me with a dollar and a penny in my pocket when Kate walked up to my table with a smile, waving over two others behind her. She was a beautiful and bubbly girl in my grade with long blond hair, who came from a very well-off family and cheered at almost every football game in which I had ever played. It's never a secret in high school as to who's fond of whom, and it was no secret that Kate told her friends, who told my friends, who told me. As Kate and her entourage got closer, I recognized another familiar face under a hat—Jonathan, as in pee-hat Jonathan, whose entire being still repelled me.

Jonathan and his new girlfriend came into focus just as The King was finishing "Can't Help Falling in Love." Jonathan pranced up to my table dressed to chill like Duran Duran in their *Rio* tour, trying way too hard with the New Wave look and short-sleeved Madras plaid button-down shirt synched with a thin black leather tie. He plopped down opposite me in the booth, leaning back to observe me smugly while singing "Hungry Like the Wolf" as if he had fucking written it and snapping his fingers for the waiter to hurry up. I really hated that kid, but I actually liked Kate, especially with her hand on my thigh beneath that table. But going dutch just wasn't in my blood, and affording a girl like her was not yet in my economic plan. My mind could never escape Jane anyway, and I wanted them all to go away. I just wanted to be alone.

"So sorry we were delayed," said Jonathan as he doffed his wannabe 1940s Dean Martin fedora right on the table between Kate and me. "We had to listen to my sainted mother carry on about how our housekeeper put the Mottahedeh in the dishwasher." I had neither a housekeeper nor a dishwasher, except my own sainted mother, and hadn't a clue

what Mottahedeh was, but assumed it must be a living being, perhaps a pet lizard or hamster that would die trapped
in a dishwasher. I could not take my focus off that goddamn hat near my food. Jonathan was now in college, drove
a brand-new BMW, wore exorbitantly expensive clothes, and
let everyone know it. About the time I landed his piss-sodden
Nothing Runs like a Deere up The Pole, his dad struck it rich
and I guess new-money Jonathan expected to be revered like
a rock star, though he was an unoriginal Frankenstein in de-
signer duds. He had attempted a few sports, mainly the tennis
team at the country club, so he had slimmed and switched
hats. But he still found opportunities to let me know he had
the potential to be a threat in my life, at least financially. My
self-worth was steered initially by stupid things like the economic difference between Jane and me, and by people like
Jonathan.

You know, I'm embarrassed that I was embarrassed about
being poor. Hell, I don't even like using the term *poor*, because I wanted for nothing. My parents provided all of the
basics and more than enough love. It was far more than I
could've ever asked for. And as far as the things that I truly
value in this life, they gave me more than any other child I
knew. But I learned to wait. I knew that Jonathan's bank account would slowly deplete, but what my family had given
me would pay dividends my entire life. I trained myself to
avoid the chafing social situations where my economic short-
comings would be obvious. I had accepted the world that my
lowly high school income placed me in, but I could not fucking stand it when it was thrown in my face.

Jonathan picked up his ridiculous Dean Martin hat and
flipped it around like he'd practiced it in the mirror a thou-

sand times prior, and then dropped it again right next to my plate on the table. I had not even taken a bite of my hot dogs yet, so my attitude was teetering on the edge as I fought it to a close-decision victory against jamming a fork straight into his fucking eye socket. I had to take a minute to collect myself, then I simply pointed to the coatrack at the end of each booth.

"Yup, that fedora cost me over a hundred and fifty dollars. It can reside right here where no locals can steal it off the rack." He then lit up a Dunhill Red and exhaled at me. I wanted to want to be a gentleman, but that hat was something my Grandaddy would never allow on a supper table, and I really just wanted to shove it straight up that pussy's ass. Some guys feared Jonathan, thought he was powerful. I thought he was derivative, an unoriginal piece of shit, always impersonating a prepackaged trend, like Lilyth with her perfumes but with a newly loaded bank account.

"Sad about your neighbor, Mrs. Milan, Mickey," Kate tried to redirect gracefully.

"Cancer for how many years?" Jonathan's girlfriend asked pertly like, *Would you like a mint?* As if she gave a shit.

"I can't imagine suffering like that. I'm so sorry, Mickey." Kate squeezed my thigh under the table, and I wondered, as her hand crept slowly up the inside of my thigh, if my body would react to her even though she was not Jane.

"Really nice, the Milans," I said, emotionless.

"Probably somethin' in the water in that part of town," sneered Jonathan. Kate shot him fierce eyes. "What? I'm just sayin', really. At least at the golf course we know which reservoir our home's connected to."

Three chili cheese dogs gave me an excuse to do most of

the listening, so I was silent the majority of the time, but I was slowly losing control. In two hot dogs' time, Jonathan had already asked me if I wanted to join them at Marisk, where he had reserved a bottle of aged Dom that we could split four ways at $250 each, and that Kate absolutely loved that place, and that it would be no locals and only *good stock*, and that maybe we could take my car because his 450SL was on order and he didn't like driving that "bus of a BMW," and that he desperately needed to find a new tailor for a new Armani suit he'd just bought while in New York at fucking Fashion Week, and did I "know anyone good?" and wasn't I glad that I no longer had to work at Church's Fried Chicken anymore? I knew he knew that I still worked there most days, and that I was still in high school. I knew he knew because that piece of shit would come through the drive-through window at least once a week and order something stupid with a car full of my classmates and mock me without having the balls to *actually* mock me. And he'd ask what year The Toaster was, every single time, feigning interest.

But right now I had a mouthful so I did not respond. I couldn't. I could tell by Kate's face and the way she was squeezing my thigh that I was not alone in feeling like his remarks were deliberate, but his girlfriend did not seem to have a clue. I wanted to know if he was like that guy driving down the road that flips off another driver and motions for him to pull over, and then acts shocked when he gets slugged in the jaw. I wanted to know if I was misreading things. It was possible. I knew I had a financial insecurity. I genuinely wanted to know if he was trying to insult me, or if he was just stupid. My insecurities were horribly inflamed. He had embarrassed me enough already, but I had to know. So, I asked.

"Um," I said. But that was it. Silence. I had to think. I had to be very specific with my question to him in order to get the right answer, or I knew that I would crack that douchey fuck right there at the table. And *please* don't do that, because good stock would *never* do that. I wished that I could have controlled my emotions and just thrown some witty comment back at him, but I was far too literal even then as a senior in high school. And in that moment of insecurity, I was only capable of asking him a very honest question, even if it made me look pathetic. I knew that I could destroy this kid in any arena. Any arena, that is, except the pocketbook. And that's where he was choosing to retaliate for that fucking John Deere hat. I hated feeling helpless, but what he was doing to me at that moment was a lot like shooting the finger at a man without arms. I wanted cool, but I did not have access to any. There was never any cool in me during those moments. Grandaddy's cool could have helped me, but I could not muster it.

"Usually something follows an 'Um,' unless you're stuttering. Spit it out boy-o," said Jonathan, and right then my blood started to curdle like cream. I could feel my bottom lip start to tremble, my cheek twitch and my fingers twitch just a little bit, the same way they always did when all of my faculties were called on and rallied together at once to keep me from erupting. But, God, please don't cry. The last thing I wanted in that moment was to fight away tears like a fucking pussy, but I guess it's just my design.

"Can you stop talking for just a minute, please?" I said. "I just need to know if you're trying to hurt my feelings on purpose, or if you've done it on accident?" I took Kate's hand off my thigh and brought my shaking hand with a napkin in it up to my mouth, less to wipe chili off my face and more to have it close and ready to make a fist to slam into that glider's face depending on how he answered. But he said nothing. That's just what gliders do. "You know, if you were trying to hurt my feelings I'd rather you just say you wanna go outside and fight than beat around the bush. But if you're not, that's okay. Just apologize and we'll be done 'cause I'm getting the feeling that you're not actually being nice to me. But if I'm wrong, just tell me."

"You can't be serious. Good hell, look at you. You look like you're about to cry. If you don't want to go, just say so. But, in the meantime, when you fetch your car from valet, get mine, too, will ya? I'm gonna hit the closet." He spun his valet ticket onto the table and I watched him wind his way around the corner and straight into the men's room.

The closet? Yep, the fucking *closet*.

I heard Kate spout something about not really wanting to go to Marisk, and that we could just stay here, and blah, blah, blah. But I just stared at that restroom door until I finally looked down at my plate and cut off a bite of my last hot dog. Anything to not look up. I didn't want anyone to see my eyes, because they would tell more about me than I wanted anyone to know...anyone except Jane. I could feel Kate's sympathetic eyes on me, but I just wanted them to go away.

Finally, Jonathan's girlfriend drew Kate into a much more important conversation about utter nonsense. She was carrying on about reservations, and who was to be there, and then giggling, and then pointing out the window at someone cool that just arrived, and then more giggling. I wanted to vanish, but my pugilistic hatred rooted me to the spot. Also, Kate had me wedged into the inside of the booth against the wall.

I sneaked in an "Excuse me, could I slide out real quick? I'm just gonna run to the restroom—be right back" in between cheerleading gossip and Jonathan this and Jonathan that.

I saw his feet when I walked in, flung open the door to his stall, and found Jonathan sitting down peeing like a girl. He looked up at me as I waited for him to zip up and stand. My first punch grazed his eye, and the middle-finger knuckle on my right fist actually impacted the sharp Formica corner of one of the walls of his stall. It opened up, just like his face. I don't remember how many times I jackhammered Jonathan's jaw, nose, and eyes, but I certainly felt better, contrary to what my watering eyes were indicating. I left him and that stupid fedora in a puddle of pee just like I had found his hat years earlier, and stared into the mirror as I pressed a wet paper towel on my knuckle to stop the bleeding. He was a glider then, and he is probably still a glider today. I knew puppy love was bullshit, but he made me realize that so is puppy hatred. So, Jonathan...thank you.

His girlfriend did not even stop her mouth for a tiny beat when I arrived back at the table. I had not been gone long, but it could have been an hour and I do not think Mint Girl would have noticed a thing if it was outside of her immediate sphere. Kate started to get up to let me slide in, but I dragged my plate with half of a chili cheese dog on it to the outer side of the booth and quietly told her to just scoot in. I finished my food with my left hand, but I could tell that Kate knew something was wrong. Her eyes went from what's-her-name to me repeatedly, until, "Kate, are you listening?" would drag Kate's focus right back to that irrelevance.

Finally, I felt Kate's eyes go down to my lap and rest on the knuckle that I was trying to hide. It had to be the last cubic centimeter of air from her lungs that spit out that "Hoh," because it sounded like a mixture of desperation and revile. I didn't look up. I couldn't. I didn't want her knowledge of my actions to put me in the "bad stock" category. Still, I could feel that she never took her eyes off me as she pulled a paper napkin out of the dispenser and gently wrapped that torn knuckle while that Tourist continued to spew their glorious night's itinerary. I finished my plate, and I swear I tried to wait for a pause in that girl's diatribe, but it just wasn't there. So, I let "I think I'm prolly just gonna head home, Kate, but it was really good seeing you tonight" roll right over her friend's sustained prattle.

"Stay, please," Kate blurted out as I started to slide out of that booth. I told her that I really just wanted to go home, and I rose and finally turned to face her. Only then did her eyes tell me that I was right about the "desperation," but categorically wrong about the "revile." Kate's face that night was the first to show me that those violent primal instincts, publicly denounced but still hidden at the core of just about every boy I've ever known who was worth a shit, were actually privately adored. I turned and walked out as I heard Kate telling her friend, "Will you please just shut up . . . and go get your boyfriend outta the bathroom? He's an Asshole, and I want to go home!"

Yeah, fuck *good stock*.

From early on, my Grandaddy had taught me to have compassion for all, but to always be ready to *not* have any as soon as a situation required it. The situation with Jonathan required none. I am ashamed of nothing I did that night, except not holding that car door open for Jane. My Grandaddy never once told me how to live my life, he just lived his correctly...and he let me watch. And I remember the exact day that he showed me what both having and not having compassion was—the lesson that Jonathan probably wished I had never learned. It was at my favorite cafeteria in the world, which might not have meant much since I had only ever eaten at one. But in my Grandaddy's opinion, there was only one cafeteria worth going to, and we went just about every week. Next to my Grandaddy's porch, that cafeteria came in a close second place as far as wisdom delivery locations with him were concerned. It's why just a little part of me, despite their heavenly chocolate, resents Baskin-Robbins—because that is what replaced my Grandaddy's Piccadilly Cafeteria when it got knocked down.

I was eight. It was early summer, just before I discovered Jane, and my Grandaddy had given me a bloody pocketknife as a little gift resulting from an altercation he had had on the job. While we were sitting there, me examining the dried blood on the blade, Grandaddy looked up, sensing something in the air. Now, only once was I ever allowed to have two helpings of macaroni and cheese, and when I was, it was not the extra dish that stayed with me—it was my Grandaddy's message. It always was. On the odd Sunday every now and then, after church, the men and women went in different directions, so it was just Grandaddy and me. This was necessary, he said. He spoke differently. He painted different pictures. And he always closed with, "Now don't tell your Mamau." I never did. Nor did I tell my parents about the double helping of mac and cheese.

My Grandaddy was a creator. He told me at a very young age that most of the people who could not find what they wanted in this life just had not had the system explained to them properly. He was the deputy sheriff of Lake Charles, Louisiana, and then again in Galveston, Texas, back when that meant a lot more than handing out speeding tickets. He was a father to everyone not lucky enough to keep one around long enough. He was a real man, long before they were outlawed.

The Piccadilly Cafeteria was always a treat for me, and I loved sliding my tray in front of all that food. It smelled like everyone's best home-cooked meals I'd ever been to on a Sunday all rolled into one. The first station after silverware was always the assorted colors of Jell-O, and I loved the look of the "lucky" green. I would only get the green Jell-O if they were out of chocolate pudding, and that Sunday they were. I was always more intrigued with the motion than the flavor, but I had to be very economical in selecting my dishes. I could get any single dish from each food group on a "men's Sunday," but I had to eat every single crumb. I always found myself forcing down that last cube of green wonder. Grandaddy said green Jell-O was a fashion model. It always looked great just sitting there. "Whereas compared to your Mamau," he said, "... well, tha' unicorn th'very best woman in all the world, y'Mamau like the entire dessert section and the hot meals all throwed in a mixin' bowl."

We sat in the round corner table right by the window as we always did, and I think I grew more during those hours with Grandaddy than I did the entire rest of the week. My macaroni and cheese bowl was almost completely clean as I used my honey-butter dinner roll to mop up any evidence of it ever having been there when I heard the first scream. It was Miss Shelby, the cashier, hollering for help as a man sprinted toward the exit door with a handful of cash. I had seen the man eating not five tables down from us and apparently, after his meal, he had gone to the cashier to pay and just grabbed a handful of cash from Miss Shelby's open drawer and run.

Now, The Piccadilly Cafeteria was a bit of a maze to navigate, and probably a firetrap, too, by today's standards. The front door just brought you into a breezeway, which was like a little glass box of about fifteen feet wide and about eight feet deep that ended with two doors to the cafeteria. So, when you entered, there was a door to your left that took you into the cafeteria, and a handleless door to the right that was an "exit only" by the cashier. Well, this man had run from the cashier with a fistful of money all the way around to the door by the entrance that was handleless on the inside, and only opened inward. He was frantically banging on the door, as if it would open if he just ran at it harder.

"Open the goddamn door, nigga-bitch," the man screamed at Miss Shelby, who was black.

"Git yerself another macaroni, boy, I'll be right back," growled my Grandaddy long and low. Never taking his eyes off the thief, my Grandaddy walked calmly to the correct exit, slowly folding the napkin that had been in his lap, and handed it to Miss Shelby. "Miss Shelby, don't you listen that now. He a thief. And you's a lady. Hear?" She smiled gratefully at Grandaddy and let him take the keychain that was clipped to the belt on her pantsuit.

The man immediately saw my Grandaddy exiting into the breezeway and started sprinting around to the only exit that allowed freedom. The man came busting into the breezeway just as my Grandaddy pulled the key out from the dead bolt that locked the final door to the parking lot. I made my way to the entrance, where the thief initially tried to exit, and watched as my Grandaddy sat Clint Eastwood the fuck down, the way he dealt with this man. Now Grandaddy was in his fifties at the time, and this man was fit, and in his early twenties, and had just screamed at Miss Shelby to "Unlock these fuckin' doors NOW, nigger!"

"I'm the nigger y'gon' talk to right now, boy," said Grandaddy as he clipped the keys to his own belt. "Now y'gon' go back inside, and apologize to that beautiful woman in there, that's Miss Shelby. Then pick all the money you dropped while you was runnin' the Piccadilly, hand it nicely back to Miss Shelby, and then we gon' talk about how you can pay fer yer meal." I had my face smashed against the glass watching as Miss Tillman, one of the servers, tried to pull me back to the safety of the kitchen, but I would not budge. The man took a moment to think about it. I knew that he was about to do the right thing...just as he did the wrong thing. He leapt at my Grandaddy, and was met by a huge left hand that latched on to the front of his collar and held him at a safe arm's-length. The man tried in vain to release the hand as we both heard, "Well, what're you gonna do, son?" The man then seemed to relax for a brief moment, sizing up his options. He stared into my Grandaddy's eyes, and then exploded, throwing wild punches that were just out of reach. Grandaddy balled up his empty hand, held it by his right ear, and yanked the man's face toward him by his collar as he threw that giant right fist. They met in the middle with a violent crack. My Grandaddy repeated this three more times. Blood flung onto the window right above my face as he dragged him by his collar to the corner of the breezeway right in front of me and dropped him with all his stolen money in a heap.

Grandaddy turned and walked back into the cafeteria. I was back at our table before he was, and Miss Shelby and Miss Tillman were in a panic next to me. He sat down, asked Miss Shelby for his napkin back, and told her, "Tell that boy when he wakes up to come get the keys from me and he can go." He palmed his big glass of ice water over the rim and turned it upside down over my empty bowl of macaroni and cheese. After all the water drained out, he dumped the ice into his napkin, twisted the edges, and wrapped his knuckles saying, "Your Mamau sees the swellin' otherwise," and threw a spoon into his pinto beans. My last cube of green Jell-O swiveled as my Grandaddy finished his beans, and I watched Miss Shelby and Miss Tillman talking to that man through the glass. He finally stood up and entered through the door he initially tried to beat down, and walked up to our table. My Grandaddy unclipped Miss Shelby's keys from his belt, held them up without looking at the man and said, "The gold key in the middle open the front door. You can put that money back in the register and let yourself out, or you can sit here and talk to me." I jumped in my chair as the man grabbed the keys in a whiff and bolted to the front. He fumbled with the keys until he found the one that finally unlocked the door while sporadically looking back to make sure that my Grandaddy wasn't coming after him. He then ran out into the parking lot.

My Grandaddy just looked over his shoulder and said, "That just really hurts my feelin's. Boy's garbage. Garbage's what's wrong with the world."

"Charlie!" Miss Shelby yelled. "He's coming back in."

We both looked up to the front door and sure enough, the man was back in the breezeway looking right at us with two fists full of dollar bills. My Grandaddy pulled out his huge index finger and threw it looping over his head indicating for the man to come over to our table, and went right in for another spoon of beans. Miss Shelby beat the man to the table and offered to take me away, when my Grandaddy said, "Not necessary, boy's gonna stay, he needs to hear this. Boudin for my great-granbabbies." She just looked at him kind of shocked and slinked away. The man arrived coated in defeat and blood and opened his mouth to speak when he was met with, "Have a seat, son." The man slowly took a seat, and my Grandaddy removed his soaked napkin from his knuckles and handed it to the man and said, "Go on, clean yerself up." The man began wiping off his face with wells of tears in his eyes as Grandaddy asked, "You steal 'cause you ain't have money to eat, or you steal 'cause you's an ass?"

"Bit of both I s'pect. I'm sorry, sir. Woman in the lot says you's the law," the man said. I had just seen this man violently throw himself into a glass door to try to escape The Piccadilly with a handful of stolen money, curse out and attack my Grandaddy, but I truly felt horrible for him. He hurt. He hurt badly.

"I can fix the job, but you gotta promise me you gonna fix the ass," said Grandaddy. "You gonna clean up here at The Piccadilly, then you gonna clean up next door at the Piggly Wiggly till they tell ya you done every day for a month, then you'll be clean. I'll have Miss Shelby give ya' three hot meals a day here and I'll tell 'em to keep you least for the thirty days, but if you really wanna rid youself of the ass, then you make them wanna keep you."

"How do I do that, sir, when I just tried to steal off 'em?" he said.

"Miss Shelby!" Grandaddy called out, "Bring us a pen and paper placemat, will ya?"

Miss Shelby rushed back to the table as if summoned by royalty, laid a placemat and pen on the table, then drifted back to the front door as a patrol officer finally showed up. I saw the uniformed officer walk briskly in through the front doors with his hand on his holstered weapon, then he called for my Grandaddy.

"Fine, Macky, no need, go back ta business," my Grandaddy responded without even looking up. "Now, what's your name son?"

"Lenny Frank, sir," said the man.

"You write, son?"

"Yessir, a bit," he responded.

"Write this down. It's three things you gotta do every day. My own daddy gave me these. Three easy shit little things and I promise you they's gonna wanna keep you here at The Piccadilly Cafeteria. You ready?"

"Yes, sir," said Lenny, as he picked up the pen with his hands shaking like he was freezing to death.

"Number one, you gon' show up early." My Grandaddy took another scoop of beans as he waited for Lenny's pen to catch up. "Number two, stay late...and number three, volunteer for the hard shit. You do them three, and you already ahead of the whole field. You do those three every single day for that month, and they gon' ask you ta stay and they even gone pay you. Now, you wanna know how to stop cleanin' and move up in this company? One simple rule: For every dollar Mr. Jarman pay you here at his Piccadilly, you give him two dollar of value. You understand me? I come back here next month and you don't work here for pay and I'll know you's lazy garbage. You lazy garbage, boy?" asked my Grandaddy.

"No, sir, I'm not," answered Lenny.

"After I come back in three months, you still cleanin' and not moved up, I know you just lied to me . . . You a liar, boy?" he asked the man whose hand still shook like it was diseased.

"I'm not, sir," responded Lenny.

"Three simple things to tell a boss you'll do, and you get any job in the world . . . and one extra if'n you wanna be a boss," said Grandaddy leaning in toward Lenny, whose face was now down practically touching the placemat ready to write. "Shake my hand and get yourself home, you gonna be here shit early, son." The man's hand came up in front of my Grandaddy. "Ain't no shake you don't look a man the eye, son. You look him in the eye and you give him the truth're you don't shake at all. You give me the truth, boy?" my Grandaddy asked him. Lenny's head slowly came up from pretending to write on the placemat. Two full eyes of tears and he offered my Grandaddy his hand. My Grandaddy scribbled on the blank placemat, stood up, shook his hand, and said, "Now get outta here, lemme finish my beans with my boy . . . you tell your momma you had good talk with Charlie and that shit gon' change . . . but leave out the shit, you don't curse your momma, hear me?"

"Sir," he said, and the man held his gaze for a moment and slowly walked for the door.

"You get your second macaroni, son?" my Grandaddy asked me.

"No, sir, I forgot," I said.

"Finish that green plastic sugar cube'n we'll have Miss Shelby get you one ta go. Double macaroni don't come around enough." My Grandaddy turned and gazed out the window as Lenny walked across the Piggly Wiggly parking lot. "And don't you tell your Mamau what we done today."

"No, sir, I won't," I promised.

Lenny was working at The Piccadilly Cafeteria every single time I ate there until it got bought out by the ice cream chain. I wish I could control my emotions when it's time to not have any compassion, like my Grandaddy did. He was cold and calculated, and he still had access to his logic and reasoning. But instead, my fists had a sort of physical Tourette's when my emotions got the best of me. To this day, I don't think I've ever struck someone in hostility without a tear in my eye. Where my Grandaddy was the definition of cool in those moments, I just turned into a vicious infant. In this way, I thought my Grandaddy's rattlesnake analogy was a bit flawed, that the cool had somehow skipped my generation. Emotionally, my dad and my Grandaddy were both very different than me, or so I thought.

I know how lucky I am to have had strong men in my life like my dad and my Grandaddy. But I was far too emotional to be strong like my father, and cried too often to be as tough as my Grandaddy. They did have a bit of rattlesnake, I thought, and I always wanted a little bit for myself. I had never seen either of them cry the way that I so often couldn't help myself. But, there is always a moment in a child's life when he realizes that his father is as big as life itself, but not actually larger. We're all the size of life, and maybe my dad was just a more pronounced version. He didn't take up any more space than I did, but he did it in a much more profound way.

My dad shrank to a mortal size and I saw my lineage accurately defined the night we returned home from seeing snow for the very first time. It was soon after Lilyth's return from being "away" and after she cut my tassels, ending our truce, and right after the trip that was intended to be a family reunion for Mom, Dad, Lilyth, and me. No mention was made of Lilyth's baby Charlotte or the nuns. The endless drive back from the wonder of snow in Taos, New Mexico, put us in late to find my buddy Kim from next door slumped over my handprints in the cement step, crying. Kim had been feeding Steve McQueen for us and letting him out to do his business, and didn't know what was wrong with him all of a sudden. My dog's stomach looked like it had been inflated with a bicycle pump. Wheezing, Steve McQueen waddled stoically into the kitchen and his knees just kind of buckled at my feet. I knew something was really wrong. No Grunt came as I did not even try to stop the tears that showed up, seeing the look of apology in my dog's eyes, like he was ashamed that he hadn't run to the door and jumped on me like always. My legs buckled, too, and we met on the floor.

My dad immediately slung Steve McQueen in his arms, told the girls to stay by the phone, and told me to get in the back of the car and hold Steve steady and calm so he could race us to the vet. My mom kept saying, "It'll be fine," and patting Steve's head, *nice dog*, every time Steve released a brittle whine. She closed the door with tears in her eyes, her palm remained pressed flat on the glass until the car pulled away from her. As my dad and I drove, my dad kept assuring me we'd be at the vet soon, his voice steady as usual. My best friend never took his eyes off me as my dad drove and told me to be strong for Steve McQueen.

"We'll get him the help he needs, son. But you hold him tight, boy, and let him know that we're right here and ain't going nowhere."

I wanted my dad's strength. I wanted my dad's control. My dad spoke to me the whole way to the vet's office, just like we were at the dinner table discussing dodging open field tackles. Steve McQueen had spent every single moment of his life with either me or my dad. I wanted my dog to know I was there for him just like I knew my dad was there for me. I wanted to be strong for Steve, but I was completely overwhelmed by the possibility of losing my best friend in the world. And that level of grief punctured my chest like a pointed helmet charging at me for an open field tackle. Where was my rattlesnake when I needed it? I needed to be cool for Steve, like my dad was. In his moment of pain, Steve did not need to worry about me, and see my chest heaving so severely that I could hardly get an "okay" out at each of my dad's instructions. I was truly a child, but my dad was a man.

"Almost there son, tell him we're almost there."

And that was the first time I looked up from Steve. I left his eyes and caught my dad's in the rearview mirror as he drove. He was still talking to me with the strength of a real man, but I saw that his eyes felt the same thing I felt. I saw his cheek twitching, the same way mine did as tears fell from his red eyes. And I could see him collect his heaving breaths before stoically throwing a sentence of strength back in my direction. I saw my dad that night, and he was no different than me. I saw his hand occasionally come up and wipe away the flood of tears, but his voice never once acknowledged their presence. My Grandaddy was right about us all being the same. But he was wrong about there being no rattlesnake. There wasn't no rattlesnake in either of them, there was maybe a couple scales and a fang in each. They cried, too, and they were the realest men I've ever known. I wasn't a rattlesnake, because my mom and dad were not rattlesnakes. That was the first time I'd ever seen my dad cry, and it shook my core. He was not sure my dog would live, and it tore him to pieces that matched my pieces. He was my pillar of strength. We made it to the vet but Steve was already gone. As a courtesy, the vet pronounced him dead and ceremoniously removed Steve McQueen's collar and prepared his body for burial, but I did not want to let go of him. My whole body could not stop crying and I remember clenching his collar to my face and inhaling my friend for the last time. My dad told me that all the years of loving him would speak far more eloquently than anything I could try and tell him now.

"He knows, son."

And I let go of my best friend. It was well after midnight when we finally drove home with Steve McQueen's empty body wrapped up in the backseat.

And I remember there was a tall building just off the freeway whose top floors were completely engulfed in flames. My dad pulled off the freeway about a block from that blazing building as fire trucks screamed by. There was a police car sitting sideways in the middle of the street right in front of a House of Pies deflecting what little traffic there was at that hour. My dad pulled into the lot, told me to stay in the car, and walked over to talk to the cop. I wondered if any people had died in that building on the same night that Steve did. And I wondered what my dad was saying to that cop. When he came back, he reparked the car, backing it into a space in that empty parking lot facing that flaming building, and just said, "It ain't time ta go home yet, you hungry?" I waited in the car until he came out of that House of Pies holding a large box. I climbed out and onto the hood as my dad reclined on the windshield right next to me.

He opened that box to reveal a large orange pie and said, "No chocolate, pumpkin's all they had left." That night, we sat on the hood of his car and ate an entire pumpkin pie as we had one of the longest conversations I've ever had in my life with the fewest words. Around three in the morning, long after House of Pies had closed and the firefighters had rolled up hoses to go home to their families, I was slowly drifting off to sleep from the emotional exhaustion of Steve's departing. I heard my dad say, "It goes by so quick, son . . . please tell me you'll take care of it." I took a minute to think about what he meant, although I knew I already got it. And as we pulled out of that parking lot, that same officer whose cruiser had been sideways in the street waved our car over and stuck his head next to my dad's open window.

"You know, I spent the last three hours over here just watching you and your boy, and I seen his tears. I think you already know you got a good one there, sir. But sometimes the young'ns don't know till too late who their daddy is. All night long, only one car stop'n ask if they's somethin' they can do. That your daddy, son." And then he offered his hand out to my dad, who shook it in kind. "Pleasure to meet another who don't just keep driving by in a time of need. Y'all have a good night and God bless."

"God bless." And we drove. He knew exactly who my daddy was . . . and so did I.

"I will, Dad."

My dad and I watched the sun come up in the front yard, because it had taken us another couple hours to bury Steve. We put him right at the foot of the bean tree where he had always waited for me to come down. There was a Steve-sized circle of dead grass where he had been lying beneath me in that tree for years and that is where he lies still. Before I finally fell asleep that morning, I vomited up every ounce of pumpkin pie that I consumed.

When I woke up later in the day, I found that Lilyth had already found a way to punctuate my grief in her own uniquely sociopathic way. Every bit of Steve McQueen was in the trash: his bowl, his chew bone, his blanket from my bed, his brush.

"What, y'retard, don't look at me that way, y'ingrate, I was being helpful. Mom!"

"Oh, darlin'!" Mom came in from the garage followed by Dad. Lilyth burst into tears crying loudly, so Mom hugged her instead of me. "Aw, Sug, it's *fine*, Lilyth didn't mean it bad." Dad looked bewildered and fatigued. I headed for my room.

"Paul, fish the dog's things out the trash, darlin', will y'?"

"Mickey blames me for everything! I didn't kill his dog!" Lilyth wailed, tearing away dramatically to rush off to her room in hysterics as if she had been misunderstood. As she stomped past my room I saw her through the crack in the door. The hair on the back of my neck stands up even today as I recall the look of hatred in her eyes as she winked at me, dry eyed, and whispered with a smirk, "Your dog stunk up the house. I'm glad it's dead."

I was powerless, immobilized by fury. She had been gone for months and home had felt safe and easy. Now I was right back to where I had been all my life, on guard, waiting for Lilyth's proverbial shoe to drop.

Steve McQueen had been my companion and guardian since I was a toddler. It had been this gargantuan Weimaraner who buffered the mail truck's blow when I chased my toy fire truck that Lilyth had deliberately rolled into traffic for me to chase. Though I did end up in the emergency room that day, it was Steve McQueen who had taken the majority of the blow by putting himself between me and the oncoming vehicle. When Mom had left Lilyth alone with me in the hospital room that day to "keep me company" while she was out in the hall with the doctor, Lilyth had leaned in real close with that look in her eye, hissing the four most terrifying words a toddler could try and wrap his little brain around: "You stole my mother." Lilyth, then age six, punctuated with, "Steve McQueen's gon' die, y'know, y'lil retard, all 'cause'a you." Steve lived to protect me and never left my side. It was Steve who first revealed Lilyth for what she was. He knew. I don't have a single memory from my childhood that Steve McQueen is not in. And it was Steve McQueen who helped me see other truths, like my true lineage displayed that night in that rearview mirror.

Each time Lilyth elected to rend the fabric of my childhood with her fine-tuned sociopathy, I took a step back before going forward without her. I retreated further from my sister, learning to deploy strategic forethought before I would tell her anything at all, and I became more covert in my actions whenever she was watching me. Lilyth was the opposite of Jane, but truly a motivator to me. I credit Lilyth with my keen ability to spot a con-artist or a freeloader. Thanks to Lilyth I never did rely on a bully's charity to not get my lunch money stolen, but I had also learned to behave as though absolutely anyone could potentially kick the shit out of me. Except that day at hole seventeen. That fight with Andy I wanted to neither finish nor start. That fight I have always been ashamed to tell you about. But here, you know, I had to tell you. And I've adjusted. I hope I've made my Grandaddy proud that he taught me right. Grandaddy's *Right*, that is, according to The Law. And that he'd recognized ten corrections. Still, I could not hit my sister, though at times I wanted to hit her more than anyone else.

Lilyth was my point of departure for understanding women, and because of that, maybe I was gun-shy and misunderstood the signals from other girls in high school, including Jane. Where Lilyth was lawless, Jane was flawless. Flawless, but a misunderstanding left unchallenged, nonetheless. Misunderstandings left unchallenged have wrought isolation between me and the people I care for on more than one occasion. And I hated that. When I was sixteen and my pal Eduardo was seventeen, he had me meet him at the Utotem to show me something "really cool" before heading off to college. He had been on every one of my sports teams. And although we were not best friends, we had each other's back. I liked and respected him. He pulled up in a badass primered '68 Chevy Nova SS and got out beaming, as I circled the car in awe. Man, I knew more about that car than he did. I saw that it had the highly revered 396-cubic-inch engine rated at 375 horsepower under the hood attached to the rare M-21 close ratio four-speed manual. We spoke about our dream cars just about every day in school, and this one was a fast and very rare bird for some small-town Texas boys. He told me that his dad had bought him two Pioneer #6905

6X9s for the back, a couple smaller Pioneer five-inch door speakers and a "blue light" Alpine in-dash stereo with a cassette player, and he wondered if I would help him install it in my driveway.

"Hell, yeah!" I said. I knew that the angle of the rear window in that Nova would produce some killer acoustics. I circled the car, taking in every inch, and he finally said with a smile, "So what do you think?" I just looked at him and shook my smiling face back and forth knowing that he already knew the answer to that. I could see him crushing that four-hour freeway drive all the way to his college in Kingsville with that Alpine deck throwing out Zeppelin all over the I-59 South. I finally stopped gawking and pulled away from that gem, looked up at him.

"How much?" I asked.

Eduardo took a moment before his face just went blank.

And he climbed into that beautiful Nova and slowly drove away from the Utotem—and me. I never heard from him again until I saw him at Firefly's bachelor party years later. I asked him why he had left that day, and why he had never spoken to me since. He said, "Shit, Mickey, you just really hurt my feelings, man. I asked you what you thought about it, and goddamn, man, no one knew cars like you did, and you took a long time to answer, and when you did, you just said... 'It's not much.'"

"Holy shit, Eduardo. You're wrong. I've run that scene in my head a thousand times wondering what happened that day, and I can even tell you how I'd planned to mount those 6905s on your back deck to project directly to the driver's seat, or how that cam made that 396 lope. No, goddammit. I asked 'How much?'" And I did. I really did. I figured his silence was just compassion for my Toaster next to his SS. Some lessons come early, and some come late. More compassion. Fewer misunderstandings left unchallenged.

———

Friday mornings in high school, I'd see Baxter, for whom I had absolutely none—compassion, that is—until after the Chevy Nova conversation with Eduardo. Baxter sightings were rare and mostly on the school bus, which I only took on Fridays when we didn't have swim practice. I'd get on and Baxter would acknowledge my presence but I'd overlook him, Jane and disdain flooding my mind as I'd aim for the back row. Over time, Baxter had grown even fatter until he pretty much took up an entire seat, his butt hanging over the edge into the aisle. And every Friday, on fish stick day, Baxter reeked of what he ate that day, so I'd hold my breath until I got past him to my seat in the back row. The very last time I rode the bus before Firefly and I finished building our VW was also one of the days that I wore my favorite Britannia shirt, and I recall it because it was also the time that Baxter vomited in the aisle of the school bus. To this day, everyone who was on that bus ride refers to it as The Poseidon Adventure.

It was a smell I'll never forget, and kids all hung their head out the windows, gasping. Much as Baxter himself always made me feel like throwing up, I did not want to humiliate him by covering my face with my shirt, so I just sat there focusing on the feel of its soft terry cloth slit-neck collar, and looking down at the mix of green and brown horizontal panels on the torso with white sleeves and white band at the waist. As Baxter's puke sloshed back and forth each time the bus slowed down or sped up, eventually Baxter's river of fishy spew reached the 95s that I had bought with my own money, and a perplexing feeling of almost-compassion for Baxter arose in my heart. And that surprised me. Hell, I even considered offering Baxter my second Reese's but decided that would be a waste.

The next time I saw Baxter, it was just his fat head above a crowd outside the country club waiting to go in for some event. I scouted for Jane as I headed to swim practice after mowing their neighbor's lawn by hole eighteen, but none of Jane's family members were around. My Fonzi T-shirt that mom had appliquéd was soaked in sweat and clung to me. I had four days' worth of clothes and I looked well cared for, though maybe a little disheveled at times. But Baxter, fat as he was, always looked like his mother had spit-polished him into the latest brand-name attire. He was a walking catalogue in XXL.

Baxter's mother waved and came at me, scoped me up and down, put her hyper-red manicured meat hooks on my shoulder, and slithered down to my bicep where her touch lingered an uncomfortable moment too long.

"You!" she said, gushing like I was her very own Baxter. "I just have to thank ya for inspiring my Baxter to be a fashion maven." She released my arm only to pull Baxter out of the cluster of club members to place his lump in front of me. There it was, the twin of my Britannia shirt I so loved, stretched beyond recognition across Baxter's girth. He looked ashamed. I felt sorry for him. "You musta paid a fortune for yours, boy. I had the darndest time findin' Baxter one just like yours...boy." Mrs. Parsifal never bothered to remember my name, and I never wore my Britannia again. Sadly, the fact was, Baxter had no inspiration, none, everything was handed to him, and he had no desire to try, trapped as he had chosen to remain in his fat suit. "Why don't y'all come *dahn* with us at the country club. Special event! C'mon, er...what was your name again, boy?"

I just stared at her. I wanted to ask why she chose to overfeed her son and why Baxter chose to eat fat sticks in front of the TV. He might have told me to fuck off or he might have said he was perfectly happy leading a sedentary life, despite his wheezing and lack of mobility. Maybe if we had all known then what we know now—maybe then, Baxter would have bothered. But back then, we didn't know. I just knew Baxter was a lazy, cheating turd.

"Y'know I was a teen bride when I had Baxter. That makes me old enough to be your big sister." I had no idea where Mrs. Parsifal was going. "So you let me know, boy, anytime ya wanna dahn at the country club. Baxter's so bored there. He'd rather sit home on my bisque suede Henredon eatin' Velveeta outta them new squirt cans writin' his college application essays than anything else. So diligent, ain't ya, baby boy. You look like you're goldurn diligent, too, boy." The harpy squeezed my bicep again and let her hand slide down to my waist. I took a step back, and then another. I knew if only Baxter would join swim team, Coach Randall would whip that tub of shit into shape. Coach would make Baxter learn The Oath. But hell, I didn't really feel it was my place to be preaching the gospel while Mrs. Parsifal was cougaring me outta my Sears layaway jeans, up and down with her false eyelashes lined in bright blue.

"And it gets so frightfully lonely sometimes dahnin' all

alone at the club. Y'know, with Baxter's daddy an airline pilot and all. He's gone fer days on end, especially when he flies t'places like Japan. You know they got geishas there in Japan..." I despised this family. So, with all the politeness I could muster, I excused myself. "Unless you'd rather dahn at our home, boy. Right over there by Jane's house at hole eighteen. Hole in one, boy!" Mrs. Parsifal winked a cluster of mascara talons at me. There was no misunderstanding here, and I certainly did not let it go unchallenged.

"Y'know what, ma'am, I don't think I belong here, in your company." I was sickened to hear Jane's name come out of that harridan's mouth.

"Well, course y'do, darlin'." I felt sorry for Baxter, with a mother "like my big sister." Like Baxter's malodorous bus vomit, her acrid words clung as I jogged away toward the wrought iron fence to climb through it to the pool.

"No. I don't," I hollered over my shoulder.

"Perhaps, y'could mow my lawn, boy? Pay you double overtime." That unrelenting pig of a woman was Baxter's fish puke incarnate. I ignored Mrs. Parsifal and waved to Coach Randall in his Speedo talking to the Titly-est waitress at the Snack Shack. The second I was a few strides away from Baxter's mother, she motioned flirtatiously to Coach Randall.

"Other side of the fence!" I heard someone yell, as I arrived at the barrier.

It was not till I noticed the fat Santa manager of the Green Beans Yard Crew eyeballing me from his red Rolls-Royce golf cart that I felt an odd kind of relief. He was always there, turning up at my swim team meets, and other moments in my life. Maybe I was paranoid? But he was always tracking me with his laser gaze. His lock'n'load look was like an intervention as if I were a drug user. Like I didn't belong near that crowd going into the country club, and I didn't belong near those fancy houses, even if I was there mowing lawns. I didn't belong. But that was *fine*. I was done there. I was going someplace *nice*.

"Seedlin', out on the porch!" So out I went. "What could be *nicer*'n here, Seed?" My Grandaddy was sitting in his lawn chair on our porch and looking out over the horizon right next to James when I got home that night after swim practice. "I know you wanna start thinkin' 'bout college and ya own life, but just know that most folks born the way you was is gonna look out from they porch at all the land and silence and say, man, one'a these days I'm gon' get outta here and move to the city and make a fortune. But make no mistake, dees same people, when they older, gon' be lookin' down from they big office with all they money and say, man, one day I'm gon' buy me a little place away from it all with a porch, just looking out over God's green land…and I'm just gon' sit there and enjoy the silence. So, you know what, son? I'll meet you right back here."

"Yer Grandaddy know, boy. Listen up," said James, without ever taking his eyes off of my Grandaddy's horizon. My Grandaddy was the first to make me see, even before going out on my own into the world to see it for myself, that most people spend their twenties, thirties and forties trying to make money. And once in their fifties and sixties, these same people inevitably end up spending the majority of their acquired earnings trying to prolong that same life that they exchanged for that money in the first place. My Grandaddy might have never heard the term "rat race," but *damn*, did he sure know what it was. And yet, it was Grandaddy and Mamau who drove me to scout college campuses because Dad was working so much and Mom was dealing with Lilyth, who had gotten weirder and meaner since she came back from the nuns. Driving to see college campuses, Mamau would jabber and Grandaddy kept saying, "Goldie, woman, you're dingy, quit flappin' y'jaws and waggin' y'tongue." But she just kept on in the backseat, smiling at me driving and waving at me in the rearview mirror and holding Grandaddy's hand sitting right beside her. I loved driving Grandaddy's car. Every three to four years Grandaddy would get a new Cadillac to drive to church, though he and Mamau lived in a shack. The foot pedal to change the radio station was on the floor, right by the dimmer switch, but Mamau didn't know. So when I was driving them, I'd change the station and pull Mamau's leg. "I have these special powers," I'd say as I pointed to the radio while pressing that button with my foot on the floorboard...and the station would change. "Oh my God, Mickey, tell your Mamau, how you done magic, electron-ifyin' this vehicle's radio," my Mamau would exclaim. And Grandaddy would bellow, "Goddammit woman, it's the car's own *elec*ronification system. Seedlin' ain't got no powers, 'cept his own God-given self. Now, hush it and let him pull over an' get out. Leave the air on, boy, for y'Mamau so she don't dampen." And with that, I pulled over to the curb and met my Grandaddy's outstretched fist in the blistering heat on the sidewalk where he dropped a small matchbox in my palm.

"Listen, Seedlin'. You see how y'Mamau think you 'lectric and I know you ain't? I know you always understand me.

Hell, even on the football field that day that devil-pussy crack you in tha head with his helmet back when you was a tiny. I also know y'momma hollered at you about the same thing you know I was proud of. Well, they's some truth in the both of us. I give you this 'cause I want you to put it in my great-great-granbabbies. This is the stuff I want the future to see, so make sure the future hear it. Your wife gonna disagree, and sometime you gonna disagree with her on what a child need to hear to be raised up right, but it's important that your baby hear both sides. You got a wife who agree with you all the time, then you choose the wrong one. Choose correct, goddammit. Let the mirror tell ya. Look at ya mouth. Where them corners pointin'? You pick tha one that give you a smile you tryin' ta hide, 'cause the love smile the only one that tryin' its best not to. All the other smiles don't give a shit, 'cause they ain't scary. I seen it on you before and you best go get it. Don't lead with the trouser worm, least not for a wife. You pick a good momma for my great-granbabbies, and then you fill in all the holes of the stuff she leave out. Can only come from a man. Ain't no other way. These lessons got a long way to travel, and it's important that they path don't get interrupted by somebody that don't give a goddamn. So, you give a goddamn, and you keep giving a goddamn. I knew someone once who didn't, and I ain't cared for him much. My daddy gave me these and I want the future to see 'em, so I gotta hand 'em off to you. Seeds in that little box I wanna keep alive. Daddy was the best man I know. He was James's daddy, but mine, too. It's complicated, but someday I'll 'splain to ya, that Almond Tree. And your daddy's the best, too, I saw to it. You gonna be next, so pay attention. Sometime ya baby need ta hear that he 'lectric . . . and sometime he need ta know he ain't. I love you. You got a tree an' a nice bowl of gumbo with big chunks'a Boudin, so don't take a crap in it."

And with that nice bowl of gumbo, I prepared to go off to college—a period of intense work punctuated by fewer and fewer Jane sightings, and more than a few returned letters from The Dancing Mailbox. So I set off into a new world with the hope that if I went someplace nicer it would be fine for Jane to join me. The last time I saw Jane before I went off to college was senior year at prom—well, actually, I saw her as she was on her way into the country club where her school's prom was being held. I was plugged into my Walkman's earphones, listening to "Only You" by Yaz and skimming the pool for Coach Randall, but all I could hear in my head was a frustrating cacophony of "I'm Not in Love" by 10cc blaring from the country club, mixed with the static AM radio rendition of "Love Hurts" by Nazareth pouring out of what looked like Jonathan's BMW as he quickly rolled up the tinted window and sharked past. I loved each one of those songs, but they each required their own solar system, and not being able to separate them frustrated the hell out of me.

Jane's long brown-black hair hung straight down around her bare shoulders, and she wore a flowy purple and gem green paisley-print hippie dress and a new pair of 95s. There she stood, radiating at me, my flower with a tinsel heart. But she was with a Brooks Brothers tuxedo who sounded like he had come down from the North, maybe New England. Christ, besides Mr. Pink Pants, I had only ever heard people talk like that on fuckin' *Masterpiece Theatre*. I stared at Jane and Jane stared at me. She took a step back, then forward, but stopped after the first step when that guy—probably the honking, non-door-opening 911 douche—handed her a cup of punch. I really hated Jane's preppy little escort. But I hadn't a hope in hell of competing with his social economics. He had a 911 and punch, and I had a dirty pool skimmer in my hands. As the line of gussied-up teenagers gradually filed into the club, Jane glanced back at me a couple times, smiling like always and forever at me, then turned that generous smile and tinkling tinsel-bell laughter to her date. He obviously knew how to make Jane laugh. The entitled asshole turned to see what Jane was smiling at. He looked right at me. Then he turned to Jane with a nod, and I couldn't tell if he said something to her or not, but she nodded back. Again, the son of a bitch turned toward me, this time looking squarely at me, and he fucking smiled. He didn't smile wickedly like Jonathan would have. The fucker smiled broadly at me, like there wasn't a question in the world that I was not a threat to him, because there wasn't a question in the world as to what side of the fence I belonged. I felt like I was a fire hydrant and he had just lifted his leg. He had simply planted his flag on the moon and I'd always just be a cosmonaut. As they filed in, I forced my attention to skimming the pool. Jane smiled back at me over her shoulder as she was propelled inside the country club by the tide of teenagers in line behind her. "I'm Not in Love" blasted louder from the country club with its open doors, but I could turn up "Only You" on my Walkman even louder, and drown that shit right out. Because, it wasn't just a silly phase I was going through.

Chapter Nine

After college, I came home for a short time to regroup and pack my dad's old green Gran Torino he was letting me use for my trip out west. Mandy, my Irish setter, leapt to follow on my bike over to Quail Valley and down the golf course path where I needed to stop by Jane's one last time before I left town again for good. I'd heard she had moved to another part of Houston, down near the arts district, but I hoped if I went in person she might be visiting her parents, or at least they might tell me where she had gone. As I wheeled past the ninth hole Halfway Food Hut, I noticed the red Rolls-Royce, but that fat man was nowhere to be seen. In a strange way, I missed that man. I inhaled the newly freed chlorophyll. The place I recalled so vividly with gemstone colors was washed out to pastel. My childhood color palette had been through a hyper-realistic lens of a Fuji Velvia, but now it had faded to old-school Kodachrome. Vibrant memories. But it was like a red filter had turned all my blues to black.

When I reached hole eighteen, I rode all the way around

to the front of the butter yellow house, but it was quiet. I propped that old Schwinn Sting-Ray against Jane's forest green mailbox curbside, and I never once looked back to see if it looked impressive. I knew it looked impressive. I still loved that bike. And even having already been out of college, I hadn't a concern in the world about riding that old Sting-Ray over to Jane's. I no longer cared about all the things that had nothing to do with who I was. That day was only the second time I had ever rung her doorbell, but this time no one answered. The trampoline was completely rusted. My WD-40 from the card shark's suitcase in The Ditch was still tucked in between Jane's springs, with my initials I'd scratched into its painted surface still there. I tried to give the springs a squirt but the can was beyond use. I biked home and passed her old house on Sandpiper Drive, with a herd of kids in the yard, and on past the Milans', overgrown and in need of care, and absent of one aluminum lawn chair. I ran into my dad's garage and fired up the push mower one last time before I left town for California.

I never did learn what became of Mr. Milan after his wife died, but I never saw him again. I swept up the husks under my giant bean tree so Mom wouldn't have to do it, busy as she was raising Lilyth's little one. I was finishing packing the Gran Torino for LA when my sister stumbled by.

"I shoulda killed you when I had the chance," slurred Lilyth before she passed out in just about the same spot where Lew Hoagie had lost it the night of the yard sale.

I kept right on packing till little Charlotte came out of the house followed by my mom, looking worried and trying to keep Lilyth's daughter from seeing her own mother that way. I saw the look of desperation on my mom's face, and I hoisted

Lilyth off the lawn and slumped her in her bed. That night, I counted 143 unopened letters stamped RETURN TO SENDER sent to the wrong address and postmarked as early as 1973. I had kept sending letters to the same wrong address, as it had become a sort of therapy for me. The next day I left Houston, car packed to the gills, and drove by the art supply store where I had heard, quite by accident, that Jane worked. And sure enough, I saw her through the art shop plateglass window, way in the back where she was smiling, gorgeous, heart-stopping, helping a customer. I mailed a good-bye letter to her in the freshly painted mailbox right in front of the art store. This box had a dent right in its gut, and a jagged ring of rust bled through the new federal blue paint job. I wondered if that dent, like the leg of The Dancing Mailbox, had been Kevin's handiwork.

And you know I couldn't bring myself to go inside that art supply store. Hell, what would I say? *I'm leaving. Come to LA?* Too much time had passed. I had let too much time lapse between us. Maybe the fat groundskeeper was right. Maybe I didn't belong in her world. We had shared a ditch between two fences is all, and she was from somewhere else. With Mandy riding up front with me, lolling her tongue out the window, I drove away; still, I was hoping Jane might see me, come out of the art store, and tell me exactly what she wanted in life. As I kept on driving and got on the interstate for LA, "Wild World" ignited that Torino's old speakers, and I wondered if Jane preferred Cat Stevens's or Harry Chapin's version. I wondered, too, how long my letter would sit in the mailbox in front of Jane's art store. And if she had seen me out there. Or if she even cared. Or if she'd somehow get the letter and come find me.

Jane,

I'm going to Los Angeles and I still love you. Madly. I'll look for you out there. Everywhere actually. In everything. You really defy logic. It would be almost stupid to tell you at this point, but I've been in love with you from before it was supposed to be possible. Nothing's changed. I've outgrown nothing. The books are all wrong about love. Written by idiots. I never cared about their nonsense. Only yours. I knew I loved it all. You made sense. We agreed. With you, everything was right. You made me realize that this thing that the adult mind calls "puppy love" is just a taste of what we'll be chasing for the rest of our lives, but unfortunately we'll then be armed with a newfound adult logic and thus fatally ill-equipped to ever find it again. Because finding it requires a certain abandon from the same things that we must devour to become just that: grown-ups. It's the "adult" things that preclude us from ever seeing what we've waited for adulthood to see. It was only ever limited to a taste because youth discourages the natural inclination to gulp. And with you I only ever wanted to gulp.

My memory of Jane remained my driving force. I still hoped maybe, someday, we would run into each other somewhere. I got a good job in LA and I loved it, but I never really fell in love with another person. I always hoped Jane would track me down somehow, but she never did. I just couldn't cut Jane's siren anchor loose. Work kept me busy, but I felt there were few people I could truly connect with. I had grown up in a time and place where people greeted you with "good morning," courtesy was built in, bred in, compared to the Hollywood Hills, where even after a decade I had met only two neighbors on my street, one of which was the house-keeper to the first. I knew it was the transient nature of city life and industry, but I still wished for a place and a home like I'd known.

Grandaddy came to visit me one time in LA, Mamau at his side. Mandy and I picked them up from LAX in my dad's vintage '77 BMW 530i, Dad's trophy when his small business finally took off. I had restored the Bimmer's origi-nal silver paint, red leather interior, and even the meditating groan of that 3.0 liter in-line 6 that sounded like no other car on the road. Yelling over the throaty engine as we worked our way down La Cienega toward the famous Sun-set Strip, I pointed out sights until we were forced to stop at a blockade at Santa Monica Boulevard. I had completely forgotten that it was parade weekend. As all the rainbows and dress—and lack of dress—passed in front of the car, I could see my Grandaddy's face in the rearview mirror tak-ing it all in. My Grandaddy just chuckled and shook his head as my Mamau got more and more excited by all the festivity that she clearly misunderstood. We all watched as a group of about five men in white boots, white Speedos, chef hats, and nothing else slowly approached holding giant silver platters of food that random paraders would occasion-ally approach and grab a snack.

"LGBT," remarked Mamau, noticing a few paraders' T-shirts. "Is that a type of sandwich they's advertisin'?"

I explained to her what LGBT stood for, and Mamau gasped and clung to her large bosoms. My Grandaddy just watched as it all passed before him.

"Hell, every man like his own sandwich how he like it. And I reckon they can throw they trouser worm wherever they wanna, long as whoever where they's throwin' want ta get throwed at. Don't know if it require a goddamn parade, though. BLT, that's my favorite. Just plain old BLT," said Grandaddy wryly, and he gave Mamau's hand a squeeze. I could see he was thinking, but there was no familiar horizon for his gaze to rest on here. "All them official ti-tles . . . and they offended if ya call 'em somethin' different. Hell, I don't wanna hurt no feelin's. I'd call 'em nickel if they want, but then we gotta come up with somethin' new for five cent. Ain't nobody can live they life proper these days without worryin' 'bout who they gon' piss off. I tell ya, ya cain't take a shit these days without people worryin' 'bout hurtin' the goddamn feelin's of folks born without assholes, and when they feelin's get hurt y'cain't even tell 'em to go fuck theyselves 'cause then you's offendin' the goddamn self-sexuals!"

My Grandaddy never could come to understand what all the fuss was about what with the new distinctions publicly explaining sexual orientation. Just then the platter group in white passed right in front of my Mamau's window, and I saw my Grandaddy's face lose all hope for the future when he could clearly see that the platter that each of those chefs carried down by their groin displayed numerous sausages, the closest to them being their own. They had cut out holes in their Speedos and laid their own genitalia next to an assortment of wurst for all to see. Grandaddy quickly took my Mamau's face in his hands and turned it toward his and away from the parade.

A year later, when I arrived at my Grandaddy's wake in the Louisiana bayou where he had grown up, I was not surprised to see over a thousand people lined up to pay their respects. There I saw a rough-hewn wooden cross in the backyard out by the bayou that had been split in half by a pink-blossomed tree coming out of the ground beneath. Two men's names were carved in it, but one was too scratched out to be legible, the other was James's father. At Grandaddy's wake, I saw a middle-aged black man crying his eyes out off to the side of my Grandaddy up in the front. After the service, as the sun was setting, the man approached me and asked me to take a ride with him. I recognized him from somewhere and he seemed to know everything about me, and my Mamau seemed to know his whole family, wife, kids, granbabbies and all. So I climbed into his brand-new Lincoln Town Car, and he drove me away. That man's eyes wept the entire time we drove, until we arrived at a huge Ford dealership. He took another tissue out of a little plastic pouch, wiped his eyes one final time, and said, "C'mere, gotta show ya somethin'." He got out and walked me up to the front door of that display room with a fleet of new Ford and Lincoln and Mercury cars, took a key out of his pocket, inserted it, and spun the lock what seemed like five full rotations until the giant glass door was free and he swung it open, motioning me in.

"Yer Grandaddy gimme somethin' long time ago. Kept it in my pocket for years. He gone, and can't see...so I wanna show it to you. Ain't gonna live in my pocket no more."

A huge white wall served as a backdrop for all the display cars in that front room. And when he switched on the lights they seemed to flicker on, one by one, all the way down the line until the very last one at the end of that wall. But when that wall lit up, I knew exactly who that man was.

"You was there when he give me this, but don't know if you remember."

But I remembered everything from that day. On that giant wall behind those brand-new cars was painted:

At Frank Ford, we show up early.
  At Frank Ford, we stay late.
  And at Frank Ford, we always volunteer for all the hard stuff that no other dealer is willing to provide.

And sure enough, there was the climber, as my Grandaddy had called it:

For every dollar you pay Frank Ford, we'll give you 2 dollars of value.
                                                                    —The Law

"You must be Mr. Frank, sir. Lenny, I believe. I met you a long time ago at The Piccadilly Cafeteria."

And with that he broke, and hugged me with enough tears for the both of us. It was Lenny who had sent all the Ford LTDs for Grandaddy's cortege at no expense to the family. I thanked him—for everything. And I thanked him for having kept my Grandaddy alive in his dealership showroom. My Grandaddy was one of the best people I ever knew, and I miss him every single day. And that advice worked wonders for me. But I had no answer for Jane. The rules of love seemed to be different from anything I understood.

There's no glamour in grief. While I never forgot Jane in LA, I found myself embedded in an industry in which a large majority of my coworkers credited misspent youth, absentee parents, drug abuse, child abuse, sexual abuse, and various other types of childhood turmoil to explain the brilliant origins of their craft. Some even wore these experiences like badges of honor, as if tragedy were necessary for the creation of any type of art. Grief is a hurdle to be leapt over, not bragged about.

I had absolutely every opportunity provided to me by a loving, caring, doting family, but was taught to leap, just in case. I owed everything I have ever achieved in my life to my mom and dad, Grandaddy and Mamau. Looking around me in LA, I realized that nothing of any value in my life could have been obtained without my family. Nothing. In Texas, growing up, I always thought it was my "right" to have good parents. I expected it, and thought everyone had a pair. But it's not a right at all. And some just say it's a kind of genetic luck of the draw. But rattlesnakes breed rattlesnakes, so there's really no luck involved at all. My Grandaddy showed me that hard work, discipline, and good parenting is what promotes children who expect more of their parents, just as it promotes parents who expect more of their children. Well, I was given the world from my family. They all taught me that life was a continual demonstration of value to yourself and to the world around you, and I did not expect it to be some arbitrary definition of fairness. My family wanted me to have an unfair advantage by *their* definition. Their main objective was making sure that I was sent out into the world with an almost certain chance of survival and ultimately procreation, or at the very least *creation*. They put this in me, and unless there had been a design flaw, it would always be permanently encoded in my DNA. I did not want to let myself or them down. And I hoped I wouldn't. But I knew I had a Boudin recipe.

My Mamau passed away only eight days after my Grandaddy. They were inseparable, and I don't think she wanted to live without him. I grieved the double blow of their passing by immersing myself in work and wishing I could sip a cold pony with my Grandaddy on his porch, looking out at our horizon, listening to his stories, fried chicken diluting the smell of Grandaddy's Pinaud on the porch back home ... and Jane. The day my 187th letter was returned was the day a girl called me from Houston.

"Can you come home?"

"Uh ... who's calling, please?" My mind reeled.

"Lawrence is going to marry me, and I've heard so many stories about you two, I know he'd want you here," she spoke gently into the receiver.

"I'll be there."

Shit, I hadn't seen him since we both left for college—a decade at least. I flew home to Texas for Firefly's wedding.

I was excited to see him at his bachelor party inside the belly of a whale. His familiar Moby Dick living room was full of guys yelling "SURPRISE!" and offering congratulations, and two drunks perched up on one of the giant oak crossbeams, chanting *Lor-ents, Lor-ents,* one of whom I recognized to be Andy. I looked around the Tudor-style room at Firefly's groomsmen, most I recognized: Trent, Eddy, Timmy, and Eduardo. Some were camouflaged by the pouchy pink doughiness of chronic alcohol consumption, and others, like Firefly, had a resilient glow.

"Holy fuckin' shit! Is this pussy eyeballin' me? Huh, fuckhole?" Firefly picked me up in a bear hug, then put a Miller into my hand. "Ha!! Mickey, you little sack of shit! What the hell're you doin' in my huge-ass nigger-cockin' house all the way from LA?"

"I don't know, somebody told me you're gettin' married?"

The front door opened, and my question was answered as the stable of groomsmen quieted down respectfully when a stunning blonde, years younger than any of us, stole center stage in her yoga outfit. She wrapped herself around Firefly.

"Mic, this is Felicia. My woman." Firefly smirked.

"I bet my lucky seven that someone would get ahold of that cocksucker!" The freckled guy sitting up on the beam above me cackled, beside Andy. I did a double take.

Andy nodded in friendly recognition when I glanced up. I raised my hand just like that day on the golf course and he did, too, and a bolt of regret shot through me, wondering if he had forgiven or just forgotten.

"Okay, you found him," said Felicia. "Did y'all get some pie? It's pumpkin! Firefly tells me that's yer favorite." Firefly and I exchanged a laugh.

"Holy shit, I wondered why you made that nasty thing!" exclaimed Firefly. "Did YOU tell him I was get'n married, woman?" asked Firefly.

"WE! I told him we are getting married, shit head." Felicia kissed Firefly very affectionately, and he lit up.

"Oh, you know what I mean, sugar britches. Come here ya little buttermilk doughnut." He kissed her, then turned to me. "JEEZUS! I haven't seen you in like...well, too long, damn it! So, you went to LA to become a faggit? Clatterbuck tried to tell me you're gay!"

"BULLSHIT COCKSUCKER!" hollered Clatterbuck, lumbering down off the ladder from his seat up on the split-timber beam overhead, his eyes pouched and red from drink, and about seventy pounds heavier than when I had last seen him.

"Oh, don't lie, ya little turd, Clatterbuck!" said Firefly, then turned to me. "I said to Clatterbuck, shit, Mic's weird but he ain't gay! You're not are ya? HA! Just kidd'n!" Everyone laughed as Felicia stepped in.

"Mickey, I'm glad you could come. He never shuts up about you." She smiled, delighted that Firefly was happy.

"Bullshit, I hardly even recognized him!" Firefly laughed, knuckling me in the ribs.

"Okay, I'm outta here, fellas. Mickey, make sure he behaves himself!" Felicia shook my hand and gave me a polite hug. "And, no sleazy lap dancers!"

"Only tasteful lap dancers!" bellowed Firefly. Felicia shook a finger at Firefly, no manicure, no makeup, just beautiful. She kissed him tenderly. "Oh, don't you worry my little potato dumplin'. Tomorrow you're my wife!" shouted Firefly as the door closed behind Felicia. "Okay, bring out the peelers!" Suddenly the door popped back open and Felicia stuck her head in. "HA! Just kidd'n, baby. I don't even like peelers, can't stand 'em. MAKE 'EM ALL LEAVE!... See there."

Felicia broke into peals of laughter at Firefly. I hoped Firefly would always make her laugh like that, because he looked like he'd be lost without her and he'd never get another one so pretty and smart who could tolerate his nonsense.

"He's an idiot, but I love him." Felicia smiled at all of us and pulled her head back to close the door behind her.

"She makes me do frickin' yoga," said Firefly, staring after her. "But for her, I'd stick my head up my ass, if I could bend that far."

The party migrated from Firefly's turreted manse on the golf course, and we tailgated as close as we could park to the football practice field. I felt right at home as I read the sign, HOME OF THE BEARS. Everyone drank beer from kegs that were set up on the back of Clatterbuck's pickup truck parked out on the mound near The Hole, right where Kevin used to park his Firebird. More guys accumulated, buddies from high school, and college friends of Firefly. I noticed the cement scar where The Hole had been filled in was now built over with a pop and burger vending station. I wondered if anyone knew that my friend had died underneath it.

I was having fun catching up with the guys, and roasting Firefly, until a black-and-white wool houndstooth cap appeared, and the air sucked right out of the atmosphere around me. Andy nudged me and gestured discreetly when Jonathan adjusted his Donegal tweed cap like he was an erudite book publisher. I tried to make eye contact, if only to indicate I didn't give a fuck anymore how big of an asshole he was, but Jonathan looked away. Aside, Clatterbuck and Andy took turns filling me in that Jonathan had been Firefly's college dorm proctor who permitted heavy-drinking parties, and was now on his way to replace his dad at Texas Instruments. Jonathan's wife had left him, walking away with not only the Mottahedeh wedding porcelain but half of Jonathan's inheritance plus the estate, a Bentley, and a kid.

"What the fuck's he doing here?" Jonathan murmured under his breath, as Eduardo eyeballed him to back off. Hatred blistered in Jonathan's eyes, and I actually felt compassion for him for a moment.

"There's a Porta-Potty over by the bleachers," Clatterbuck laughed. "Why don't you two girls go powder yer noses?"

"Bathroom break, fellas!" Firefly saw where things were headed and stepped in, maybe 20/20 hindsight to right the Quik wrong he set in motion with Andy, once upon a time over my spilled chocolate milk. "Hey, you eyeballin' Mic? Cut the shit, Jonathan, this is my day, this party's about me, shit head. Me, me, me. And you gotta know by now that that boy will fuck you up while crying!"

Firefly tackled Jonathan and hugged him like a grizzly, laughing like a child.

"Get over it, Jonathan," Clatterbuck echoed.

"Mic never woulda done it if you didn't deserve it," said Andy, and I smiled.

Firefly broke in with self-deprecation, "I ain't ever gotta worry then 'bout Felicia leavin' me, 'cause I ain't got a pool t'piss in. C'mon fellas, Jell-O shots for old time's sake!"

Everyone dove for the tray of Jell-O shots, purple and pink like at our swim meets, and Firefly stuck his finger in every single shot before anyone could grab one, laughing insanely that he hadn't washed his hands after the Porta-Potty.

"All right, when's the last time you've gone out with just the boys?" asked Clatterbuck. Firefly could not recall.

"That's all right, we get it. We're just not important anymore."

"Firefly's pussy whipped." Jonathan's air of superiority had not tempered with age.

"Bullshit, that's just bullshit," said Firefly, searching to find the words to explain. "I wanna wake up next to Felicia, I just wanna wake up next to her, that's all, and I'd never do anything with you guys at night that might jeopardize my mornin's with her." Firefly looked up mischievously. Then reached for Clatterbuck. "AW, HELL, SOMEBODY HOLD THA C-BUCK DOWN, I'M FEELIN' ROMANTIC!!" The guys busted up laughing, as Clatterbuck wriggled out of reach. "Hell, Clatterbuck even managed to get laid. It took him till senior year in college, though!" announced Firefly.

"Bullshit, I was just picky. Besides, all the chicks were head cases," declared Clatterbuck.

"Hey, here's a weirdo!" injected Jonathan. "Who here went to Quail Valley? Anybody remember that love child Jane?" And with that, I could not move, I just stared at this intruder. All other noise faded away as Jonathan's mouth continued to move. Jane's name on Jonathan's lips was blasphemy enough, but he then proceeded to address the whole group with some other shit he called language. "I heard she's got cancer," said Jonathan.

I could not move my eyes from Jonathan and I felt my lungs shrinking. I had never wanted to club the consciousness out of a person more in my life, but that claustrophobia had now spread to my fingers, and I could no longer make a fist. I hugged Firefly quickly and started running, his voice behind me shouting about "where the fuck was I going?"

I found myself hyperventilating in my rental car and fumbling with my cell phone. It was dead and I had no charger. I pulled over when I found a pay phone out in front of the Utotem. The polished chrome face staring back at me on the pay phone, I dialed. A homeless man sat on the Utotem window ledge about ten feet from the phone, watching me intently.

"Hello?"

"Hey, Mom."

"Hey, Sug."

"What are you doing?"

"I was sweepin'."

"Sweepin' the kitchen floor, or *sweepin'* in your bed?"

"The kitchen floor."

"Liar." I chuckled.

"You still coming over tomorrow before you leave?"

"Yeah, of course."

"Sug, didn't you go to Lawrence's party?"

"Hey, be cool, man. You got any change?" asked the homeless man. I stared him down.

"No, sorry."

"You didn't, why not? I thought you were excited."

"Uh...yeah, no, I went. Sorry, Mom, I was talking to someone else here."

"How was it?"

I kept looking down, but occasionally met the eyes of the homeless man.

"Good, Mom, it was good."

"Weddin's tomorrow morning?"

"Yeah."

"Well, we'd love to see you after, Sug. Come by? See the

new house? Your father's done so great, Sug, you'd be proud. And he finished restorin' his MG. And in lieu of babysitting Lew, he took up paintin' my portrait, too, you gotta come see, I look twenty years younger, just like my old self."

"I bet it's pretty, Mom."

"Aw, Sug."

"Hey, where is he?"

"He's right here, can't you hear him?"

"No, is he snoring?"

"Here, I'll put the phone closer."

"Damn, Mom, how do you sleep with that?"

"Oh, Sug, I can't sleep without it! If he goes racing for the weekend I don't sleep at all. Hang on, let me go into the kitchen so I don't wake him up." My father's sawing cordwood at the other end of the line made me smile. Mom hovered over his health like a twenty-first-century helicopter mom.

A Jamaican Utotem guy came out the front door and approached the homeless man. I wondered what had become of Samir and his music.

"Hey, you!" yelled the manager to the homeless man. "You know what time it is?"

"I try not to," replied the homeless man

"Well it's late. And I think it may be time for you to move the hell on. There's nothing free here."

"Sug?" asked my mother, concerned.

"Well, I am. I'm as free as a bird, man. And this bird'll never change," murmured the homeless man as he got up and gathered his things.

"Sugar, you there?" As the homeless man shuffled around the corner, he turned and looked right at me...then he slowly disappeared from view.

"Yeah, Mom, sorry. I'm here."

"You scared me, 'cause I could still hear people talking."

"No, sorry, I'm here...Um, listen, I might be kinda late getting in, okay? There's just, there's just some things I think I need to do here."

"Is everything okay, Mickey?"

"Yeah, Mom, I hope so."

"Okay, well, call us when you know when you'll be arriving."

"I will."

"Mickey, one more thing, Sug. Your sister's really hoping you can make it by while you're in town. You know she's just a block from the old house."

"I don't know, Mom."

"Charlotte's grown up since you last saw her. Ya won't recognize her."

"Course I'll recognize her, Momma." I wondered if my niece would be more like Kevin or trashy like Lilyth.

"You know she'll be twenty-five next month, and her own little Genie's already eight years old. Your niece grew up without a father, Mickey; she needs you in her life. Come by after? It'll be *fine*. Lilyth's so *nice* now."

"I understand, Mom. I, we'll see, I just..."

"Hey, is there anything I can do for y'darlin'?"

"No, I promise, I'm fine. I'll call you when I know more."

"So nice hearin' your voice. I love you, Sug. You sure yer fine?"

"Yes, I'm fine. I love you, too, Mom."

About an hour and a few phone calls later, I was outside Jane's hospital room trying to control my heart rate before telling my hand to knock. I remembered Kevin's words the night we had sat in the stranger's driveway hiding from the police. And I remembered standing at Jane's door the day Mr. Troy Bradford had opened it to a shy little boy. I felt my arm positioning itself to knock. I glanced at a muscular arm, and the large fist of a man. It was my own. My God, how had so many years gone by?

Jane's mother opened the door with her lips moving, but no sound coming out. I touched her hand as I walked past, and I saw Jane on the bed seated Indian-style, looking more beautiful than I could have possibly remembered. And I could hear the bass of my heartbeat just like Kevin could that night in his car, and I could hear hers. Barefoot, pedicured in purple, Jane was seated with perfect posture and an arched back in a graceful lotus position, one hand rested in the other, palms up. Jane's thin frame was wrapped in a winter-white cashmere cowl-neck sweater scooped enough to allow her delicate clavicles to peek out. Gray knit silk warm-up pants covered her long, shapely legs. A black wool beanie cap topped off her long, dark brown hair she still parted in the middle. Purple flip-flops were under her hospital bed. Glittering and gorgeous, Jane looked at me as if she couldn't believe her eyes, soft and green-brown as I'd memorized, and her full lips broke into a wide, welcoming smile.

Then she said it: "Mickey." And, at that moment, the viscosity of my blood changed and I was locked in place. She not only remembered me, she knew my name. Her hands flew to her mouth just like her mother's had when I walked in, and I saw all the things I ever wanted in her eyes. In that moment, I understood everything that she wanted me to know. I just stood there until she said, "How'd you know I was...?"

"...I just..." I didn't even know how to get from that door to her arms, but that's where I needed to be. Jane's little giggle poured out of her like tiny Christmas tinsel bells, and she held her arms open for me. For me. With tears welling up in her eyes, I slowly approached her and we hugged like we'd never let go. In the window's reflection, I could see Mrs. Bradford standing by the door watching, holding steady a trembling lip.

"Oh my God, Mickey, how did you even find..."

"I just...did."

"Well, I think I'll go down to the cafeteria and get a juice, let y'all talk. Mickey, it's really wonderful to see you, darlin'."

I saw her mother slip out of the reflection and we were alone. Jane felt so wonderful in my arms. She wouldn't let go, and neither would I. I couldn't think of anything I wanted to say, but I knew everything I wanted her to know. Jane's lips were touching my ear when she whispered, "Thank you." Regret wrapped its noose around my throat, and I took far too long to loosen it enough to finally tell her what I wanted her to know. None of the emotional training ground of my youth could prepare me for this moment with Jane. My Grandaddy had always told me to look for truth in behavior, and not words, and everything that I saw in those initial moments gave me all the information that I needed. I knew right then that Jane was where I had always belonged, and she with me.

"I shoulda been here a long time ago," I whispered back. And then I felt her face hide in my neck as her whole body tightened around mine. I felt her lungs quickly spasm the way mine did when I was a child when my grief from Steve McQueen had given me a heaving, silent sob. I felt a Jane tear follow my neck all the way down my chest, and I knew. I was right—I should have been here a long time ago. "I came in town for a friend's wedding, and I, I just overheard that you might be here."

Jane glanced into my eyes, and shook her head, then pulled me close again. I knew that what we saw in each other's eyes was that same look of wonder and fear, that maybe as children we had just misinterpreted. I saw a look of wondering endearment in her, and hope, and all the things I had always wanted to see forever. You know, that night I prayed. My God, did I pray.

"I'm glad you came, Mickey. I didn't think you even, I mean."

"Well I did. I spent my entire fourth grade trying to work up the courage to tell you, and then the next couple years."

"You . . . Really?"

"Jane, I remember the exact day I found you bouncing over a fence across from mine, and the exact day you stopped."

"Oh, Mickey, I used to walk home in front of your house just to try and see you, and I even remember one time you just appeared out of a car trunk, like magic . . . and I just . . . I just wanted to . . ."

"So did I."

That night Jane and I spoke for hours, and made up for years. I told her all the times I watched her bounce, and that I thought about stealing her *Charlie's Angels* T-shirt from her room while their house was still under construction, and she admitted responsibility for leaving the copy of Yaz's "Only You" on my doorstep that year for my birthday, and that she had gone back and removed it because she thought it might be too weird, but then put it back and prayed that I would like it and *know*, and that she had read all of my school papers that her mother would bring home to grade, and that that bastard who took her to every festivity and even the Gary Numan concert was her cousin David because all the other boys thought she was weird, and that I was the only one David had ever given the "nod" to when he first saw me skimming the pool that evening when they went to her prom, and that she saw me standing in line that Halloween at her haunted pirate ship and jumped behind the Cap'n Bolan barrel so that she could be the one to hold my hand and place it in the bowl of oily grapes while whispering in my ear that they were eyeballs, and that she had felt the scabs on my knuckles that night and had known what they were from, and that she'd watched me ride wheelies in front of her house from the bottom-floor living room window, and I told her that I always looked up at her second-floor window as I rode by to see if she saw, and that I had run to *her* in that yellow dress for my first touchdown, and she told me that she had wanted me to keep on running, and that she watched me cry in my bean tree as her father drove past my house and that she just wanted to give me a kiss, and that she saw me place her 95s in her mailbox and prayed I'd knock, and I told her about the note I left under the insoles, and that I'd wanted to knock—that I *really* wanted to knock, and that I watched her paint, and she told me that bouncing high gave her a better view into my yard, and into me, and that she was angry that she'd missed out on so much of my life, and why the hell didn't we talk to each other sooner?

I didn't have an answer for her. I had known Jane my entire life, and she wasn't a rattlesnake, either. She was something else—the same *else* that I was. Before she fell asleep, I told her I would send her a box that contained the last twenty-eight years of us inside. I leaned over the pillow that she was dreaming on and kissed her good night at 6:43 a.m., having promised to attend her gallery opening in two weeks, after a brief return to LA. In that hospital I experienced the most intimate moments of my life. I had never felt closer to nature, never felt more comfortable. The gold standard exists, I experienced it, and I nod in appreciation. When I FedExed the 187 RETURN TO SENDER ADDRESSEE UNKNOWN letters from LA to Jane's hospital room in Houston, all were still sealed. I had never opened them, never reread them. Had I opened them, I somehow felt that it would have let something escape. Keeping them sealed all those years, I guess, was my way of keeping the hope locked inside. And I'm glad I did.

Chapter Ten

J ane died on November 10th, eight days after I had seen her. Her mother apologized for not accurately communicating the fragility of her condition, and also the danger of her upcoming procedure. The one that I had thought was just a formality. She said that Jane had received my box of letters, and that she read every one of them. Mrs. Bradford gave me the information for Jane's memorial service, and told me that when I was there, she would give me a package that, she said, Jane had wanted me to have. You know, I was welcomed into this Jesus time-share experience when I got here. And I knew some stays would be shorter than others, but somehow now I felt betrayed. Jane's stay was short, but she drove her point home, straight into my heart. When I returned to Houston for Jane's memorial, the crisp smell of autumn was in the air. The service was a blur of words, just a lot of kind words I could not hear, spoken by people I never knew loved Jane or even knew her. To me it was a continuum of blurred silence—Jane's silence. Jane's silence was mine, and I didn't want to share anything of ours with any of them.

She was gone. And I would live. I would live with her plank shoved straight through my grille. It hurt seeing her mother and father hurting. It hurt when Mr. Troy Bradford came up to me and shook my hand with both of his, the same way he did on his front porch so many years ago when I still had time. "Sunshine Superman," he murmured, drawing me into a fatherly embrace. It hurt more than I could have ever imagined it could hurt.

After, there was food to be served in the rectory. I couldn't stay. I wanted to go home. But first, I had the cabbie stop by The Pole. And that's where I was. The taxi driver had grown impatient and actually followed me down the long gravel road all the way to that schoolyard flagpole. Although he was only about five feet from me, I did not come out of my dream until the horn honked.

"Hey, you coming or what?" yelled the cabbie.

I was glad he had waited, but now I had to climb back in and tell the cabbie where I really needed to be. I just needed those memories back...at least as many of them that would fit in my pockets. Out the taxi window I stared at Grandaddy's horizon of open fields, cattle, horses, and subdivisions in various stages of construction. Crops were dying, like they had given up and died with Jane. No rain was expected. There was even some water rationing for showers and lawns that was supposed to ensure the harvest would not die, but I couldn't care. I drank some Gatorade in the taxi to nurse my dehydration, and my lifetime with Jane welled as a cloying bitterness like the residue of a pumpkin pie. I choked and spat it down the front of my clean white shirt. And it didn't matter. I felt like I was hungover from grief, like it had poisoned every loving cell in my body.

I told the cabbie to drive by Bentliff Street. In my lap, I hugged the box that Jane's mom had given me, as we passed the Milans'. It was boarded up and overgrown. A mangled aluminum lawn chair stuck a jaundiced elbow through the long grass, a corpse reaching up from the grave to grasp whatever became of happier times. At my old house, my bean tree was the first to greet me, bigger than ever. The dirt of Steve McQueen's grave had long since blended with the untended yard, where our lawn had prospered. Mom and Dad had moved to Galveston after Dad started doing well years ago. It looked like no one was home, so again, I asked the cabbie to wait. I got out and climbed my bean tree still in my suit and sat on the same giant branch where I'd slept after Kevin. I'm not sure how long I sat up in my old tree, nor how long its new owner watched me.

"Hey, what're you doing in my tree?" a kid yelled up at me. He couldn't have been more than eight years old. I wondered if that boy was anything like me, and then I wondered if I had said it out loud, like I did back in the boys' room to Jonathan over Jane's 95s. "What the fuck do you mean, weirdo? You spilled some shit all down your front didn't you? Pig. You better get the fuck out of my tree, mister, or I'm calling the cops. I ain't shittin' you, pal!"

"No, you're nothing like me, are you?" I heard myself mumble toward the kid.

The kid ran off, stomping his Nikes on my tiny handprints in the top cement step, yelling at the top of his lungs.

"Mom! There's a crazy fucker in my tree!"

He didn't know that Steve McQueen was buried here under that tree. And he didn't have any clue that Steve was a better friend to me than any friend he'd ever have in his entire life. He didn't know that it was my fucking tree.

But it wasn't. It just wasn't anymore. None of it was. I no longer belonged there. I slumped back into the taxi, under the gaze of the driver in the rearview.

"Where to?"

I told the driver around the corner down Sandpiper Drive, and I clutched the box to my chest, trying to slow down my heaving lungs.

"Kid's right, mister. You look like shit."

He drove to the intersection of Bentliff and headed around toward Sandpiper and stopped at the new red light. We waited. There on the corner was my mailbox. When the taxi turned the corner, I noticed it no longer danced. It looked lame. The old bent-in leg was gone. Shorn off. An amputee that leaned lame, and farther over than ever. And immediately, no Grunt. Just tears.

"Sir?"

"Turn around, can you just turn around?"

He eyeballed me in the rearview and pulled a U-turn and headed away from Jane's. I directed him to The Ditch, where the eight-year-old me had waited so many times for Firefly, and Kevin hid from the world. I asked the driver to wait once again as I got out to see. The waste near my old home was perhaps the only thing that got bigger with time. Under that tiny bridge, where people would at one time dispose of small items and Jack in the Box bags, were now refrigerators, lawn mowers, and even a Ford F-150 truck bed. It was dirty back when a much different me would crawl down in the creek with Steve McQueen searching for crawdads, but now it was a wasteland. I looked under the bridge where Kevin used to hide and saw the same sentences written about girls. *Lilyth* was replaced by *Charlotte*. Rattlesnakes, I guess.

My heaving chest calmed a bit under that bridge. I heard kids playing somewhere. There was life here, but I recognized none.

As we passed the Utotem on the way to the airport, I saw a tiny little record shop with a name that led me to believe I might know the owner. It read SAMMI-R'S SOUND HOUSE. So, I asked the driver if he could pull over yet again. I wondered when time had decided to accelerate. And why I hadn't been notified. I was a man. But I was a man who wanted his Grandaddy. Finally, I realized my taxi had stopped in front of the store and the driver was looking concernedly at me in the rearview. I wiped my eyes.

"You okay, buddy?" I saw him looking at me in that rearview with the same emotion that my father had tried not to show the night I held Steve in my arms as he drifted away.

"Yeah, yeah, I'm fine. I'll just be a second, okay."

"No problem. You can just leave your box on the seat. It's okay."

Inside the little shop I scanned the two tiny aisles for a familiar face. Seal was on the sound system, and a tan-skinned old guy behind the counter was bent over unpacking merchandise and singing, "in a whirlpool of people only some want the cry"—fucking up the lyrics. The smell of the place was hitting me, as I was about to call the man's name. The smell in that little record shop was a spicy-sweet incense, exactly like Jane's, and it engulfed me. All those years only Jane had smelled of this inexplicable intoxicant.

"What is that smell?"

The guy behind the counter leapt up in surprise from unpacking merchandise. He took one look at me. Suddenly he was upon me, embracing me and laughing and holding my hands. And it was wonderful to see him.

"Mic-mic!" All these years since the Utotem, and Samir had managed to save up and get his own shop. "Your timing to enter my shop is perfect, my friend, what is means 'whirlpool of people cry'?"

"The song's about dreamers, Samir . . . and that they're rare. Hey, what's that smell?"

"Smell is Nag Champa, my old friend. Oh the shit, I miss you, Mic-mic! So many songs you must tell me. But, Mic-mic, sister baby-baby my new friend!"

"Are those lyrics, Samir? I've never heard that song."

"No! Just like you, she is loving the music."

"Wait . . . who?"

"Your sister baby-baby. Little Genie . . ." Samir riffed the song, then explained, "She is reminding me much of little Mic-mic!" Samir told me more about Genie's love of music. He showed me two CDs that Genie had come in and ordered from the UK and asked if I wanted to take them to her.

"Actually, Samir, I don't really . . ." And I didn't, really. I didn't even sort of. But I knew I should. "Yeah, sure, Samir."

That little record store felt warm and familiar. And Samir was a wonderful constant in that town of change. Samir wanted to pretend fight me for fun, and serve me tea, and talk about bands that most people had never heard of. But I had to go. I hugged him and took the two CDs. And then I left smelling like Jane and I hoped that scent would never leave.

"You're looking like shit, man, what you are doing to yourselfhood?" Samir's Bollywood accent extracted a wan smile from me, as he inflected syllables where there were none, and arranged their tones like the sound of a calliope.

"You know, I'm not really sure, Samir." He tipped his head quizzically. "I gotta go, man, take care."

"Don't forget Samir, Mic-mic. You come back, my friend. My door is always here, is open for you." Samir stood there hollering and waving.

I went full circle. Across the street from the address that my mother gave me, I asked the cabbie to pull up. It was about four houses down from the Carvel Bridge over Kevin's ditch, where I had just been. And all the kids' voices that I had heard while down there were in my sister's front yard, play-ing football. The driveway served as an end zone and had a familiar car up on blocks with a For Sale sign in the back window. There were five boys around ten or twelve years old scrambling around the yard, another younger one on the side-walk, and three girls watching from the porch. Little Genie was obvious. She was a clone of Kevin. Introspective and shy, she sat apart from the other two girls on the porch. I didn't remember her birthday, or even the year she was born, but she looked to be about eight. I watched her watch the game, and then I watched her watch that boy on the sidewalk, until he watched her, and then she watched the game some more. And I knew about them as much as I did not know about myself as a child. They were both separated from groups that I hoped that they would never join. I watched Little Genie for about twenty minutes just sitting across that street parked in that taxicab, and I knew she was different. I could see so many questions in her eyes that had never been in Lilyth's, so many ideas, secrets, and dreams. I couldn't believe that she was Charlotte's daughter—who was Lilyth's daughter.

"How much do I owe you?" I asked as I collected my box.

"You sure you want me to leave you here, mister? An hour ago we were headed to the airport. Shit man, you sure you're all right?"

"Yeah, I'll be all right. I've got a car here. How much do I owe you?"

I walked across the street with my box and Genie's CDs from Samir's as I heard the cab drive away behind me, and I breathed in the same neighborhood that had raised me so many years earlier. I imagined how I would sit on that porch with Genie and watch the game that I had played so many times before, but a cautious little girl stared back at me as I approached.

I took a step back. And then I held up The Verve's *Urban Hymns* and Portishead's *Dummy* and she knew.

She patted the step for me to sit, and I told her everything I knew about porches, and I think she understood. And then I went over to that boy sitting on the sidewalk and introduced myself. He was everything he appeared to be, clearly cut from a different cloth than that neighborhood usually produced. He shook my hand like a gentleman, and looked me in the eyes. Periodically his eyes would flicker over to make sure that Little Genie was still on the porch, and I could tell that he was petrified of her catching him looking. He told me his name was Porter, and even at eight years old he told me that he understood his name's meaning. And although he had never heard of a porthole before, he promised me that if he ever saw one, he'd jump through it immediately.

Then I walked up to the door and knocked. My sister Lilyth was forty pounds heavier and leering at me like a banshee until her eyes focused. I stepped back in the same moment she reached out to embrace me. My sister had been a huge influence on my perception of people: what I want no part of, what I don't want in my life. From the fire truck she rolled into the street when I was a toddler, to the scar on the inside of my elbow and all the other crap for which I was never allowed to physically retaliate, so anger and powerlessness were still there, but so was disgust. Lilyth did not have my back then and, I was willing to wager, probably not now, either. And I was sure Lilyth resented me.

But then my sister opened her arms even wider for me with a smile that I decided to neither trust nor fear. I took another step back.

"Oh, for fuck's sake, Mickey, are you eight years old? Get the hell over here." I stood there and hoped for the horizon, wishing Grandaddy were there to tell me what to do. "Get over here, I've changed, I've been saved by Jesus Christ our Lord, already, fuckin' A! I'm a nice person now. I'm fine." Snake-eyed, Lilyth studied me coldly for a reaction. I didn't believe her for a second. If that was her Jesus she was on then, no thanks, I'd take my own. The gleam in her eyes was not fun or playful or even wickedly mischievous, it was disturbingly like that of a sociopath, like the TV interviews with Charles Manson in prison. Reluctantly, I stepped forward to hug my sister and followed her inside, too numb from grief to feel the cold autumn wind that made it hard to close the door whose haunting clunk reminded me of Steve McQueen's tail hitting my bedroom door. But that smell. I walked straight to the back sliding glass door that was just like ours from years before and opened the window to dilute the redolent bouquet of Lilyth's latest perfume disaster that mixed with the bubble gum effluvium on which she gnashed furiously. The rush of cold air caused her pink Bazooka gum bubble to burst, and the brittle membrane enveloped her nose, hiding its booze-enlarged pores. "Fuck!" exclaimed Lilyth. My sister had arranged the kitchen just like our old house. I stared out the window at all the decay as Lilyth and Charlotte sat at the round kitchen table and explained all.

"Charlotte's wise like Grandaddy, and a slut like me, fuckin' DNA; figures, right? But her daughter ain't a slut, case you're wonderin', Mickey. My granddaughter's out front, she's as good as Goldie. A swimmer, too, Mickey."

"Mom, will you fucking stop already with the oversharing!" Charlotte's edge sparked against my sister's.

"Oh, darlin' it's *fahn*, he's ma' dumbass lil' brother," Lilyth slashed back at her.

"Be *nice*, Mom."

There they were again, the *F* and *N* words.

"I am *nice*, Charlotte. You know, Mickey, Genie's even got Totter this year. Can you believe that shit? He's probably still talkin' about my bra, that fuckin' perv! Miss Flinch left him for Coach Randall, boy can she swim now, looks hot as him. Hey, you dickhead, you're setting my shag on fire!"

I turned around to detect where the smell of smoke was coming from, and for the first time noticed a man lying on the couch in front of the TV flicking a cigarette into the shag carpet. He must've been there the entire time, but hadn't spoken a word. And I immediately wanted to drag him straight into the front yard and kick the fuck out of that piece of shit.

But Lilyth smacked him and poured his Budweiser on the smoldering hole in her old white shag carpet.

"That's Genie's father," said Lilyth indifferently. "Piece'a crap, but at least he sticks around and pays rent."

Genie had a chance, and I didn't want it ruined by garbage that should have been collected yesterday. But I realized that some children, the few survivors, have the uncanny ability to self-parent, and Genie was one of them. This idiot would not stop her. She was already an alien in that house. Some parents show you exactly what to be, and others show you exactly what to flee. Genie had plans. I could see them.

I asked my sister why she was selling the car in the driveway and tried to convince her to keep it. But I knew she wouldn't. She just wanted it gone. I told her I would pay her whatever she wanted and take it with me so it wouldn't be scrapped for junk or left somewhere for dead. Then that slimy fuck on the couch sat up and started to tell me what the car was worth. My fingers and cheek both twitched and I left the window, but my sister saw my eyes and Lilyth jumped up and told him to, "Shut up and sit the fuck back down!" He opened his mouth to protest, and then Charlotte shouted, "My uncle will smear your face on the fucking driveway if you don't shut the fuck up and sit back down right now!" My God, they were exactly alike. But Charlotte was right. In that moment, I would have. And he slumped back into the couch.

My sister drove me to an ATM and I paid her for the car. She then loaned me her tiny little rusted-out Geo Metro to run back and forth to the auto parts store as I collected the parts to get the car running. I couldn't fit the wheels and tires in the little Metro, so I had them delivered. From the porch, together Porter and Little Genie watched me work until the sun went down. Then I drove the boy home about two miles away. Not once had anyone called to look for him, nor did he have a bike. I asked him how he had gotten to the house, and without missing a beat he said he had run and that it only takes him eighteen minutes when the crosswalks hurry, and could he come over again tomorrow? I knew I would be gone tomorrow, but I told him that I hoped he would. Like Genie, he would be okay, despite everything else being anything but fine and nice. He was a climber. When I got back to Lilyth's driveway, I got the car to fire after fluids, plugs, and a battery, but it still would not idle. So, I spent about two hours adjusting the floats and cleaning the carburetor. But when I was done, it shook the driveway just like I remembered.

I slammed the hood and saw that the relic text ghosted through an off-shade of red spray paint: *I was based on a true story.* A rotting piece of wood, much smaller than I remembered, was peeking through the cracked grille.

I woke up with the sun and Little Genie tapping me on my cheek as I had fallen asleep in the front seat of her Grandaddy's car. I told her that I'd return it to her, where it belonged, completely restored on her sixteenth birthday, and yes, I'd come inside for some Eggo waffles. All I could think of was what James would say to my own Grandaddy, every time we'd eat waffles for breakfast at The Piccadilly Cafeteria. James would pour about half the syrup bottle onto his plate before my Grandaddy would say, "Goddammit, save some for Seedlin' and me." But James would just keep pouring with a big toothy grin and sing out, "Aunt Jemima . . . and I ain't ya daddy neither!" After breakfast, I said my good-byes in the driveway. I hugged Little Genie and whispered in her ear all the things I hoped she would remember. She asked me what was in the box on the passenger seat. I didn't know. She took a moment to really look at me and then asked me if I wanted to. She was a beautiful child, and really was based on a true story—Kevin's. Lilyth yelled something from the porch, laced with profanity that I did not quite understand, and then blew me a kiss, of all things.

"God, it's okay, Uncle Mickey, don't listen to Granny," squealed Genie flipping her wild blond hair, the texture and color of Kevin's. Everyone else had gone inside as I drove her Grandaddy's red Firebird away, and Little Genie just got smaller and smaller—a colorful blossom on my horizon, still waving in that rearview mirror. My mom was right about Lilyth's house being only a block from our old house. For the last time, I pulled up alongside Steve McQueen's grave under the bean tree. I had wanted to see all the places of my youth, to pack up my memories to take with me, but they just didn't live there anymore. I pulled slowly into the driveway and brushed myself off as much as possible. But I was a greasy mess in a suit, with Gatorade slopped down my chest. You could still see the patchwork in that old garage door from when the Firebird's grille had plunged through. And this was where all the memories lived. I wanted that door to raise and see that gorgeous Schwinn Sting-Ray again. I wanted the "Free Bird" to fall out when I opened the car door. But mostly, I just wanted to see her again from my own backyard. I knocked on the front door and explained myself to a lady that appeared far too nice and understanding to have raised a child like her feral son. I told her that the tiny hands in the concrete under her feet were mine, and that where she lived was my vantage point of everything important in my life, and could I just sneak into her backyard for a moment and I'd be gone? "I can go 'round the back. I don't have to come inside, ma'am."

"That's the crazy one, Mom, don't let him..." And then his protest suddenly stopped. He just gazed at me like there were things he recognized and questioned at the same time.

His mother smiled after a cautious look, and then opened her door to me. I ignored the boy as he followed me the whole time in watchful silence, and I stood just outside that sliding glass door through which I had first seen Jane bounce and I had the emotions of a shy, little eight-year-old all over again. But the fence was much closer than I remembered, and I imagined the few remaining rusted-out pieces of her trampoline where she had bounced could no longer propel her skyward. The bushes were gone from where I had first filmed a stunningly beautiful young girl floating gently above her rear fence. I stood impossibly close to what once seemed so far away, and it hurt. And I just wanted a fucking do-over. It's all I wanted. I felt a warmth touch my palm and I looked down. The foulmouthed boy that I couldn't fucking stand stood quietly beside me looking out at my horizon, holding my hand...and I could stand him. After an impossibly long moment, I patted his head and I let myself out the side, saying good-bye to a house I no longer recognized.

I had only ever ridden my bike to Jane's new house, cutting across fields and fairways, even when I dragged my mower bungee-corded to my sissy bar, so I had to guess at directions and navigate my way down streets I had never been on before to finally pull up in that Firebird. Jane's butter yellow house did not seem quite so fancy anymore after all the years, but seeing it made me want it, even the rusted trampoline crouching in the backyard by the sand trap that protected hole eighteen where I sold my first golf ball. The house had a Century 21 key lockbox on both doors, and looked completely desolate, so I took my box out back to the trampoline and sat. Wherever Lew Hoagie was, I knew his balls were out, because I could smell the rain coming. The clouds moved visibly, and a cleansing Texas drenching was near. But with 1,600 miles of I-10 between me and home, I couldn't wait.

The fragrance of Jane's Nag Champa exploded in my face when I used the Firebird's key to slit open the cardboard top and look inside. I think you know an important part of me fell out in Jane's backyard that day as I recognized the box's contents. My whole body became pressurized as I pulled out a familiar, but partially rusted Charles Chips container that I had last seen the morning of my parents' yard sale. When I was finally able to bring myself to open the tin, I felt a compression within my chest unlike anything I had ever felt, and a Grunt that would contain nothing. I slowly and carefully lifted the lid and stared into the can. I found inside it everything she had not already said. The box was what made me understand. My dad's silver stopwatch and its brittle leather thong. Jane's cobalt blue feather and a 45 of Simon and Garfunkel's "The Sounds of Silence" with *Mickey + Two = Us* written in the center in purple Crayola. I reached into the tin, and touched a reel with about a hundred feet of slightly yellowed Bolex-geared film that I immediately knew was of an eight-year-old Jane, intermittently rising above a six-foot wooden barrier—defying gravity just as long as she could—until gravity finally won and called her back down, her hair the last thing to disappear. The box contained all the looks and thoughts and gestures that Jane and I exchanged on the hospital bed. The box completely crushed me. I recognized all of its contents, all but two things: a purple upholstered book with a brass lock and a small canvas painting tucked underneath it. Beneath the Charles Chips can a postage stamp from Mom's butcher-block drawer in my old kitchen stared back at me, postmarked and condemned, RETURN TO SENDER faded to poltergeist gray. I flipped through the stack of letters I had written when no one was looking, unself-consciously real, recalling stamps I had pilfered from school that were intended for letters destined to some congressman with rallying adolescent cries against fur trapping or oil spills... or whatever. A few of Jane's letters I had mailed without a stamp. I'd forgotten that. And yet the postman had elected to *waste taxpayers' money* and return even those.

Not knowing what was coming out of each envelope, I paused, stepping back before stepping forward. I read my letters, with the bittersweet perspective that Jane's eyes had graced each and every one. Most of them I had written with a blue ballpoint Dad brought home from his job at GE, a pen I'd had to warm up by drawing circles over and over again, or it stuttered and globbed up. The Write Brothers' jingle echoed in my mind, "Write on brother, write on, with my nineteen-cent Write Brothers pen." A few were written in a deeper navy blue, more of a blue-black, a liquid ink that seeped into the paper and, over the years, had bled to unreadable. For those, secretly I had borrowed dad's Montblanc fountain pen he had won from GE for his sales record. I remembered the heft of that pen; it felt expensive, important, fluid. The paper I had procured for Jane's letters ranged from the backs of torn envelopes, to a Shakey's Pizza placemat, to all kinds of random paper that still told me stories of her, but there was nothing ornate. It was whatever was there, whatever was necessary—perforated spiral ring, a report card edge, a Juicy Fruit wrapper. I had considered every inkable surface as a potential vehicle to communicate to Jane. The content of my letters to Jane, too, meandered to every conceivable topic. Some were like old friends, some mundane, and some tormented me. But I remembered the girl to whom I had written all of them. And she was exactly whom I'd thought she was.

I needed that box, and everything in it, only because Jane was gone. Mrs. Bradford was the one who had called to tell me that I was everything to Jane, and always had been, and then Mr. Troy Bradford got on the line with us, saying he had known from the moment he shook my hand on his doorstep on Sandpiper Drive that I was the right one for his daughter. And my soul collapsed on itself. And there was that painfully familiar Grunt from deep within my throat. That sentence from Mr. Bradford was probably the most painful thing I have ever heard. I don't know why, but hearing him speak of what he knew about his daughter and me hurt so much it made my ears stop working. I just wanted that feeling to go away.

My letters in that box were about *that* girl. The one that I was right about. The one whose plank I still carry. As I lifted them carefully from the box, the pages of my letters smelled of youth, that magic; sometimes they smelled of regret, like the residue of Baxter's vomit, that you just cannot shake. Some letters made me laugh aloud and some just really hurt. The child who wrote those letters was so pure, so unselfconscious. They were written to a girl I met long before I heard "I love you" in a small hospital room. And though it was killing me to read my letters, I discovered that I was a kid I liked a whole lot.

Jane,

I really think your nonsense suits my nonsense.

Jane,

I don't like you. I like chocolate. For you it's bigger.

Jane,

My Grandaddy says that love is a poison that lives inside us. And we gotta give it away to survive.

Jane,

You're the common person in my dreams. All of them. My mom says everybody has one.

And there's one with a (bad) drawing of Jane's wooden fence with a little grass at the bottom that read,

Jane,

I saw you today. My mouth didn't work, but I was shouting with my eyes. You hesitated for a moment. I liked that.

Jane,

Big people say that your life will be divided in two by something really important. I think you're my something.

Jane,

I think it's been too long. I try to not think about you. But it's like trying to not hear a fire engine that's screaming by.

And another, written without any quotes or apostrophes when I was nine years old,

---

Jane,

I think theres more included in my I love you than in anyone elses.

Jane,

I'm from somewhere. But we're from somewhere else.

Jane,

Where are you going? We're not supposed to know yet, but if you can tell me I'll meet you.

Jane,

Sometimes I have to chase the dreams away with a switch.

Jane,

Olly olly income free.

Jane,

It's not like falling at all. It's more like floating.

Jane,

You can have my Bull-Yawn. All of it. Always.

The last letter at the bottom of the FedEx box was dated my birthday:

Jane,

My Grandaddy says that the first half of finding happiness for yourself is giving it to someone else. So I just wanted you to know that you're halfway there.

Eight days with Jane. Now she was gone.

Miss Jane Bradford
33 Lieu Lieu Lane, Houston, Texas

RETURN TO SENDER ADDRESSEE UNKNOWN stared back at me and I cried like an infant on that trampoline until I remembered it.

———

Beneath the stack of letters was the fat upholstered book. It was Jane's diary, hand-stitched in raw purple silk. I read everything about a girl I had loved for far longer than eight days, and I loved her more with every word. She described finding my can and hoping I had not chosen to sell it, and then concluding that I must not have known, after having seen my film of her, and that she had waited. And waited. For me to reach down. But a shy and insecure boy never did. A photo of Jane slid from the fragrant, spiced pages into my scarred hand. It was chased by a rubbery little insole that flopped into my lap, exposing bled ink on its bottom.

enaJ I made out the first word.

!ti htrow yletinifed er'uoY

But my reality was used to being inverted, and it quickly recombined the words in my memory, and I was at the top of The Pole again, and, yes, Jane still was. The note I had stuck under the insole of her 95s the day I tied the laces perfectly and placed them into her mailbox had long since disintegrated along with her sneakers, but the phantom letters remained on the insole, indelibly stating what I had known since the first day I saw her—she was worth it. I continued to read Jane's most intimate thoughts, hopes, and dreams about a life she had hoped to lead with a boy just beyond two fences and a ditch. A boy whom I know had missed his porthole. The rest is private and I shall keep for myself alone.

Under the purple book, and wrapped in waxed paper, was the completed oil painting on canvas of the field of green that I had once seen Jane painting in her garage and then again in her vacant bedroom on the golf course. There was now a fallen empty lawn chair with yellow and green webbing right in the foreground above those same detailed blades of grass, and a young naive, suited-up boy standing perfectly still under the white H uprights looking straight at me through his facemask, his arms raised and waving to what I knew was his family, the number 24 on his jersey only partially visible behind the football that was glued securely to his chest with Stickum, and an empty field of hash marks stretched out behind him.

Epilogue

Lew's rain was starting to mask my tears as I climbed into the red Firebird in front of Jane's old house and I drove away from my past. But it was on that trampoline in her backyard that I first asked for help. I got about thirty yards down her old street when something shook the undercarriage of Kevin's old car like I had just run over a cinder block, until the back end sort of lurched and pitched the car sideways and I skidded to a stop on the wet street. I climbed out to see what I had run over, and there, in the street, about ten yards behind the car was The Plank. As rain continued to soak me to the bone, I lifted the hood and inspected the radiator. But nothing leaked at all. In Jane's street by the golf course I realized that that plank had gone through the grille, but never actually pierced the radiator at all. It just dented it in a few inches and lodged itself there, taking all of these years to work its way free on its own.

The car idled perfectly, and none of its lifeblood escaped. I left that plank in the street in front of Jane's house. And I climbed back in and headed home.

You know, I think grief compresses you into a manageable volume so you can operate, be functional while you landscape your emotions. Mine had been clear-cut and strip-mined. But I'm okay. And I hope that she knows that I'm okay, even though it hurts like it was *then*. Some people in this modern world may question why I talk to you. Well, the reason is simple. It's because you've always been there, subtly nudging my conscience. I could always feel it, even at my worst, like that day on the golf course when I bludgeoned Andy when I was so young. The day the fat man played that song. I wrote down the bits I remembered on my social studies homework from my three-ring binder while leaning against that house on the golf course with those bloody banana leaves at my feet. I still have those homework pages today. I pull them out occasionally just to be sure. *September 19, 1975* is scrawled across the top next to my name in the undeveloped handwriting of my youth. The lyrics I wrote down questioned where your love went when fear stretched time. Even then I knew it stayed right where it always was...where it lives. I loved that song. I went to numerous record shops and sang what I remembered but no one recognized it, not even Samir. Two months later, on a date that would eventually house my grief, a ship went down in Lake Superior that would be the impetus for a melody that I'd heard just a bit too soon for logic. But I now know that love doesn't live in logic. So, when I peer into my mailbox to check, it's not because I don't believe. It's because I do.

I sent 187 letters to Jane and prayed that somehow they would find her, and that she'd know. I wanted her to know everything. One hundred eighty-seven sealed letters were returned to me through the years, undelivered by an angry mailman who missed 187 chances to do the right thing. It was not until after Jane left that I truly understood my flaw. I had prayed and asked to put something in your hands that you'd already put in mine. That's not how you work, is it? I should never have asked for you to deliver Jane a message that I could've simply whispered in her ear: 187 little secrets I wrote when no one was looking, and I could've told her each one, 187 little wounds that slowly dug the hole in my chest where Jane's plank had been.

Windows of opportunity really are portholes, and I had missed mine. I understood, but I knew I had one more letter to write. I needed Jane to know everything that I thought I had more time to convey—how she moved me, how she changed me forever, how the mere recollection of the sight of her will forever be incomparable, how there's nothing I ever wanted to do without her, how I wanted to hold her and never let her go, but mainly just how I loved her. Oh God, how I loved her. And so I wrote. And I mailed. And I prayed again.

One hundred eighty-eight letters sent to the love of my life. You know it's modern-age blasphemy to talk to God. Hell, it's even modern-age blasphemy to believe. But I believe. You've always listened. I know it. And I just want to thank you for listening again—and apologize. I asked you for 187 favors for Jane, favors that I could have done for myself. I'm sorry for that. But now I understand, and I just need to patch a hole.

I realize now that I only ever needed your assistance on the 188th. So when I walk out to my mailbox every day and look, it's not because I doubt, it's because I don't. I know it won't be there. I know that letter will never be returned from 33 Lieu Lieu Lane. It's been ten years since I stopped writing when no one was looking, and you've never let me down. I just wanted to thank you for the delivery...and to thank you, Lord, for Jane.

Amen.

Acknowledgments

To three girls,

   I met an invaluable developmental editor on the Internet named Ghia Gabriela Szwed-Truesdale. I needed help. See, I was left a box of almond seeds, and the sun was always there...so was the rain. Thank you, Ghia, for throwing them in the dirt and sprinkling some pabulum. It seems a Boudin Heirloom needs more than just one pair of hands.

I suppose there's always an intersection in which an opportunity lies to follow your future. The one that counts. The one that holds it all. The one that not all roads lead to. I'd like to thank a girl named Julie McCullough for pointing a wandering boy in the right direction...to a Happy Ending.

And to the one who deserves the most...I'll write nothing. I've learned. I'll simply whisper it in *her* ear.

—*Sean*

About the Author

Sean Patrick Flanery is an American actor, born in Lake Charles, Louisiana, and raised in and on the outskirts of Houston, Texas. He graduated from John Foster Dulles High School in Sugar Land, Texas, and then attended the University of St. Thomas before penning his first script and heading off to Los Angeles. He has appeared in over one hundred movies and television shows, some of which he hopes you've seen, and some of which he hopes you haven't.

He lives with his family in Los Angeles, California, where he loves his life, works in the entertainment industry, writes, and owns and operates a martial arts academy, Hollywood Brazilian Jiu Jitsu.